The Filly

The Filly

Ivor Herbert

Heinemann : London

William Heinemann Ltd
15 Queen Street, Mayfair, London W1X 8BE

LONDON MELBOURNE TORONTO
JOHANNESBURG AUCKLAND

Collin's
6,37
Nov/77

First published 1977
© 1977 Ivor Herbert

SBN 434 32761 1

Printed in Great Britain by
REDWOOD BURN LIMITED
Trowbridge & Esher

For Kate and Jane

I

'D'you think that you and I together will really be able to save her?'

The old man drew two lines with his stick, the first forceful, the second trailing away, through the ash of the fire. But he did not look up at his son.

Mark patiently watched the pigeon-coloured smoke. It lipped the green and cream carved urns of the marble fireplace. The chimney had been impeded for years by jackdaws' nests. The smoke smelled soft as old apples, for they had hacked these branches, twisted like crones' arms, out of the overgrown orchard. In the great hearth the fire was kept alive all year, basking on a mound of ash. Its smoke wafted up through the rents in the high ceiling right through the storeys to the stars. Where there were no holes the smoke stained what still remained of the beautiful plaster patterns on the ceiling.

The boy knew better than to attempt to prompt his father. The old man could usually be played like a pike below the mill-pool. Now, with shoulders hunched and jabbing with his branch he was seeking another trial of strength to emphasise the wisdom of age. Peeved by the boy's perception, his father spoke sharply and glanced up with his wide-apart blue eyes. 'The mare is bound to come back to her foal if you leave it.'

The boy, kneeling on the ash-deep marble surround, shook his head.

'Why not?' demanded Lincoln testily. 'Nature's way.'

'The foal's here,' said the boy. 'She's next to the new calf. I brought her in.'

His father, having the holly stick in his hand, thwacked him across the shoulder. Though Mark's shirt was torn, the blow of pique was only hard enough to smart, not bruise. Old Lincoln sprang up with the hobgoblin elasticity which his son envied. 'How?' demanded the old man. 'How did you get her here so far alone?'

Mark had come upon the foal that dawn. He had been hunting

I

across the old parkland, swinging his silent catapult after baby rabbits. These bobbed about profusely in the overgrown garden of the collapsed keeper's cottage by the east gate. They danced upon the graves of their ancestors' persecutors, and both Mark and his father enjoyed the thought. Beyond the track which was now thin grass over old flints, the invasion of the bracken began. Miles of its curling leaves and rank green smell washed up the slope to the shadows of the forest. But in the fringe of the bracken above the track, warmed by the rising sun, Mark had seen some animal flicker, a russet quiver. He had drawn back his catapult with a round black pebble from the brook, poised to loose it at a crouching leveret. Then he saw the liquid movement of an eye. It was twice as large as his. It regarded him directly. It was encircled by a slender ring of white. The pupil, in the shade of the low bracken, was expanded.

A fawn, the boy had thought, stepping barefoot across the flint foundations of the old lane. But it had been, to his astonishment, a very young foal. The creature stared at him without instinct of alarm as he climbed the bank. Then, with a little grunt, it pushed out its fragile forelegs and hoisted itself up. It flicked its tiny brush of a tail and arched its furry neck as full grown horses stretch. But the boy saw that the foal was at the most only four days old. He saw too that it was not the offspring of a pony, cob or workhorse. The filly foal was without doubt a young thoroughbred. Its ridiculous legs, like a clown's stilts, inclined inwards at the knee, then swerved out again, in danger of doing the splits.

The appearance of this cultivated, delicate creature out in these wilds astonished Mark so much that he froze at the foot of the grass bank below the foal. He was listening so hard for people or transport that his ears worked like a dog's under his long dark hair. He sniffed for a whiff of dirty diesel. The nearest road still in use was an hour's walk distant. He thought: truck broken down, no, accident more likely, mare and foal from some official stud got loose, run off . . . But there was no breath of man about, no calls, no far-off throb of an engine. And the foal had plainly slept the night out. Mark stared down the track and listened on the air. Nothing. He knuckled his forehead.

Believing that the filly foal would totter off to find its mother, who must be somewhere close in the sea of bracken, Mark did not try to be quiet. He scrambled up the bank on hands and feet like a monkey. He pushed through the bracken fronds, expecting the foal to turn away and move off. But she took two steps towards him. Her eyes were enormous. Between them lay a thin pale blaze like an exclamation mark. Her cocked ears were as furry as two ginger mice. She stuck out her muzzle, silky as worn, grey velvet, and she licked his hand with her pink tongue.

The boy knew that this was no sign of remarkable affection, but of a basic craving for the salt in his skin. He extended his index finger. The foal took it with her little mouth, half tilting her head by a reflex, as if still under her mother's teats. She started to suck his finger. Mark was nearly sure then that the foal had been abandoned. But he slid back down the bank on the leather-patched seat of his trousers. He squatted on the track opposite the foal, beneath the canopy of honeysuckle and dog-roses and among the trumpet standards of the foxgloves. He watched the filly foal and she watched him.

No mare moved in the bracken. Some young rabbits quivered on the brink of the keeper's garden and then hopped out to play on the track between the boy and the foal. But the boy would not loose a stone at them lest he frightened her. He rose. The rabbits scattered in a silent burst of white bob-tails. The foal remained on the bank top, still standing, still staring.

Or the mare could have died, Mark thought. Delicate thorough-bred mares did sometimes die foaling, so his father said. But the expanse of green bracken undulating away was like an ocean. If the mare lay in there she was buried deep as any sailor. But why then wasn't the foal still beside her, hanging over the body as animals will, believing that lick of tongue and warmth of needful body can resur-rect the dead? The sun's shafts on his own head answered him: the filly foal had come to the edge of the bank to keep still hidden, but to be warmed by that glow. 'She's clever!' Mark exclaimed aloud, sur-prised, for he had it from his father that thoroughbreds were idiots.

The boy walked backwards through the park's stone gate pillars, watching if the foal would either move away or follow him. She gave an experimental thin, high nicker, and stepped forward till her tiny forefeet perched like horn inkwells on the bank's brink. The boy waited. But she did not attempt the descent.

Mark ran at stretched speed the shortest way home, leaping through the long parkland grasses so that his thighs were soaked in dew and his trousers clung to them like cold dead hands. He found his father on a stool milking a cow, and told him the tale. The old man, disconcerted as always by anything alien, inexplicable and therefore threatening, had been both sceptical and grumpy. He tugged upon the cow's teats for emphasis.

'No thoroughbreds. Anywhere near here. And where's the dam? Dead? Whisked into heaven on a magic carpet? Where's the body?'

Mark's lack of answers irritated his father further. 'Won't be mixed up with blood horses again.' He tugged away at the cow's teats. The milk spurted. He butted his damp head against her flank. His grey beard wagged. 'It'll belong to some great official place.' The word 'official' possessed for them both a special meaning, combining menace with the smack of envy, as savages on other continents had thought of lions or of ancient kings. 'Thoroughbred foal. Can't be *wild*, Mark, now can it?' Then old Lincoln said very sharply, 'Leave it alone. Alien. Dangerous.'

But Mark, taking a bucket of the skimmed milk his father put out for the pigs' swill, had run back again praying he would still find the foal. She was there, sleeping. He had dipped his fingers in the milk and slipped them into her mouth. She sucked the milk from them.

'But how the hell,' demanded his father now, bustling crossly ahead of him through the hall, 'did you get her back here? Carry her?'

The owl, whom they called Ozymandias, swung away like a ghost. He dwelt in the top of the hall where the ivy covered the broken glass panes of the cupola. Normally he let them pass below unstirring. But old Lincoln's sharp tone, the tap of his feet, and the vibration of tension rose up to the owl like the dust off the chequered stone paving. Ozymandias vanished, white as a spirit, through the empty rooms of the top floor where he would swoop upon small rats.

'I had to. Down the bank,' said Mark. That his father had again called the filly "her" not "it" boded well. Perhaps when he saw her . . . 'She hated being picked up,' said Mark. 'Fought like anything.' He had tried to hoist her over his shoulders as his father carried calves, but her neck was like a serpent and her sharp little hooves, thrashing about in front of and behind him, had slashed his thighs. He had dropped her. Then before she could escape, he had put a shoulder and both arms behind her quarters. Before she could kick him, he barged her down the bank. She shot down, forelegs braced, amazed. And waited for him. Both were panting from effort and

4

from fright.

'Then she followed you? All the way back?'

'Followed the milk in the bucket.' Mark was honest.

'Ah, she would,' said old Lincoln quickly, but he was surprised. She must strangely have known that she needed the boy to save her.

They went quickly together, side by side now, over the moonlit cobbles. Several paths wound through the enormous shrubbery which had once so neatly fringed the drive and screened the farm buildings from the mansion. The old man had a notion, sprung from distant days of military service, that it was an important guard against observation from the air to avoid making beaten tracks. He constantly urged Mark, particularly when uneasy (he could smell threats as surely as a fox) to take different ways through the woods. He was less careful himself; he possessed, too, a fox's bravado. The last time Lincoln had been arrested had been just after a helicopter had whirred across the place. He had blamed Mark's slack field-craft, although the police had made no mention of aerial observation. For the first few weeks after his release, father and son had been like beaten dogs, doubly careful to slink about.

Old Lincoln unhooked a lantern from the side of the stone barn, lit it, and pushed into the calves' byre. The filly foal was not lying down, but standing as close as she could to the black and white calf. The thick stone walls of the byre had kept out all the heat of the day. Now in the evening the coolness inside felt like a larder after a warm kitchen. The sun had been baking the cobbled farmyard all day.

'She's cold,' said the old man critically.

'Perhaps she's never been beneath a roof before,' said Mark.

'It's a good thatched roof,' his father started. Then, 'How d'you know? Must have been foaled on some grand stud. Born under cover naturally.'

The boy did not answer. Never having seen any stud, he was trying to envisage not only it, but his filly being born there. Electric lights, he supposed. Squads of grooms in smart uniforms. Instructions being barked. Foals promptly being dropped in scrubbed boxes stark with disinfectant.

Remembrance of the smell evoked his two schools. In both, first in the now abandoned village, then in the glassy sprawl on the town's edge, the reek of disinfectant had predominated. His nostrils, attuned almost as finely as those of animals to the nuances of the countryside,

5

had been so smothered by the artificial hygiene that in the evenings his 'nose' was lost for hours.

His contemporaries had held their noses at the smell of pigs driven past one morning invisible in a truck. Mark showing, he hoped, some enviable ability had told which breed they were, how old and what they had been eating. The others, jeering at his knowledge had named him 'Dogg', and it had stuck.

He supposed his father's stays in prison were much like school, but worse because of having to sleep at night with urban strangers in cells. Captivity made the old man shriek and sweat in the black hours one week long after he came out.

Lincoln was intently studying the filly, head poked forward from his shoulders, holding the lantern closer. It was an aid to his concentration, not his eyesight which could see a moth furled on a flower at a hundred paces.

The filly's eyes shone in its yellow beam. She edged away, leaning against the calf who, fearing it would be squashed, darted out from behind through the bed of straw.

'You've put more straw in,' the old man complained. 'Too much.'

'You've always said to make a deep bed for mares and foals,' said Mark correctly. 'Even with the ponies and the carthorse foals. And she' – diplomatically switching from a statement to a question, 'And isn't she a thoroughbred?'

'Racehorse if ever I saw one.' His father blurted out the hackneyed phrase, and could have bitten his tongue off when he saw Mark grinning. 'And that's why she'll be far too dangerous to keep.'

To emphasise his decision he flung up an arm. The oil in the swung lantern spurted. The light flared. The foal, jumping back, banged herself against the wall. Recoiling, she leaped past old Lincoln like a buck and dashed through the doorway into the night.

The father collared the calf with one arm and flung it back cursing. Mark shouted, 'You frightened her!' and was gone. The foal's small hooves scrabbled hornily through the yard and faded into silence. Lincoln came out, slamming the door on the calf. The clap reverberated. Bats flashed from the barn against the moonlight. Mark heard pushing, and the squeak of branches and the crackle of leaves in the undergrowth. 'She'll eat some yew!' he swore, running after the sounds.

The moon's rays were fragmented by the foliage which moved

jerkily in the night breeze. Beneath the trees, patches of dazzling white alternated with pools of pitch. In these Mark was blind. Trees loomed up at the last instant as he blundered forward. His face, head and arms knocked into low branches. Some, killed into brittleness by the ivy jungle, had stabbing ends like dirks. Mark heard ahead of him the scutter of the filly's feet. By her hoof-fall she was trotting. Then ahead in the dark came a crash, and prolonged scrabbling, a snort of alarm, then silence. Mark, pausing and holding his own breath, thought he could catch the foal's quick breathing beneath the branch creaks and leaf rustles. Somewhere ahead lay the circle of holly trees and once clipped yew hedges which had, in the old days, enclosed a formal garden of statues gazing round an ornamental pond.

That earlier owner of the place, who had constructed the Palladian façade, had been captivated by formal gardens. He had commanded one to be created in a summer, ordering the full force of labourers from his fields in the break between haysel and harvest. Water colours, painted by a cool daughter, '*Erecting Garden in the Italian Style*' had been passed down the family.

'The foal's stuck in the old pond!' Mark shouted. 'She's in the bloody marsh!'

The pool's edges now opened onto a swamp where yellow irises bloomed wild. Among them Mark heard the foal's legs squelching. She must be in deep. Her legs came out with a long suck, before the plop. Her panting was now distinct. She was terrified. Old Lincoln was moving as softly as a squirrel. He reappeared and wafted a hand beneath Mark's nose. The scaly, tanned claw with its long fingers smelled of the magic unguent he used when breaking horses. The concoction had been given him years back by a passing gypsy scurrying from the authorities.

Lincoln would not yet let Mark use it. 'Learn the basics first,' he would mutter maddeningly. Both knew that the unguent was only another enabling device to prop up the father's dwindling superiority.

'I'll have her,' whispered his father with that glee which any sort of hunt ignited in him. 'Stay here, so she can't break back.' He vanished.

The foal, terrified by the false ground, stood quavering in the marsh. She was over her elbows in front and nearly up to her stifle behind. Her small belly pressed into the mud, disturbing it so that it

7

reeked of rotten vegetation, black slime and her sweat. She was within an instant of plunging still more deeply in when she smelled the old man's magic, snuffled and stood still. Stepping firmly across the firm tussocks and broken masonry he had a foal-slip round her head with a flick of his wrist.

Ah, he was quick still. 'Well done', Mark breathed, guarding the gap in the dark holly wall through which the foal had burst.

His father, leading her out with crooning murmurations, said, 'She's a chestnut. Hot. Difficult. But with fire. She'll take a lot of handling, you'll see. But we'll do it. We'll try, anyhow. If not, well, when she's able, we can turn her away near the town. Someone'll find the little treasure.' And he cackled.

Mark knew better than to fawn with thanks lest his father, now involved, might think he did a favour. 'Good', said Mark crisply, following them back out of the undergrowth and into the yard. He was annoyed not to have recaptured her himself.

'And no more fingers in the milk', his father commanded. 'There's a bottle with a teat on it in the cow parlour. Feed her now. It'll make up for my frightening her. Idiot!' He meant himself. Mark smiled. In that way, if in nothing else, the old man was honest.

2

But the foal did not take happily to the bottle. She did not thrive. The disturbances of the night had upset her. She purged. She would no longer settle with the calf, but shifted uneasily and sprang about whenever Mark looked in. Mark criticised his father squarely. The old man nodded. But he was too enchanted by his general way of life to bemoan set-backs. He knew that the gods kicked down whiners. Hubris was one thing: very dangerous. But the gods, he had learned, did not like the opposite either, and scorning those who complained, frequently gave them extra cause. So, beyond remarking that it was a pity that their circumstances made it hard to find a foster-mother, he did not apologise. He said, 'I'll go into the hills for a few days', sprang on his cob, whistled up Rip the brindle lurcher, and rode off, pack and gun and headcollars strapped across his back.

Sometimes he would come back from these expeditions with a deer shot in the cool fringe of the pine forests where the trees petered out on the grey mountain slopes. Sometimes on his way back he would 'free' a sheep, milk-cow or bullock from a far, large farm. 'To free' was his established euphemism for stealing. He liberated things, as well as animals 'cooped up in those new boxes in the town.' Things there, seldom glanced at, begged him to free them into the wildness of the woods. There, because they were needed, they would be loved.

A few pony herds grazed out until the winter on the foot hills. They belonged to associations of hill farmers, but were tended with a slackness that provoked the old man. Animals should be cared for. He hoped to find among the herds a mare who had recently dropped a dead foal. She would thus be still bagged up with wasting milk and in need of freedom.

Having travelled across country all day, he spotted the main herd where he expected it: grazing beyond the lake. They were at the foot of the mountain which kept off the north-east wind. They were cropping in the narrow valley watered by a stream. The stream spurted from a spring high on the mountain flank in a stone cave believed – when those ideas persisted – to be holy. It had been the abode of a hermit. The water was certainly delicious. On its leaping path down to the lake, the stream collected minerals and deposited this largesse richly in the valley grass. The ponies knew from accumulated herd experience that they could satisfy their cravings there.

The old man tied his cob to the arched bole of a willow. He spied out the herd with his old copper telescope. He counted a dozen foals, but the older ones were already forming play groups of their own. There was one mare standing a little apart who had about her a mourning air. Could be, thought the old man.

First, he examined the whole of the far bank for any trace of mankind. He went back to his cob, and whistled up Rip with a hiss through the gap in his teeth. The sound was scarcely audible to human ears. Then he rode briskly off through the lake's edge. The water splashed round Benjamin's hooves and the dappled stones gleamed and rattled beneath them. The sun swiftly descending, flashed on the moving corrugations of the water with tongues of flame. He would have to hustle.

He reached the head of the lake and turned towards the mouth of the brook. He took out his telescope again, found the mare he wanted, saw she was still alone while the others had their foals back with them now. He saw that she had a full tight bag. Then the sun, whose sinking had brought the foals to their dams, dived beneath the mountain ridge. Mist rolled into the valley. The pony herd, legless in the still white surf, seemed to be swimming. They were moving away, dark heads and necks like chess-board knights, because of the cold kiss of the mist.

Using it for cover the old man pressed resolutely through and up the side of the hillside to the hermit's cave. He unsaddled Benjamin and fed him, flung Rip the bone slung across the pommel and unrolled his blankets on the dry ground of the hovel. The noise of the spring in the inside cave chortled and boomed, so that it seemed that the water spoke by tapping and that ghosts through its resonances replied. Superstition kept people from the hermit's perch at night, but the old man understood the ancient man who had, some still thought, worked cures as well as curses from the holy well. Lincoln felt comfortable in the cave. He unfolded from a grimy scarf his home-ground loaf and cheese. He drank deeply of the water which, though so chilled that his yellow teeth ached, instilled optimism as if alcoholic. With Rip across his feet, he slanted over into sleep.

3

The foal was ill. Mark agitatedly knuckled his brow. Gazing at her in the calf byre he bit off shreds of nail. She panted. The dark sweat patches staining both sides of her neck felt clammy as he stroked her. Her little rib cage squeezed in and out too quickly. They were like bellows worked to keep a fire aglow. Her furry ears were clammy. Round her eyes, which shone excessively brightly, were patches of encircling moistness where the skin lay as thin as silk over her bones.

Rummaging through the muddle of the medicine chest Mark cursed his father: for driving the foal into the bog, for keeping nothing where it should be, for being absent when needed, and for teaching him too little.

He finally found the thermometer between some old tins and bottles all with indecipherable labels. He greased it, then stretching wide to hold the foal's head with his left hand, slid the thermometer under her tail with his right. She sucked it in so deeply he feared he had lost it. But its tip just showed. Having no watch he counted the seconds to two hundred: 'Higgledy-piggledy one, higgledy-piggledy two, higgledy-piggledy . . .' The foal's left eye glanced back at him, and her left ear twitched. She was soothed by his incantation. So I'll stay with her talking, he decided. It helps her.

He secured the slippery end of the thermometer and contrived, at the third try, to withdraw it. He ran with it to the daylight, peered and gasped: the mercury had been pushed right past the danger line. Mark turned it round, hoping he might have misread it. The verdict was reiterated and terrifying. The fever was very high. Colic, Mark thought. Or worse, a stoppage in her gut? He burrowed through her bed, searching for droppings to prove that her intestines were not blocked.

The foal lay down again. She turned stiffly onto one side so that her ribs bulged upwards. She stuck her neck out, and panted dreadfully. She's dying, Mark thought, and stood there staring down, mesmerised by the rasp and roar of her breath which he felt was itself blowing away the guttering candle. He hated his father for leaving him in ignorance and himself for his inertia. He knew that up on the slate shelf stood the bottles for drenching against colic and the tin trumpet through which he could pour the medicine down her throat. But with colic horses were in pain; they pawed, tried to roll, twisted their heads round and back, their necks like striking snakes, nuzzling at the flaming pain in their guts. The foal lay still. Certainly she had a fever and should be kept warm. But should she be made to drink, given sugar to sustain her, alcohol, or not? For which things was drink bad or good, curse it?

Mark rushed away to ferret through rows of unlabelled bottles for what might be a fever drench. He uncorked them, sniffing. The fever drink should stink of turpentine. None did. And after several he could smell no more. Fearing the foal might be now on the ledge of death, he dashed back to her again. He must warm her. The calf was of no help. Worse, its instincts warned it of impending doom. It crouched away from the foal and stood lowing from the back at the prostrate

11

body. More calves, thought Mark, more body heat to warm the byre. He climbed over the partitions, lassooed two, lugged them round protesting, stiff-legged, and thrust them into the foal's box. They cannoned over her to join the younger calf. The foal tottered up, swayed and went down again buckling over at her knees. The calves clumped together, staring with the bland immobility of spectators round an accident. The byre was far too lofty, Mark saw, glancing up to the rafters, for their bodies to warm the air at all.

There were sick animal drugs somewhere in the house, freed by his father from a chemist's shop. Mark ran across the cobbles. The pigs, seeing him, squealed for their food. The chickens squawked: their water trough leaked and they were parched. Single-handed, the day's essential tasks could only just be concluded between dawn and dusk if all ran well. There was no time for illness. The creatures caught his anxiety as he ran past and set up a special, maddening clamour.

Mark found no drugs where he had expected, in the dank gloom of the cellars. Because potatoes and sugar-beet were stored down there, too, the rats stole in. He heard them squeaking and scurrying and saw red eyes pass like dots across the piles of beet. Sugar, he thought.

He ran upstairs again, found some honey, put a pan of water on the slumbering fire under the marble mantlepiece, blew upon the flames, fed them with brittle pine twigs . . . The fire awoke and blazed. The water heated slowly and the honey dissolved. He scurried with the pan across to the yard. Again the chickens clucked from behind their wire compounds. A raw egg. He slipped in, seized one, broke it into the pan. Strengthening, and should he add milk? A little might help. Into the milking parlour for a pan. Was cream too rich? Out again. He tore off his jersey as he ran, and ripped off both its sleeves.

The foal was lying very still. But she was still breathing. Mark chivvied all three calves out and left them to gawp in the yard, bellowing for their fellows. He knelt by the foal's head. Her upward eye watched him with what he feared was terminal resignation. He raised her head, pulled his jersey over it and down to her shoulders. But there was no way, he discovered, in which he could insert her ridiculous long legs through the sleeve holes. He could neither pull her thin limbs far enough forward nor flex them. As he tried, she sighed, and a shiver went through her as if she might try to struggle up to evade his attentions. He ripped open the front of the sweater. The foal started

12

at the rasping. But he could ease the jersey back now over her small shivering body. Under her belly he linked the edges with twine. It looked so much a cross between a tramp's waistcoat and nineteenth century lady's corset that Mark let out a grunt of humour, of relief that he had at last done something for the foal.

Using the tin funnel he tipped the milk, raw egg and honey-water into the pink pouch at the side of the foal's mouth. He rubbed her throat, urging her to swallow. All the time he murmured to her, trying to suppress the urgency in his voice, so that he sounded soothing and confident. He heard his new voice booming ridiculously in the cow byre.

But swallow she did. More than half the pan went down her and only a little spilt through her mouth onto the straw. Mark kneeling, felt suddenly cold. He was simultaneously struck by fatigue. His legs ached. He realised he was now bare from his trousers up. I'll keep her warm, he decided, and she me. He sat down behind her back and put his arms around her neck, hugging her to him. Within a minute warmth flowed between the two bodies. He wondered drowsily, but with such interest that he resented the swamping fatigue: Do I warm her only? Or does she now warm me? Convinced that the question was all-important and that its answer lay just round the corner of another thought, he stroked the filly's neck with gratitude. His hand stayed still. He felt her pulse beating. She felt his breath on her ears.

4

The darkness in the hermit's cave did not prevent the old man stirring exactly when he had decided. He had dozed fox-like, with his eyes half open though rolled back, so that the slightest growth of light registered on his pupils.

He kicked Rip off his feet and flung saddle and bridle upon Benjamin. To his delight he saw the pony herd had moved up during darkness towards him to graze above the white band of mist. This was now creeping away like a giant's breath, curling over the trees by the waterside. Lincoln had corn in one pocket and a spare headcollar over his right shoulder. He would get that mare within half an hour.

Down the slope of the mountain he rode. Enough pale light was blooming in the east to reflect the shimmer of the dew on grass stems and shining rocks. Halfway down he felt on his shoulder blade the touch of the breeze which was shifting the mist. His sound and smell were thus borne down on the ponies. One head, then another was flung up to face him. The tip of the sun leaped over the ridge and loosed two golden rays towards the herd. He clearly saw the foal-less mare out on a flank. Her bag was so stiffly full that she waddled like a pregnant woman.

'We'll soon ease you,' murmured the old man. He contemplated the thoroughbred foal's future with delight. He had hatched a plan, but he would not let Mark know of it for a while. Let him come to it by himself. They would break that filly and make her and try her. And if she had speed in her at all, they would train her together, he showing Mark how it was done so that the boy might learn the rudiments. That done, why, they'd take her away over the hills, clear of their own part of the world, and run her in a race. They would run the first time quietly, feeling their way, letting her learn that racing was a joy. Then if all still went well and she showed great promise (his hands hooked round Benjamin's reins, feeling the power and zest of a restrained racehorse at the far end of them) they would, by God, have such a wager on her next time that they need never starve again. And no one, thought the old man, as foolish as always in his dreams, need know whence she came.

There was a sharp crack-bang! from the mist of the lake. The old man heard in the air above him the whistle of some device. The ponies instantly whirled and galloped off with a thunder of reverberating feet. The old man paused. In the second during which the missile was screaming over his head he considered the idea of dismounting, lying down or digging a foxhole. He took a firm hold of Benjamin's reins, and bent right down to shield his head and shoulders and to grip Rip by his collar. An explosion erupted. A fountain of brown earth shot into the air. A shower of pebbles sprayed swiftly, then heavier clods fell within yards of him. Mortar, he surmised. Lucky it fell in the stream's boggy patch. The ground had soaked up the force of the explosives. Now if that had been in a concrete town, he thought, feeling himself again blessed.

Then he saw below him the line of red flags hanging limp by the lakeside. He cursed. The army were out on one of their exercises, firing live ammunition to battle-test recruits. In the silence which followed the explosion and the disappearance of the herd, he heard the squeak and rumble of tracked vehicles. He heard, too, some bellowed injunction through a loud-hailer. It ended with a coarse oath. In a lull in the breeze Lincoln heard clearly the mockery of the soldiers. He flushed so that his tanned face glowed like a chestnut. A disadvantage of their solitude was missing governmental proclamations.

His heart, which had tripped and banged, steadied. He had envisaged himself obliterated by a pattern of mortar shells, parts of himself and horse and dog flung up like those brown sods. But that one shot had been a warning to get out. To hasten him a short rattle of automatic gunfire now spattered across the slope, followed by more braying through the megaphone. The combination of himself, cob and lurcher would be unusual enough to be reported anyway. He swung off at as fast a gallop as Benjamin could muster, urged Rip ahead and crossed the next ridge into a fold of mountainside. He left behind a burst of derisive shouting – 'stinking old tramp!' – and there was another plop of the mortar firing. The next shell fell close to the first, but fragmented on an outcrop of rock. Slivers whistled. The old man, perched over his cob's withers, crouched like the jockey he had been long ago. His thin legs drummed against the cob's flanks. He sped onwards, scurrying away. Benjamin grunted beneath him and Rip, galloping alongside, lolled his red tongue looking sideways and up, as if laughing.

When he was out of shot of the military Lincoln took a wide sweep over the uplands searching for the pony herd. The ground became softer. Heather sprang. There blew towards him the lovely smell of peat and over the next ridge he came upon a peat-bog still being worked. Slices, as if cut from a chocolate cake, neatly patched the landscape. The wind was changing. Lincoln sniffed and studied the sky. A huge cloud, dazzling white, towered up like a castle of the fairies. Wind and rain would come. But the old man was gazing in such rapture at the cloud that he halted Benjamin and raised a hand, first to feel the outline of its wonderful shape, and then to recognise its beauty by a salute.

The wind, circling like a hunting dog, brought on it a percussive crescendo of shell-fire, the rattle of automatics and then gasps of the animal raspings of the soldiers as they practised the hearty murder of

15

one another. The instructor's megaphoned shrieks of 'Kill! Kill!' whistled across the uplands.

The old man grimaced with loathing.

5

His son, wearied by a sleepless night, was pouring powdered aspirin tablets, hot milk and a little brandy through the tin funnel into the foal's mouth. The foal was still sweating. 'Sweating out the fever,' Mark had thought at dawn. But her temperature remained as high as ever.

He had therefore, on a forlorn chance, hunted for aspirin. His father disapproved of human medicines. He was rarely sick and when he was, took some old elixir distilled from herbs and wild flowers and freely stiffened with brandy. 'Juice of the grape gives you heart!'

Mark suspected that alcohol might not soothe a soaring temperature, but the foal needed to be given heart. Unsure of the dosage, he calculated that the foal must weigh, if fit, about one third of his own weight. Knowing that she could not vomit, he measured the brandy and the aspirin on the low side. As the brandy went down, the foal spluttered and snorted and tried to rise. Mark laid his hand on her heart. It was fluttering beneath his fingers like a trapped sparrow.

6

The old man passed all habitations cautiously, at a distance. He had resigned himself to returning this time without a mare in milk. But he knew a quarry which was such a garden metropolis for rabbits that they called it, from its hanging terraces, Babylon. There, silently, Rip might snatch up a couple of sweet youngsters.

He rode up to the quarry into the face of the late afternoon breeze.

The smell of the rabbits hidden beneath its lip wafted so strongly towards Rip, that his nostrils quivered like blackberries. He began to drool. The old man, murmuring, urged stillness upon his dog. His cob, knowing what lay ahead too, quickened his tired pace. The rabbits, fearing horses not at all, would not look upwards until too late to observe that a man bestrode another friendly animal.

Just short of the quarry's green lip and while still out of sight of the rabbits nibbling the turf, the old man flung his hand out, pointing to Rip. The lurcher crept forward. He kept so low that his deep narrow chest cut like a keel through the cowpats and the thistles. He moved to the left edge of the quarry. His brindle body lay like a log. Only his skinny tail flicked at its very end and his ears worked.

Old Lincoln kicked the cob forward, flat out, down the steep right bank to intercept the rabbits from their warren. For a second he felt himself take off over the top, then the cob's forelegs came down in a clatter of rolling stones and he started to plunge towards the bottom. The grassy floor was brown and grey and white with rabbits' bodies, ears and tails all in that instant frozen by astonishment, before panic.

While Lincoln was plunging down he shrieked at Rip. The dog swept down, ears cocked, too experienced to be bemused by the mob of rabbits dashing at him. He did not even glance at the cob's thundering arrival. He had picked out a young rabbit. He snapped his jaws on its neck as it jinked, tossed it up over his head, dead, with the flamboyance permitted for individual victory, grabbed another going across his front, snapped that back, and then coursed a third streaking up the far bank. That ducked too quickly for him into the great blackberry thicket. His speed carried him past. The rest had safely bolted into their holes.

Old Lincoln was delighted. 'G'boy Rip, g'd ole boy, then,' he cackled. The dog grinned. His tail wagged hugely. He paced over to the two dead rabbits in a grandly exaggerated trot. 'Here, then', called the old man. Rip brought them over, tossing each and pretending, with a glint in his amber eyes, that he would eat them up.

It was then that Lincoln saw at the cliff's foot a still fawn shape. Halfway up the slope something moved and a scatter of pebbles fell down Babylon. It was a scraggy donkey, staring down at the intruders and struggling for a foothold. It had been lodged on a red sand ledge. Now the ground was giving way. The donkey came slithering downwards. It let out small weak grunts of pain and terror as it gathered speed, at one instant nearly tipping over sideways, which would have broken its short legs. It reached the bottom, shaken, but on its four small feet. Without looking at Lincoln or the dog, it moved across to the fawn shape at the cliff's foot and, snuffling over it, began piteously to bray. It was its foal.

'Here!' Lincoln bellowed at Rip who was stalking towards them. 'Here!' His tone was fierce, because like any experienced creature of the woods he knew sharply the danger of moving without checking the ground. He trotted across towards the donkeys. The foal was dead. Its mother was so thin her ribs were like an empty hayrack through her tight-drawn hide. Lincoln walked towards the body and the mother let him come. Flies buzzed over the foal's extremities. Its tiny mouth was open in a snarl. Lincoln felt the body. It was completely cold. Then he saw where the black carrion crows had eaten its flesh. He spat out his revulsion. 'Get back!' he shouted at Rip who had crept close. Whoever owned the miserable donkey had left her a full week stuck on the quarry side with her foal dead below. Lincoln was in a fury. He gave his corn to the donkey and strapped on the headcollar. She accepted it. She was not wild then; she had been used to being handled. Very well, he would free her. Her bag beneath her poor thin creamy-coloured belly, was still tight with milk.

7

'Then you're old enough to *be* able to cope!' When old Lincoln was rigidly angered he stuck his fists on his thin waistline so that his elbows flapped like wings. With his head jerking forward he resembled their fierce bantam cockerels. 'Sixteen!'

'Seventeen!' shouted Mark. They stood face to face, shadows behind them, a leap of flames in between. 'And you don't bloody teach me nothing.'

'Don't nothin'' mocked the old man, snapping the words off like bites at a cucumber. 'Can't speak. Can't get a job. No good at school. Dogg!' he mimicked the cries of the boys there. 'Doggy Dogg Dogg!' He wanted the boy to rush at him, to let the row froth over. But Mark was not yet sufficiently goaded. Lincoln was weary, too. Knowing there could be no risk of it he said to Mark, 'Go off and get a job on a farm then, if you don't like it here. Harvest's coming.' Mark knew that he meant insultingly that any pair of hands would be accepted. But he did not rise. 'You couldn't cope here', said Mark calmly.

'I'd manage.' The old man flung his arms one, two, wide across his body, his action of broadcasting their seed corn. 'Cut down. Cull inessentials.' He eyed his son. 'Have to one day, won't I?'

Again Mark would not rise. He said with conviction, 'But you must have known she'd be ill after that night in the swamp. You *must* have. But you jaunted off whistling.'

'To get your precious foal a foster-mother. To get food. I leave you a day.'

'Nearly three. Two nights with the foal nearly dying.'

'*And* I bring food. *And* a foster-mother.'

'A donkey!' Mark spat. The cockiness of his father's return, old Lincoln's patronising benevolence, his flourish of the starving donkey, had made Mark explode. Acting like that conjurer once at school: rabbits here, foster-mother there! And there tied up in a stall, thin as a skeleton, with his father bowing like a governmental toady – 'A half-dead donk!' Mark sneered. His father, deft as a fly weight, darted forward and slapped Mark's cheek. The blow was light but perfectly delivered. The old man had won not only boxing contests in his racing days, but afterwards, when things went badly, had fought for cash in fairground booths. His smallness and apparent fragility deluded opponents round the countryside. His bones, though thin, were as solid and heavy as a thoroughbred's. The speed of his eye and fist, his balance and force had made him dangerous. Mark, caught off-guard and off-balance, fell back against the marble fireplace, tripped, and, as his feet skidded over the ash, slithered to the floor.

'Always blame others', said his father with venom, pressing his advantage and crowing over him. 'Like your mother.' He spoke of Mark's mother only when they quarrelled, bringing her out like a bit of broken glass bought in a moment of gross loss of taste. He spoke of her not with loathing nor scorn nor regret, but with tight lips round a light thin voice. 'Never her own fault. Always something happened, ill-luck, wrong time, someone else's fault. . . .' He opened his hands, palm upwards, but not shrugging. He looked down into his palms.

Mark was climbing out of the fireplace. The old man examined him critically, touched his shoulders and said with bite, 'Not big enough across there yet.'

The boy would now either smash at him or turn away in a sulk. Mark did neither. Mimicking his father's hands on hips (which thus expanded his shoulders) and being able to look down on the old man, he simply stood there. He seemed calm, but Lincoln was pleased to see it was a question of control, for the firelight showed the bulge of Mark's jugular vein, the raised blue vein down his forehead, and the strong beat of the boy's pulse in the slim wrist nearest the fire.

'You looked after the foal very well,' said old Lincoln. 'You did the right things. She'll be all right. Why, if all goes well, we'll –' But he did not wish yet to add breakable substance to his dreams by uttering them, so he said instead, 'Let's eat', and nodded into the fireplace.

One of his rabbits, disjointed, simmered in the smokestained casserole over the fire. It was surrounded by a shoal of peas, carrots and onions, gently stewing in the stock to which Lincoln, like a tramp Escoffier, had carefully added, whilst stirring, a quarter bottle of elderberry wine. They would eat it with new potatoes, mint and a dandelion leaf salad. Rabbits sold from shops were nothing. 'Fresh-killed and small, better than petits poussins', his father said, passing Mark the brandy left from the foal's emergency.

It had been, as so often, the quick swigs of brandy on the old man's return which had sparked their quarrel. From his childhood Mark recalled his mother glitteringly presiding over some expensive pudding, while brandy drenched it and was lit by some bold-eyed stranger's hand. He had seen his father at the table's foot dart daggers from his blue eyes at the charming gentleman on his mother's right. The pudding, after the flash, had quivered with a chilly blue light, then suddenly gone out. So it was usually with their quarrels.

But Mark now wanted to improve matters. He said quickly, 'Then let's label all those bloody bottles. There's no point in your scratchy writing with foxglove-juice, belladonna, hemlock –' Old Lincoln cackled. But Mark would not be deflected. 'All right, *you* know what's what. Now *I* must know what they're for. And now I know there were fever drinks hidden away, and me grinding together bloody aspirins, nicking the brandy –'

'Poppin' in eggs.'

They both began to laugh. 'Ought to make it up properly', said the old man, 'and we'll sell it at market: Mark's Magic Mixture, Elixir of

Mallards Court.'

They were picking the rabbits' leg-bones cleanly, wiping the pot with bread crusts and developing the project – 'would a raw egg keep in brandy in an airtight bottle?' – when the old man's eyes widened, as they did when he listened intently.

He had no need to raise a finger. The tumble of ash in the fire was the loudest noise in the room. In the fire's orange glow they saw the hackles on Rip's back rising like hedgehog quills beneath a sorcerer's hands. On the wind came softly the alarming honking of the guardian geese.

'The gangs?' whispered Mark. When food shortages in the town grew acute and supplies of work ceased, youths came into the countryside on moonlit nights to steal poultry, eggs and firewood, and broke into farmhouses.

His father shook his head. 'Too dark.' Townsmen needed bright full moon to find their way around even on farm lanes. Out in this wilderness they would not dare to come without torches. And the police, stamping on all lights abroad at night, rounded up foot-travellers and impounded them.

'Police', said old Lincoln. 'The donkey', he said instinctively. 'Tell them I'm away in the mountains buying a pony.' He slid his plate, mug and the brandy bottle into the recess behind the great fireplace. Mark smoothed the ash across. His father murmured to Rip and stepped out through the broken frame of the great bow window.

As he vanished into the dark, there came up the overgrown drive another, closer wave of honking from the next gaggle of geese. Old Lincoln maintained two guardian piquet lines across what had once been the main drive. A third flock quartered on the ruined farmyard on the southern side protected that flank against any callers. The few goslings who fell in action to the foxes, were a small price to pay for the vigilance which gave them their sort of freedom. The sentry system not only signalled intruders but alarmed them: after the swelling chorus of honk-honk-honkings, the geese would rush forward, necks stretched, hissing like cursing witches. Their great wings which could break legs beat the air with the creaks and crashes of leather coshes.

Mark, composing himself under the old blanket in the attitude of heavy sleep, heard the vehicle whining up the drive. Low gear. Heavy. Clank of metal and chains. No pretence at silence. Its headlights, turning into the pot-holed forecourt, flashed up and down the immense row of long windows on that façade and swung across Mark like the beam of a light-house. The vehicle halted. Two doors opened. Two pairs of boots landed on the split stones of the once splendid courtyard. But the engine remained on, idling. So the driver at least stayed there, Mark decided, raising himself from the floor on one elbow and rubbing his eyes as if dispelling sleep.

Two men, faintly illumined in the fire's glow, were peering in through one of the huge bay windows. One was in police uniform. The other wore a smart checked summer coat. Both swung their torches round, found Mark and fixed him in a scissor of white beams. The one in the coat slapped his palm on the window. The pane, loose in its long-rotted frame, crashed inwards, tinkling onto the floor. The man, surprised, started backwards. The uniformed figure turned him by the elbow and Mark saw it was one of the police sergeants from the town. The sergeant showed the plain-clothes man in courteously through one of the empty window frames at the side as Mark scrambled up out of his blankets like a whippet disturbed. 'Mark Lincoln, Sir', said the sergeant. 'The old man's son.'

'Where's your father?' asked the other. He was young and had a soft-edged indoors face, the colour and consistency of uncooked bacon fat. Sideboards sprouted down to the angle of his jaw bones. His hair was curly. He was astonishingly well-dressed and smelt to Mark's nose very strongly of small cigars, scent, leather and the stuffy, faintly acid interior of cheap cars.

'Went to the mountains, sir, to buy a pony.'

'Nick it, you mean,' said the plain-clothes man, pulling his top lip back over teeth too regular to be real. He took out a handkerchief and held it under his nose. 'The smell in here . . . filthy.' He began to prowl round.

The sergeant asked in his local accent, 'What did he want another pony for, Mark?'

'Oh, to deal in. Young one again to break and make, you know.'

The sergeant nodded. 'Then sell as usual.'

The officer called invisibly from the dark end of the room, 'Been gone long? Don't you freeze here? When did you leave school? Working?' Fools, he found, first answered the last of a group of questions, because their minds were like puddles too shallow to hold more. Rustic knaves like this lot would however reveal themselves by first replying to the question which they felt most threatened them.

Mark said into the darkness, 'Three days, sir.' And gave away nothing.

'Where?'

Mark shrugged. Say the least, listen the most, the old man always instructed him. It had paid off years ago in his racing, gambling days and when he played with women. Mark could hear the officer pacing about in the dark of the bow window. The boards squeaked. If he went much further – 'Christ!' shouted the officer. A board had snapped. His foot rasped through its hole.

'Very rotten floor', said the sergeant. He did not look at Mark, but his tone suggested a rural rapport between them. The sergeant found picking up old Linky for his piddlin' offences as painful to the backside as the jolts up that murderous track to this gaunt wreck. But new inspectors liked to see all round their precincts. Even into the back-woods. Made them feel real bosses to hear their whips crack so far from the station.

The inspector came back into the firelight suppressing a limp from his grazed shin and wiping his hands on the handkerchief. It was now coated with grime. He must then, thought Mark, have damp palms and therefore be as alarmed as the authorities often seemed by the strangeness of the place.

'The Hygiene Department, Public Health, Housing Ministry men been out here?' the officer demanded.

Mark nodded. 'Last year, sir.'

'Let you live here? In this filth? Like animals?'

The sergeant said, 'They made recommendations, sir. But housin' difficulties . . . the usual . . . certain doubts about ownership –'

'Squatting?' demanded the inspector, as eager as a hound for meat. Splendid powers had recently been vested in local police authorities to cleanse this scourge.

'No, sir. Certain domestic disagreements.'

The inspector asked sarcastically. 'Not a compensation appeal, surely, sergeant? They went out years ago under the new edicts.'

'Not exactly. I'll show you the report.'

The inspector had reached the door into the lofty hall. He was shining his torch around. Upwards it went in to the wrought iron of the smashed glass dome. It caught the huge white owl. The eyes of Ozymandias balefully regarded him, without blinking. His beak

23

glinted. His talons gleamed. The Inspector snapped off the torch and came quickly back to the fire.

'That's neither here nor there now', he said hurriedly. 'Your father was shot at by the military.' From looking into the fire he swung round to watch Mark's reaction. But Mark asked quickly, 'Is he all right? Why?'

The Inspector said, 'Riding about all over the firing range. Disobeying the regulations. Red flags – might as well be blind. Lucky to escape. And one hell of a waste of time.' He said crossly to the sergeant, 'Well, when are we going to look round outside? Check the animals?' To Mark, 'You come.'

As they were crossing the cobbles to step down into the central farmyard the Inspector's neat shoe tips stumbled over the stone coping. His flashlight caught the black barn. 'What's kept in there?'

'Only hay and straw', Mark said hurriedly, hoping he sounded uneasy.

'We'll look.'

The sergeant said quickly, 'I know it to be a hay barn sir.'

'Wouldn't stop it holding animals would it?'

'Oh, it would', said Mark, 'You see, they'd eat it.'

But the Inspector swung open the huge double-doors through which towering haywains had once creaked with the garnered revenue of a year's hard labour. He pushed inside the barn. It was as big as a church and beamed like one. As it was before haysel the barn was nearly empty, but the bats which hung like furry villains' gloves along the pale skeleton of beams, fluttered across the flashing torchlight as Mark had hoped they would.

'Could get in your hair, sir, those bats', said Mark politely. 'Very full of lice and fleas. The animals are this way.'

He had the lantern lit and led the policeman across to the young bullocks' byre this side of the donkey and the foal. Judging the Inspector's mood to be receptive to a warning Mark said, 'These young bulls could be made a little restive with flashlights.' The Inspector discreetly doused his glim. Mark held up his lantern. A glow of bullocks' eyes reflected its yellow daubs in forty shining pupils. The air was rich with the warmth of their bodies and their droppings. Expecting a feed, they moved forward over the stained bracken exposing for a moment the straw barricade which hid his foal and her dangerously noisy foster-mother.

But the Inspector was rapidly losing interest. What had been dramatically described to him by his predecessor as 'that ghostly place, the old mansion in the wilds', turned out to be a derelict ruin of a noisome farm. And if this polite lad's tramp of a poaching father had nicked a bloody moke, how the hell would they find the wretched thing in the dark without even one electric light?

'We'll be back again,' he said resolutely. 'Tell your father.'

'Yes, sir, when?'

'Christ knows!' exclaimed the Inspector, 'Haven't we got enough to do in the town where people *live* – without chasing round the backwoods for tinkers?'

The police vehicle's engine had remained running throughout the visit. It was what both Mark and his father expected of authority's prodigality when times were grim. He supposed it was to grant the police a quick getaway if he and a band of villains had attacked the Inspector. He smiled as the red rear-lights leaped and jolted down the drive. The police radio began to quack, but it and the complaints of engine and suspension were soon swamped by the stentorian bellowing of the first picket-line of geese.

Mark should, he knew, always wait at least an hour after a police visit before resuming any activity which the authorities might find suspicious. The dropped-off man from the noisily departing truck who quickly returned to snoop was an old dodge. But he was by his foal's box, and she had been again in danger, and he wished very much to look at her again.

The outer warning gaggle of geese finished their far honking. Nothing else, except the accustomed quiet symphony of the night, now disturbed the woods and fields. Holding the lantern steady, because of the threat of its heat to the dry bedding, he crept in behind the calf byre. His filly foal replete with milk had divested herself of his sweater, and was lying with her back to the straw wall, slender legs stuck out in deepest slumber. The grey donkey, crude as a Velasquez court dwarf by comparison and just as attentive, brooded over her foster-child. Turning her sad and moth-eaten head, the donkey regarded Mark mournfully, as if accusing him of entangling her in some drama of which she wished no part. The foal opened her drowsy eye and looked at him with what he was sure was recognition, perhaps even gratitude. Suddenly elated, he ran back to the ruined house.

8

Mark had expected that the foal, when fully recovered, would simply be turned out in the fields with her foster-mother to get on with her growing.

'Little you know', said his father tetchily. They were turning rows of hay. They had left it late. Hay seeds which should have stayed on the stems were flying loose, irritating the corners of the old man's eyes. He jerked at the rake, 'Delicate damned things, thoroughbreds. She'll be in at night all summer through. That'll mean feeding the moke, too.'

Little hay had been left from last season. This crop round their feet would be too green and fierce for the foal's belly until it had matured by autumn. Feed was short.

They worked up a row in silence. The fencing round the meadow had years ago been broken down by bullocks. It was not repaired. They could no longer stock it. The meadow now simply merged like a tattered yellow shirt into the encroaching green bracken and the blue green darkness of the woods. With no chemical weed-killers the meadow grasses were intermingled with a variety of old established herbs. Most smelled very sweet as they lay drying in the sun. The meadow danced with unsprayed butterflies.

'She's been a bloody nuisance from the start,' the old man said suddenly. What worried Lincoln about the filly foal was not yet tangible. As a horseman he recognised that some horses, like some people were born losers. If there was an illness within a mile, they caught it. Of twenty youngsters running free one would again and again pierce his foot on a flint, damage his eye on a low branch, cut himself and find the wound grow septic. For these, as his own father had taught him sixty years ago, there was one rule: get shot of the unlucky.

But this did not apply to the foal. So far, and against the odds, she was a survivor. But there are other horses which, like certain people, bring ill-luck to those they touch. 'Kiss of doom', Lincoln called across the buzz of bees beneath the giant honey-scented lime trees.

'Kiss of death.'

Mark worked on steadily. The swallows darted in the sky as high, swooping specks: it would not rain. Grey horse-flies, smelling his sweat, settled on his brow and shoulders. They landed too softly for him to feel until they pricked his skin. One from under his armpit stung deeply. He squashed it dead. It was bright red with his blood.

'She's done no harm. Nothing's happened yet.'

'Exactly', said his father maddeningly.

But Mark knew what worried the old man. Since he had found the orphaned foal there had been no inquiry about any lost thoroughbred mare and its offspring. There had been no talk of such a thing on market days in the town. The foal's origins remained as mysterious as the lack of pursuit.

The new Inspector had not yet called again, and Lincoln could not visualise this latest adversary from Mark's description. Thus he could formulate no plans for dealing with a character who remained a threat, but invisible. Lincoln had known how far he could go with the predecessor now posted to a distant city. He had known the matters which most occupied him, and therefore when the police were most likely to be otherwise engaged. But what had this Inspector got in his mind? Having driven an hour across country to investigate the trivial business of the freed jenny, having quizzed Mark about Hygiene Departments, why had no more been seen of him?

The old man was missing his careful visits to the town. But he had no wish yet to show his suspected face. Mark, with no contacts, could not cope at market. Mark had no friends in fact, Lincoln suddenly realised. He skipped over the thought as if across a slippery rock.

The foal came in with her foster-mother late at night, so that she could enjoy the flyless cool of the summer evenings. She went out at dawn, too, skipping ahead of the old donkey. She teased the stout grey lady like a red-haired schoolgirl pestering a kindly nun, running rings of chestnut round the donkey's stolid centre. She bit at the donkey's mangey rump and fastened her white teeth in the donkey's neck. She could get down to the foster-mother's bag now only by bending her knees so far that she almost collapsed. Her neck came up like a hose-pipe to let her lips lock onto the donkey's teats.

The foal was now larger than her foster-mother, 'Either you tie the donk up while the foal eats,' Lincoln decided, 'Or you stand holding her. Or you think of some other way. You must get the filly weaned as

soon as possible.' He was tired from harvesting.

There was dew on the corn till the sun steamed it away. In those few hours, Mark had time to evolve a special manger. The foal had a longer, more flexible neck than her foster-mother. Her muzzle was narrower. So Mark removed one vertical panel high up on the back-wall of the byre and constructed on its far side a small wooden pot. By smearing the edges of the panel with the foal's food he persuaded her to reach up, lick and stick her nose through. She quickly began to eat. She learned in two minutes. Mark was delighted. 'She's so *clever*.'

Lincoln regarded his son sardonically. The boy's eyes sparkled. Like a mother with her child, Lincoln thought, adding as usual, like most mothers, that is. But Mark wasn't just maternal. He had an en-thusiasm about the young filly, not yet a passion but an effervescence, which resembled the starting love of a boy for a girl. This mixture of both sexes' instincts within his son intrigued the old man. He watched Mark's hand stroking the filly's legs. It was to accustom her to having her feet handled. The hard ground was fraying her little hooves. They would soon need trimming. But the curve of Mark's back, the length of his hair and the sensitivity in his long arms and slim fingers reinforced Lincoln's thought. The boy now was half-lover, half-mother. Lincoln shook his head and scowled across the meadow at the pair of them.

The filly felt the heat and the flies. Her scut of a tail was not yet below the curve of her quarters, but instinct kept it tick-tocking. Her small hooves stamped incessantly. She darted across the yellow grass from one shade pool into another. Her restlessness caused her to lose condition.

One glance at her from old Lincoln perched on the jolting reaper had told him so. He was waiting for Mark to act.

A scratching of guilt at a tiny locked shutter inside Lincoln's mind lingered since he had watched Mark stroking the filly's legs. Heredity could not be helped, he knew: the mother's genes were in his son for ill. But what he should be doing about bringing Mark up so conflicted with his self-interest that he would not face it. Why should he send the boy away? The phrase 'Let him free', squawked through Lincoln's mind like the passage of a gaudy jay through the woods. 'Freedom's where you find it', said Lincoln aloud, slapping down the long reins on his horses' straining rumps. 'Freedom's everywhere. You make it. You keep it.' But he was muttering to himself.

Sweat from Mark's cheekbones coursed into his mouth as he heaved over the sheaves. The sun, almost overhead, laid a plank of heat across his shoulder blades. Flecks of dead skin curled off them like tissue paper. He had hesitated to suggest a change of plan for the foal, incurring more trouble and expense. But seeing how his jeans hung off his own thinned waist now, falling below his belly button into the area of white, he called across to his father with an air of confidence, 'I ought to get in the foal in this heat. And turn her out at night.'

Old Lincoln's pared body lost no weight however hard he worked. He kept his rhythm swinging over the stooks and called back, 'Good idea. . . . But take her in . . . late at night, too . . . she'll need a dry bed to sleep on . . . growing things. . . .' Though he did not smile, Mark could hear the warmth in his voice like a dash of honey.

So Mark started leading the donkey in with the foal following as soon as the sun started to scorch the pastures. He fed them in the cool of the byre and the foal slept after eating. She would fold up with the small groan of an old man, drop off with her knees bent under her and her nose on the bed, and then finally slither down flat out. By the time Lincoln and Mark were drinking tea under the hedge-shade, the sun had ceased to burn. The cattle moved out of their lurking grounds beneath the trees and started to graze again. Then Mark jumped bareback on a pony and rode back to the farmyard to release the foal and her donkey.

The foal grew bold enough to dance ahead of the old donkey, roaming into the shrubberies and crashing through the undergrowth. She filled Mark with fear that she would snatch at yew or deadly nightshade berries, or fall into some ruin of the old gardens and break a leg. The harvest was nearly all in, and the pale blue burnished summer had started to splinter. The air thickened. Firm white puffball clouds ran off the eastern rim. Behind came grey wind from the south-west, making rain. They worked at a furious pace, starting earlier in the dewless dawns and stopping when quick storms gathered. They were asleep by nine. Mark said, banking up peat hunks to keep the glowing fire in, 'Soon as we've done harvesting, I must get her leading in and out. She'll do herself a mischief.'

He thought his father slept, but a quick spurt of flame caught the liquid of the old man's eyes. 'Shouldn't I?' Mark repeated.

'Should have started months ago', said Lincoln. 'She'll be a tartar

now.' He had never used the word before, nor remembered hearing it since a friend years ago had used it to warn him of Mark's mother. 'Tartar', repeated old Lincoln, rolling the word slowly round his mouth like a cherry pip he was preparing to spit out. He looked at Mark foolishly for recognition. The boy raised his eyebrows. Oh, damn him, thought Lincoln, but he looks like her. 'To catch a tartar,' said Lincoln in the mincing tones of a pedagogue, 'An unmanageable person, ferocious, one who turns the tables!' He concluded in his ordinary voice, 'That filly will be a tartar.' Then he closed his eyes with satisfaction: for the filly, he thought, will be Mark's growing up.

9

The foal became obsessive about her foster-mother. She bullied the old donkey until she got a reaction, used her teats when she thirsted, spurned her when she was bored, and kicked her heels cheerfully into the old grey flanks. But she would not be parted from her. 'You'll have a hell of a time weaning her,' said Lincoln to his son. There came over his face such a look of tenderness that Mark asked, 'Did I mind that much when my mother went?'

'You minded,' Lincoln said.

Mark watched. The old man was putting three shire horses in triple harness to his plough, for he was off to the steep banks to till the stubble. He did everything with such nimbleness. And patience with all animals, except with me, Mark thought. Because I must remind him of her.

Lincoln said, 'You'll have to find a place beyond earshot of each other. Or the old moke and the foal will scream the place down, hollering for each other like souls in hell. And that'll bring us unwanted visitors.' He clicked to his team and they pulled away towards the hills. On the ridge facing north, the beech leaves had begun to turn. Blotches of yellow, gold and brown glowed among the greenery. Of course, Mark thought, the haunted farm.

High on the ridge inside the forest, were the ruins of a farmhouse. It had been burned down by a band of vandals twenty years earlier.

Two of the youths, larking in the blaze, had fallen through the crackling floorboards into the cellars and there been baked to a malodorous death. Their screams, so far from bringing aid, had driven their companions shaking back to the town. Their tale reinforced the old curse.

A century earlier the farmer's daughter, made pregnant by a passing gypsy, had hanged herself from an iron hook on the beam which otherwise suspended the salted hams. Her parents had naturally threatened to cast her out. In her copper-plate hand she had inscribed a curse taught her by her romany lover. This she hung on the next black hook to the rope around her neck, damning 'whomsoever shall live upon this place.' Her father and the kindly farm labourer who had vainly loved her, found her swinging. They slashed the cord before reading her testament and, galloping with her body in a cart towards the town, had turned over the ridge, and been crushed to death with the horse. The widowed mother broke down and was confined, jabbering to her life's soiled end, in the enormous red-brick institution on the town's edge.

The farm was thus shunned. Only the outbuildings were visited by day, by neighbours seeking places in which to winter cattle.

The undergrowth which had sprung up between the house and the outbuildings had protected the latter from the vandal's fire. Their reed-thatched roofs had not been ignited by the darting sparks. The buildings were snug. Old Lincoln had 'borrowed' them for his cattle till his circumstances grew more difficult. He had brought Mark up to fear neither ghosts nor the curses of the dead.

So, since the outbuildings of the haunted farm were the only ones within a morning's ride and yet out of whinneying distance between the foal and the donkey, Mark rode up on a young work horse to investigate. The green horse was alarmed by every new sight and sound. The geese, spread across the apple-heavy orchard, terrified him. Mark's long legs kept him firmly going forward, bearing in on the flank which tried to break away.

The clap-clap of a white-barred wood-pigeon's wings, the shriek of a jay, the cock-a-cock-cock of a pheasant rocketing upwards from a ditch, all made the young horse leap and snort. By the time Mark reached the ridge he was physically tired and his mind was filled only with thinking ahead to anything else which might hide another terror for the horse.

31

So when the horse, emerging on the long open meadow which flanked the haunted farm, suddenly stopped dead again, Mark was furious. The meadow, pale yellow with overgrown grasses, seemed completely empty. 'Oh go *on*!' swore Mark, driving his heels against the horse's quaking sides. 'Rotten bloody windy thing you are!' Taking a hand off the reins he slapped the horse's rump. The sharp smack rang across the enclosed field like a rifle crack. It echoed back from the farm buildings. And with it came the sound of two human voices, a man's and a girl's. The words were indistinguishable. Mark's backbone froze. Had he still hairs down it, his hackles would have risen. The palms of his hands spurted a film of cold sweat. The ghost of that farmer's daughter. He stared and stared across the bleached meadow. But his heart-beats were booming so hard inside his ears that it drowned the distant words.

The enclosure of woods made an amphitheatre. The three sides of farm buildings made an enclosed stage of the stone foundations of the burned-down farmhouse. From this like a grey monument wreathed with ivy rose up the old chimney which had once been the central hearth. Onto this stage with a clear tap of feet appeared two figures. There was a tall man, wearing a hat with a wide brim pushed onto the back of his head, and a cloak flung over his shoulders with a swagger.

The heart of the young horse thumped against Mark's left ankle. But the animal made no attempt to whip round. He had seen the movement of these people before Mark had caught it. The morning light came over the goldening trees and the foundations of the haunted farm were bright. The people were too substantial for ghosts. Being real, they could be dangerous. Mark, having the sun behind him, was merged into the shadow of the beech forest. He reckoned he was safe to stay where he was to watch. The man in the cloak was too grandly dressed to have come even from the market town. But he did not seem anything like an official. His movements round the stone oblong were curiously stiff. He swung his arms about, jabbing and lifting them like the conductor of an orchestra. Though Mark had never seen anyone from another country, he assumed from the tall, cloaked gentleman's strange manner, that he must be foreign.

The girl, presumably his daughter, looked where the man pointed, moved to a corner of the old stones and herself made angles with her arms. Twice she made a great sweep and then touched her fingers in a

bow over her head. The action summoned up for Mark an old picture: a girl thus posed was making with her arms a basket's handle beneath which her long hair blew like sheaves of daffodils. The second time the girl did this the man crossed to her as swiftly as he could, and Mark saw that he was lame.

Mark's heart had quickly settled. He caught the mood of their conversation which was of quick excitement, but not its words. But the man's footfalls on the stone foundations sounded more than uneven: they tapped across as if from a horse who had cast a shoe. The man moved and caught the girl up in his arms and Mark thought he might fall. But the foreigner was adept. He spun on his sound leg and his artist's hat was tipped off the back of his head by the girl's body turning in his arms. The man, Mark saw, was elderly. The hair where his hat had been was grey. It surrounded like a nest – and the sunlight shone on the pinkness of it – a small bald patch.

'Oh, Pop!' called out the girl in the middle of laughter.

The man's voice, slightly foreign and very forceful, came clearly across the grassland. 'Very well. We shall do it together.' The phrase uneasily echoed in Mark's mind his discussion about the filly on the first day he found her.

Neither then, nor until a long time later did Mark find the man's tone of voice unpleasant. Rather the reverse. It did not seem to possess brutality. It sounded musical even, but it was resonant with an extraordinary authority.

10

Lincoln's three plough-horses cropped the grass on the headland. Their muzzles and cheekbones pushed against one another's, and ears were laid back as their cropping-order was reaffirmed.

Old Lincoln was hopping about like a cock robin defending its territorial sphere of influence. 'Why *not* find out? Why *not*?' he snapped at Mark.

The boy had been compelled to get off the young horse. First it had minced to and fro, shaking its head so that he could not concentrate

33

on telling his father about the strangers on the ruined farm. Then Lincoln, suddenly incensed by what he saw as his son's incompetence, had shouted, quite out of character, 'And get down off my horse, will you? Who are you to talk down to me!'

This ridiculous urban attitude, legacy of mounted knights and serfs, had been for so long a joke between them, that Mark had laughed. 'Oh, come on, father –'

'Get down this instant! You can't ride one side of him anyway. And you're using what wits you do have trying to do *that*. What make of car did they have, I asked. Was the number from hereabouts? Where do they *come* from?'

'I told you: I daren't get close enough to see. How could I anyway with –'

The young horse, already excited by the events of the morning, and anxious to reach the plough horses, suddenly tugged the reins in Mark's hand, and tipped him foolishly forward.

'How the hell,' Mark demanded, 'could I know there'd be anyone at the haunted farm? I did try to get this fool horse closer. To listen for more. To look. But he *would* not go.'

'Frightened or bloody-minded?' Lincoln, even in anger, could be momentarily diverted by considering the psychology of horses.

'Frightened. Spooked.'

There were unworldly things in their own house: steps where no landing still existed; the controlled, quiet shutting of the bedroom door where one squire had neatly shot his brains out. But no door remained and the room's floorboards had long fallen down. Echoes of time took no cognizance of wood or brick. Spirits of things repeated, imprints of people and of animals long dead, were quite accepted by Lincoln and his son.

'Well, that girl's ghost's up there. The poor hanged cursing daughter.'

Lincoln's blue eyes were wide and turned upwards through the beeches to the ridge. His head traversed to and fro as if his instincts, like radar, needed to move through an arc. He asked very quickly, 'What was this girl like?'

'Very fond of her father,' Mark said. 'Happy.' He moved his free hand up and up like a fountain. 'Bubbling. No, sparkling,' he said. Then added, surprisingly as things were to turn out, 'It felt a *good* day.'

34

Because Mark had described the man in much more detail, Lincoln surmised that he had found the girl attractive and had curbed any description lest he was mocked. 'Small,' Mark now expanded. 'A lot of fair hair, but long, not thick. Fair like oats; not barley.'

Neither smiled at the simile: the countryside was their palette. But his father still expected more. Mark excused himself, 'I've no idea how old. How d'you tell with girls even close to? Anything from seventeen to twenty-three.'

'Odd figures.'

'Well, older than me, I felt that.'

'You're very young,' said his father fondly. 'And there's no harm in that.' Before Mark could pursue this line, Lincoln asked, 'And their car was large?'

Mark nodded. 'And expensive and foreign. Shiny sort of an estate-car. Boards in the back.'

'Boards? With writing? Notices?' Notices meant government proclamations, official ordinances, restrictions, threats.

Mark thought not. He'd seen no writing. 'They were stacked up. Squares and oblongs.'

The old man was shaking his head, his first hint of irritation. 'Then they came out of the buildings,' Mark went on, '*exactly* where I wanted to put the filly foal. And they walked again over the burned farm, corner to corner. As if they were doing a dance. The father with the lame leg was pacing.'

'They were measuring the bloody place up for a house!' shouted old Lincoln, face scarlet and eyes bulging. 'Here on our ridge within a few miles. Friends'll come. Ramblers,' he spat with the countryman's intolerance of urban tourists who can see landscape only as a transient backcloth to their holidays. 'Bang-bang,' mimicked Lincoln, mouth screwed up. 'Popping off at poor bloody blackbirds. And *looking* everywhere.'

'It's not our ridge,' said Mark mildly, but tactlessly. 'I'll find somewhere else for the filly when —'

'Damn the filly! If these creatures rebuild the haunted farm — and God will damn them if they do — there'll be officials sliming round here like snakes again. After us. And that'll be that, this time.'

Mark saw his father's eyes were wet from a mixture, he supposed, of anger and frustration. But Lincoln, who dreaded death for the punishments he knew awaited his soul, was weeping now from a

35

singular premonition of loss.

'All this,' he said in a small voice, 'gone.' He moved his hands and arms outwards as if placing a wreath on a memorial, and then down, as if casting the first earth handful into a grave. But the movement embraced the half-ploughed slope, half terracotta ridges, half stubble. On the freshly-turned plough the earth, smooth from the shares, gleamed like pottery. Below, towards their house, the first gulls in from the far distant sea were swooping down.

'To the gods we're grubs,' said Lincoln, 'They're just the white gulls happening to pass over, seeing the earth disturbed, swooping here and there.' He snapped his fingers helplessly.

Out of the dense girdle of ornamental trees, a wisp of pale blue smoke arose from the only one they used of the battalion of proud chimneys. Even this chimney stack had crumbled, shortened and become invisible from the far slope of the valley. The ash-blue question mark of smoke arose without a seen source. To old Lincoln it seemed forlorn, a symbol of their own impermanence. To Mark however the smoke still rising from their constant hearth seemed a slender banner of hope.

He encouraged his father in the best way he knew. 'The filly's got more sense in one leg,' he declared, 'even as a foal, than this common three-year-old's got in all his stupid frame.' He watched Lincoln's head.

His father looked round. 'Um,' he said, going to his team of horses, calling them up, and picking up their reins to raise them from the headland and to turn them round. In anger or in despair he was never other than gentle with his horses. He too much resembled them.

Mark let him turn the team. The lead horse in the centre leant upon one, pulled upon the other of his mates and round they came. It was beautifully done. His father knew it and his face lightened. He called out over the jingling, more as an apology for his outburst than as a divulgence of his plans, 'She's a nice foal. She might make something—'

Mark shouted, 'We could break her and train her and run her in races!'

His father flapped the long reins on his horses' straining quarters in what looked like a shrug. Then he turned his head back as the team walked away down the long stubble and the plough-shares clove into it. 'Well, why not?' he sang out.

36

Mark sprang up again on the youngster's back, scrabbling over the withers, finding his stirrup-irons in a flash and getting a grip on the horse's whole frame which he had not found all day.

'Ah,' he cried, driving the horse up into its bridle with his long legs. 'We will!' he shouted to his father and, making at last a good job of it, he cantered on homewards downhill. The horse's hooves swished through the stiff stubble. Then their rattling on the occasional flint died away at the foot of the slope.

I I

But, as his father had forecast, Mark had let the filly run loose too long. Unused to anything round her head, she resented the head-collar. She saw no point in being caught, collared and directed. To avoid capture she lurked behind the donkey in the byre. Then, as Mark stole forwards with his scoop of oats, she nipped at him with her teeth, or loosed out with her sharp feet. One morning she caught him achingly between his legs. Doubled-up, he cursed her, 'You bitch! You bloody bitch!' He came at her round the donkey's flanks, headcollar raised to flog her with it.

But the thought flashed: If I hit her with this, she'll object to it even more. So he slapped her high across her neck with the palm of his hand. Astonished, she squeaked and stood. Mark's palm smarted. He transferred the headcollar to it and growling at her – 'arararh!' swung at her quarters with his other palm. She sprang neither for-wards, backwards nor away, but vertically, stiff-legged, upwards. Her eyes, wide open, stared at him amazed. She breathed sharply. Mark grinned. She had not flinched. She stood still. Putting his right arm round her neck he slipped the little noseband firmly over her muzzle. She stood rock-steady. He did up the buckle behind her ears which, so far from being laid back in fear or anger, remained cocked and interested. She admires me, thought Mark in triumph.

He wanted to hug her, but again restrained himself. There would be no more spoiling. 'Good girl,' he said gruffly. He patted her shoul-der. So tall men in tweed suits had patted his mother in those days

37

when they and he had caught her vexedly in tears. They had intended encouragement. He had heard that in their voices over his head. They had been, he knew clearly even as a little boy, in his mother's team, not in his father's.

With the foal's rope in his right hand and holding the quiet donkey with his left, Mark set out for the field.

The filly walked for a few hundred yards as demurely as a novice nun. Then, opposite the plantation in which she had been enjoying regular run-arounds she gave a preliminary snort, flung up her head, tugged at the rope and began to swing her quarters round at Mark. But she was watching him now with calculation. Would he duck away? Slap her, he could not, with his left hand holding the donkey. He growled at her. She immediately ceased to pull, straightened up, and arched her neck so prettily, going forward so kindlily once more, that Mark murmured, 'You minx. You wicked minx. I love you.' The filly, by a quick dart of her eye towards him, showed that she, too, was amused. Her tail was half-lofted like a stiffly held orange brush, showing she was merry.

His father, leisurely stirring the soup in the black cauldron, viewed Mark's enthusiasm quizzically. 'You learned a little about handling women this morning,' he pronounced, skimming the film of fat from the popping surface of the broth. 'It would be better to wean her absolutely. Take her right away from the moke.' He chopped downwards with his left hand as on an umbilical cord which had not naturally parted.

But Mark wished not just to show his mastery of the filly-foal. He wanted to give her himself to depend upon, in the place of the donkey. So he persuaded her to be led for longer and longer walks. Several times Mark made his way hopefully to the farm ruins on the ridge. 'I need to check,' he explained to his father, 'exactly where I can put the filly.' But he had not glimpsed the strangers again up in the woods.

Twice there were signs of further visits. First, tyre-marks after rain one weekend and the butt of an old cigar smelling bitter as iron-filings. Then more sinisterly, white-painted markings at the angles of the foundations of the farm. 'They've been measuring it up,' said Lincoln grimly. Mark said to encourage him, 'They'll not do any building till the spring. With these frosts . . .' Rime lay like shiny salt in the shadows of the stones. Mark saw a small fur object crouched

like a stiff mouse. It was the girl's glove. Frost had made its fur erect. The leather was as rigid as a corpse. Yet inside the wool was as soft as a lamb's. Mark put his nose inside and breathed in. It smelled of the green lime-trees which the bees love in bluest summer. His eyes were closed in bliss. When he opened them his father was watching him. Mark glared. 'It's the girl's glove.' He was daring old Lincoln to touch it.

'How d'you know?' asked his father reasonably, putting out his long hand to examine it. Mark held it petulantly back, then grinned. He was ridiculous. He tossed the glove at his father like a dead mole, and said, 'Oh, it's that girl's all right.'

Once more Mark led the foal up to the haunted farm, 'to accustom her to it.' It was a morning of brilliant hoar-frost when even the pheasants' broad arrow-feet printed clearly. There was still no trace of the girl. Some of their own old wheat straw was in the barn, dry as summer thatch. Lincoln had planned that the haunted farm could be their last redoubt when the officials came finally to evict them. Mark used four sheaves to make a deep bed for the foal. She walked behind him as he made her bed. As he bent to spread the sheaves she rubbed her muzzle against him. Occasionally her small, perfectly even white teeth would nibble him lovingly as a girl might. She no longer bit. Quick backhanded slaps across her muzzle had taught her exactly how far she could go.

'I've made her bed,' Mark told his father. 'If it doesn't look like freezing or blowing tonight, I'll take her up.'

'Why aren't you off now then?' his father asked at breakfast.

Mark had prepared his defence. 'She won't settle up there by day. Cooped up in daylight, it wouldn't be natural for her.'

'But by day you could watch her,' said old Lincoln shrewdly. Knowing Mark's purpose, he was teasing him.

Mark looked shifty. 'If she's out all day first, she'll be tired by evening. Ready to sleep.'

'Take your blanket, then!' said his father, seeing through him. They both laughed.

The sun, scarlet, was flaring across the great coverlet of beech leaves when Mark and the filly-foal walked under them and into darkness. A frost, just starting, made last spring's leaf-fall crackle under their feet. Some of this winter's leaves would hang bronze but papery onto the beech-branches till next spring's winds stripped them. But the oaks and elms were already as bare as spiders. Round their tops a smokey congregation of rooks was cawing.

The farm ruins themselves would, to urban ears, have seemed silent. But the sparrows were tucking up in the tattered thatch with a thousand soft scratchings. Scuffles whispered everywhere as the mice and rats started to patter out. Silhouetted pheasants roosted on the ridge of the one bare barn. Occasionally a long tail was flicked, a wing shaken out with a soft flap. Then on the arrival of Mark and the foal one cock-pheasant, haughty as a toastmaster, rocketted off against the ruby sky expostulating, 'Uck-uck-uck-uck!'

The filly shied violently. She trotted loose across the muddy yard and sprang snorting towards the foundations of the farm. Then she spooked at its tall grey chimney-stack, and there stopped dead. 'Feels the girl's ghost,' thought Mark, stealing up on her.

He caught her swinging rope and led her into the strawed box. A blackbird which had used the old cattle manger for its summer-nest burst protestingly out of the doorway. Mark slid across the three wooden bars, turning the stall into a four-sided stable. Then he slung up the foal's hay into the old rack to keep her occupied while he went to the dew-pond to draw her a bucket of water. There was the slimmest glaze of ice on the pond's muddy lip. As he was leaning outwards to scoop up some cleaner water, the last rush of returning starlings in whirring hundreds filled the sky above his head. They made a black sweep like a waterspout as, babbling, they started to settle. Their movement, solid yet fluid from their thousand feathered molecules, put Mark in mind instantly of the girl dancing here on the stone flags. He wondered: what'll they do for water.

The foal whinneyed imperiously when she heard Mark's footsteps. He climbed in past her and put down the water-bucket in a corner. She sucked down a quick cold draught. He lodged the feed bucket in the other corner and she snatched two bites of corn, nuzzled Mark, strode three times around the straw, stuck her head over the rails again, neighed twice, and then listened anxiously. But her donkey foster-mother was too far away. The foal, head cocked, waited in vain for an answer.

Mark had not reckoned that with him for company the foal would continue her tread-mill circling of the box. He could not find a safe place to settle. She trampled over his blanket. 'Shut up!' he shouted at last, slapping her, furious that she was not content with him. The filly was affronted. She halted and stared at him. But she did not relax. She reduced her caged pacings to a slower stalk, eyeing him resentfully as if he had now reduced her to a life-time of mourning gaol. He climbed up the straw stack, lugged four more sheaves back to one corner and made himself a triangular nest in the inside corner of her box.

She paced, pushed at the rails and whinneyed. She rustled, traipsed and neighed. 'Oh shut up, for God's sake!' cursed Mark pulling his blanket over his head. It then occurred to him, as a sop to his pride, that the ghost of the farmer's daughter must be disturbing his filly. He got up to test the night-air. It was suddenly colder at the building's entrance. He looked at the ruined farm and gasped. The great chimney-stack was shining like a luminous monument. It glowed with a silvery light, then faded. Mark looked upwards. There was the faintest movement in the mist. The moon above had shafted through a gap and touched the pale stones of the stack. He waited. The dark night drowsed. Distantly a fox yapped.

He returned to the straw, stroking the foal along her little sprouting mane. She crested her neck like a cat raising its back. Mark climbed into his corner.

He dozed and was awoken by her, and dozed again. He dreamed, half-rocking, between sleep and waking, confusing the filly, the girl and the ghost from the farm, all of whom needed his help. But his aid meant too long, too cold, a stretch from his warm nest.

Dawn began in a shimmer of oyster coloured lightness through the gaps in the walls. The foal was sleeping soundly with her back to the sheaves surrounding him. He did not dare touch her, but turned and dived at last into oblivious sleep.

13

The sun came, warmed the wooden doorposts of the byre and lapped over the cobbles in a little pool. But it suffused Mark's dark corner so gradually and he was so tired that it did not stir him. The filly, too, though the sunlight touched first her folded legs and then her thinly-coated belly, did not get up. Raising her head she peered over the straw sheaves at Mark, and content now to find him still with her, stretched out again and slept.

What woke Mark was not the sun's beams at last touching his eyelids, but their sudden extinction. The temperature, as by a cloud, instantly fell. Mark blinked. The doorway was filled with a shadow. It was the black shape of a girl. The light from behind her shone through her fair hair, as it did through the ivy tendrils round the doorframe. Her hair glowed like an aureole, but her face and body were in shadow. She wore a high-collared loose coat and trousers thrust into high boots. There flashed into Mark's mind a character from his school play: a boy's part acted by a girl on the point of leaving. Mark, three ridiculed years her junior, had agonisingly adored her. He dreamed that he guarded her door and fought her dragons. She had spared his dark yearning eyes only the sparest of merry glances as she swept past him, arms linked with the two youths with whom the school said she slept conjointly.

Once at rehearsal, (he was playing – his teacher's public joke – a speechless peasant), she had asked Mark to fetch her book. He had run till his twelve-year-old ribs ached, and returned holding the paperback, to find her gone. It was a silly romance, but he read it twice, feeling that thereby he might at least enter her mind.

Mark blinked in the stable corner. He was astonished that, even when the filly noisily shot out her forelegs ready to spring up, the girl in the doorway barely moved. Though Mark could not see her eyes, the set of her head, which had just flinched at the foal's scrabbling, showed she was simply staring at what, in that long deserted farmyard, must seem the strangest of animals.

The filly, meanwhile, stared back at the girl. She, too was more interested in than alarmed by the other creature's unlikely appearance. Mark, hidden by the foal's body and his nest of sheaves, crouched still as a hare. The filly at last arched her neck and extended one long hindleg backwards in the horse's dual act of stretching. She then moved leisurely towards the three rails.

The girl breathed out, 'Oh'. There were two tones in her voice: one of a girl's delight in a pretty kitten; the other of a woman's pleasure in an exciting view. She stepped forward into the byre and Mark saw that she was indeed the dancing girl he had seen before across the meadow. Delight filled him, as when he had successfully stalked a fallow-deer, or when, after weeks of struggle, a recalcitrant horse suddenly rode sweetly for him. The girl extended both her hands to the filly. 'Oh, what a darling . . .' she said quietly. Her voice was not of the region, and sounded younger than her shape suggested.

She was confident, and therefore gentle. Mark saw with pleasure from the flatness of her palms and the slowness with which she stretched out her arms that she understood horses. Her head was now in profile against the morning light and Mark saw that what he had hoped for from that first view of her across the meadow was blessedly true: she was beautiful. Her small head was tilted forwards over the foal, making a gentle sweep of her spine and neck. Her eyes were lowered. Long eyelashes, far darker than her hair, overlapped her cheeks. Her tongue's tip had popped out in concentration to press against her teeth and upper lip.

Mark had raised himself up too much to stare at her. She suddenly glanced left, full-face towards him. Her eyes, startled, were enormous. She drew her head back and one arm. Her other hand was still extended abstractedly towards the foal. Because the girl might, like any other wild thing, be frightened away, Mark rose up as slowly as the filly, and as slowly as the girl had approached the foal. Finally he was kneeling behind the straw sheaves, head and shoulders and his old sweater showing over them.

The girl turned swiftly and called back through the doorway, not loudly, but urgently, 'Pop! Pop, come, can you?' It was the calm, firm tone Mark's father used when there had been an accident to an animal. She had called too softly, though. There was no reply. From somewhere behind the buildings Mark heard the drone of three men's voices in earnest discussion.

Before she could call out again, Mark said swiftly, 'I'm very sorry to frighten you –'

'But you didn't.' The girl smiled. 'Not frighten. Surprise. I was

43

sure you were another foal.' Then she laughed. 'A smaller one, I thought. And brown.' With fingers spread as if sketching she traced the line of his head, long hair, sweeping back.

Mark smiled. 'Well . . .,' he began.

'Goodness, your teeth are white!' She stared at him with pleasure. 'Why aren't you at school? Have you run away?'

'No.' Mark stood up. 'I'm sorry if you think I've broken in. But – we – I didn't think that anyone –'

The girl's hand flew to her mouth and cupped it. She was blushing. One cheek flooded pink in the light. 'I'd no idea! I thought, I suppose with the foal, that you were a child.'

'I'm seventeen.'

'Yes', making a movement with both hands upwards like a tree to suggest he was more an oak than a sapling, 'I can see now. But,' she complained, 'you were crouching. Only *seventeen*?' she added, with what Mark took to be politeness.

'And', he said, equally politely, 'a half.'

Her eyebrows, very mobile, now shot upwards. Her eyes opened vastly. Mark suspected that she mocked him, but when she laughed it was not against him. She made him feel that they shared a joke about his mistaken identity. 'So you work somewhere on a farm?' Perhaps, she thought, this too, was wildly wrong and equally insulting. In these wilds no one could tell who anyone was. He did not immediately reply. She tried again. 'Or are a student?' She pulled an earnest face and made scribbling signs with her hand, so that it could be a joke, if he took it so.

'Sort of.' Before she could ask anything else, Mark countered, 'Have you bought this . . . old farm now?' He had been about to call it 'The Haunted Farm'.

The girl nodded. 'To do up. For a country place.'

Mark felt pleasure so bloom in him that he smiled. Then, quick as a cloud-shadow, came anxiety. They'd be here too close, a danger. And yet not always. 'A country place' meant only for visits, surely. The rich could still do that, he had heard.

The man's voice was calling, 'Tess? Tess! Are you communing with rustic mice?'

'We've our first visitors, Pop. Come and see.' She said to Mark, making a courteous introduction. 'He's a painter. He's making a studio here.'

44

She thought with disappointment that the boy looked more alarmed than pleased. Possibilities flipped like cards dealt swiftly: he was either simple, or a crook, or a hunted gypsy. To reassure him she added a small untruth. 'It'll only be a weekend place. Those are the builders.'

Feet squelched, then clumped across the yard. Mark heard the limping foot. The man, darkening the doorway, came through. Putting his hand in that same gesture on the girl's shoulders, so that he was both supporting and supported, he asked in a ringing voice, 'Where did you spring from? Up the well? Are you a subterranean Water Baby?'

'Is there a well?' Mark asked. He had meant to be quick about Mrs Do-as-you-would-be-done-by or whoever she was, but the exact names from the book escaped him. He sounded weak, he considered crossly.

'You don't know it?' The man was genuinely surprised, not scornful. Mark shook his head, 'I'd been wondering. . . .' he began.

The man said authoritatively, 'We couldn't live here otherwise. The shaft was right in the hall of the old house. We'll pump it up with a motor. . . .' but he was looking with affection at the girl. Then, making a stiff bow at Mark while tapping the girl's shoulder, he asked with mocking courtesy, 'But you, sir, will you be staying long?' As the girl had looked, so did he sound, thought Mark, like a character from an old play.

The girl Tess did not, however, laugh. Instead, she smiled at Mark, including him.

Mark flushed. 'I'd not have stayed one night at all, if I'd known you'd come – if we'd heard that anyone had bought the place. It's been empty all my life.'

'That' said the man in the tone of a schoolmaster correcting an uppish boy, 'I *can* well believe.'

Mark was unaware that in his youth he owned age's unbuyable desire. So he could not see why he needed repressing by this man with the wide hat. He said shortly, 'It was to wean this foal.'

'We – an?' the man repeated. His accent fell heavily on the unknown word, making it into two syllables, and became quite foreign. But Mark had no idea of the man's provenance.

'To take her off her mother's milk,' the girl explained.

The painter made such an elaborate shrug of exasperation that he

45

almost toppled. 'Her? That? It? Mother?' he asked. 'What the devil is it all about, this business?'

Mark started to explain, but he was nervous under the man's stare of incomprehension. He stammered. When he came to the donkey foster-mother part he turned to the girl. She had been watching him closely. When he looked straight at her, earnestly explaining, she thought, Those eyes are marvellous, wild, innocent, and said aloud, 'I love the donkey bit.'

'Religious romanticism,' said the man. 'We shall have Chesterton next and the entry into Jerusalem!' He sounded sarcastic, but less angry, since he now controlled the situation. 'So this foal must be kept apart from her mother until they forget one another?'

Mark nodded. The girl's father was sharp, he thought.

The painter swung the girl half-towards him and said emphatically, 'And that we do understand. Very well.' The girl laughed. 'Oh, yes,' she said, 'The cursed maternal link.' Mark had no notion of what they meant. But the whole mood had lightened. Just as when storm clouds without even disgorging, roll away, the air freshened. Mark said, 'Of course, I'll take her away now . . .'

But the man interrupted him with a bestowing flourish of the hand. 'Don't concern yourself. Be my guest.' He waved round the delapidated byre. 'We can't possibly be in residence till the spring.' It was as if, having suddenly won some contest (which had escaped Mark), he was now playing the magnanimous victor. 'Can we, Mr Turpin?' he shouted back into the yard, 'Can we be living here before the spring, Mr Turpin?'

'Oh no, Mr Salerno', came the rough voice of the builder. He found his client's ideas flamboyant and Mr Salerno moved so swiftly – 'from faucet to facet' as his assistant quipped – that Turpin the builder welcomed the respite while he sorted out his plans. He called out anxiously, 'Up in these wilds, God knows what we'll find.'

'Or won't find more likely', said the voice of his assistant. 'These terrible tracks for one thing.' The younger builder had an apartment on the city's outskirts. His new block had two plane trees emerging neatly from two cement bollards. Two trees were perfectly sufficient, thought Mr Turpin's assistant. There was nothing like concrete for a clean job.

Privately Mr Turpin agreed. The idea of living beyond a town's conveniences and security, cut off by miles of dangerous forest inaccessible in winter, was enough to give him nightmares. But he was anxious to keep the renowned artist's custom. Some fame would rub off. There could be recommendations to other rich clients desiring Rustic Retreats. Turpin consequently murmured platitudinously about Nature's Quiet Corners.

The girl, putting her lips to the artist's ear, whispered. 'One thing I *will* say about Inspiration . . .'

As if in a part-song Turpin chimed in: 'About Inspiration what I *will* say is that One *never* knows where it'll spring from.' His assistant keenly took up the theme: the brainwave he had enjoyed about double-backed sanitation in the municipal buildings had come to him when squatting in the railway station toilets.

The man and the girl looked at one another, splendidly lit up by smiles, and flushed by bottled laughter. The man rubbed her hair and squeezed her. With his arm still proprietorially around her waist he asked Mark, over his shoulder, 'But we hardly know each other, sir. Your name would be. . . .?'

'Mark.'

Before the painter could press him, the girl interposed, 'And I'm Tess.'

'And I', said the artist, 'am Random Salerno.'

It was declaimed in the mock-turtle manner of public speaking introductions but, for all that, Mr Salerno awaited Mark's impressed gaze and nod of recognition.

Tess watched Mark. He said carefully, 'We've never had modern paintings at all, I'm afraid, and only one old one left.'

Mr Salerno found this so amusing that he laughed aloud for the first time. His laugh was very deep and, coming up from his belly, was that of a fitter, younger man. But it sounded genuine and was not unkind.

'Well, who knows', laughed Random Salerno, already hearing himself recount to his portly continental agent the words of this gypsy boy, 'You may win a lottery one day!' But he saw that even this made no sense to the peasant. He said irritatedly, 'I must get back to Turpin and his measurements.' He limped towards the doorway. In it, and without looking back he enquired, 'Shall you stay long, Mr Mark? You and your horse?'

'A few days, if I could —'

47

'And then do you both vanish down the well?'

Tess, partly to save Mark embarrassment, but mainly because now she did not wish to know where he sprang from, began, 'He'll be away into his woods.' It was romantic. She would not have him live in a numbered tenement. If she had possessed girl-friends, she would have enjoyed describing him to them as something mysterious. Relic from the past, she thought suddenly, staring at him.

'. . . folding my blanket', Mark was ending, 'we'll gratefully steal away.'

Mr Salerno looked round in some surprise then, nodding, disappeared into the sunlight. He immediately resumed the building discussion at the precise item at which he had interrupted it. His voice floated back, 'so, Mr Turpin, the tower round the stack will have forty risers or forty-six depending on the inner depth of the balcony . . .' Turpin could be heard in strict tempo agreement.

'The rampart,' Mr Salerno's instructions continued, 'to be solid and capped with grey copings . . .' His voice became obscured by walls.

Mark asked the girl. 'You don't mind?'

Tess, thinking about Salerno, looked puzzled.

'Our staying just a few days,' Mark explained.

'Gracious, no,' said Tess, adapting herself. 'I like it very much, Mark.' The creature was an attractive addition to the new place. He was watching her. She added, 'Will you have a little of our picnic?'

Mark said immediately, 'Oh no. I've got to get home to work on the farm.'

She saw that he had started to point down hill. That's where then, she thought. And then: but that's even further into the wilds. Probably he *is* on the run . . .

'To help with the animals', he was explaining, thinking she doubted what there was to do on a farm between winter ploughing and spring sowing.

'But the foal?' she asked.

'She's settled now. I'll feed her before I go and then come back this evening.'

'I'll feed her at noon', said Tess, 'Before we go.' She was pleased to surprise him with her knowledge. 'Better', she said firmly. 'Little and often.'

But he was not surprised at her knowing this. In his world, nature

48

and animals were naturally understood. His astonishment was that she would leave so soon. He was sharply disappointed. How could people drive from a distant city – a day perhaps further than his furthest point, their market town – and then, after a morning, turn and drive away again.

So it came easily to ask, 'When will you be back?'

The girl shrugged. 'He flies all over the world. I'm not my own mistress. But he'll keep coming back to bully the builders. You might be here still, you mean?'

'Not still', said Mark. 'But I will certainly come again.' He gave her a look of such direct admiration that she was amazed to feel herself blushing again. She said busily, 'I'll give the filly her feed then, if you'll leave it in the bucket.' She held her hand out. 'Goodbye then. For a while.'

Before Mark could say anything else and had only touched her fingers when he meant really to squeeze her hand, she called out 'Pop – I'm coming. I want to talk about that balcony too.'

14

Old Lincoln had not, he declared, ever heard of any Random Salerno. Still angered by the advance of the artist's plans and the confirmed threat to their flank, he made a broadcast movement round the cracked panels of the great room. 'We'd nothing modern here', he said with scorn.

'They were modern once, father.'

'Two hundred years ago!'

Nothing now hung upon any wall. Above the marble fireplace but painted directly onto the panelling was a late eighteenth century landscape with figures. The picture showed the house and its demesne in the height of its tended glory. The figures were those of aristocrats. A fête champêtre, celebrating a coming-of-age, was in decorous swing between those clipped yew hedges which had now revolted into their bitter, dark-green wilderness. Nymphs and shepherds appeared, divinely suspended, just above the camomile grass lawns which a score of gnarled and bent labourers had been hand-scything all that summer of the 1780's. The ladies and gentlemen included Mark's mother's ancestors. The smoke from the fire was steadily obliterating even the sharpest of their features. The pleasure which this gave Lincoln, coupled with the impossibility of dismantling the picture to sell it, had ensured its solitary survival.

Mark could recall from his childhood the glow of pictures lit by special lights in the hall, this drawing room and in the dining room. They made windows from his worried reality onto several hundred magic worlds. A book had existed in the library (where surplus hay was now stored) written in copper-plate hand in ink turned russet black. It catalogued all the pictures, listing their arrival by inheritance, purchase, or in lieu of gambling debts. Even in Mark's youth many had gone to pay accounts. His mother had taken stacks away with the furniture in those pantechnicons that misty Monday when his father had fired his shotgun at the vans and been bowled over by them like a rabbit into the then neat banks of rhododendrons.

'Yes,' said Lincoln, 'we were all modern once.'

Dusk was filtering in through the broken windows like a whisper. They had not yet lit a lamp. The fire's brightness grew.

'I'm modern now', said Mark.

'Oh no', his father pronounced with gravity, 'That you are not.'

'I'm young –' Mark began, but he knew before his father could point out his error, that modernity and youth; were far from the same thing. He could not tell from time to time whether this more pleased than saddened him. The two elements within him rose and fell.

'Your artist friends are modern', said Lincoln. 'The bold Salerno's are exceedingly modern.' On Lincoln's tongue the word became perjorative. It echoed exactly in Mark's mind a constant phrase of his mother's: 'Exceedingly common'. It had been more and more often used against his father, and uttered not in anger, but with that steely contempt of hers which Mark had so acutely dreaded. No one at school, no teacher nor bigger boy nor girl had been so capable of reducing him to the pale mute acceptance of a grub before a gaudy woodpecker.

'From all you say', his father persisted, to disturb Mark's sad-faced reverie, 'those people, with their flying about and great cars and weekend cottages and builders and extraordinary clothes, are *exactly* what being foreign and exceedingly modern mean.'

'Yes', said Mark. 'But they're romantic, too.'

Over the long nights of the passing winter his father had ceased to tease him about the girl Tess. There had been no new fuel to make the joke flare up. Lincoln supposed unhappily that Mark, too, would grow up and leave him alone in this place, running away with someone else. The boy might as well be fired by this artist's daughter as by anyone else. Mark had seen few girls since he had left school. Except, of course, on market days. He was on the point of asking Mark about the sleazy hotel in the Market Square where officials, farmers, and salesmen obtained brief relief and occasional disease when Mark said, 'I don't mean the girl alone. I mean them both flying across the world, seeing cities in strange lands. Meeting whole packs of different people, foreigners with weird names. Mixing with rich, clever, dashing people. Wearing splendid clothes. Being able to –' he spread his hands and whisked them across his chest – 'move on magic carpets.' He added, 'Which they do, hopping into different lives. As I used to, reading books, looking into the old pictures. As other people do now, I suppose, with the television.'

'It would be an extraordinary life', old Lincoln remarked, hoisting the blackened billycan of tea onto its customary marble protuberance. He gave the fire a rousting with the long coach-horn. 'Awfully lonely: city streets and concrete hotels. Not for me.' To demonstrate the advantages of their existence he selected a log of cherry wood from the broken hole in the wainscot and positioned it on the fire's pink peak. Its pied bark flaked, curled and immediately its aroma wafted out into the dark room like scented kisses.

'I should like one day to see those things though', Mark said.

Expectedly his father commented, 'If wishes were horses, beggars would ride.'

Irritated, Mark said cruelly, 'I too could marry a rich woman.'

But his father neither flinched nor rose. 'Only fools never learn from family experience', he commented mildly. Then, 'Has the girl Tess got a mother?'

'She's never there. They joke about her. Mr Salerno does her like a clucking hen.' Mark mimicked him and his father smiled. 'I suppose Mr Salerno and Tess's mother are divorced and that she fusses . . .' Mark's experience had not suggested that one divorced parent could talk cheerfully about the other. Lincoln said coldly, 'Your mother did not exactly, ever, fuss about you.'

'No.' So it fell always, the chilly and now so pointless splash of gloom. Mark would never see her. Or might I, he wondered, if I too could ever get away? He wouldn't try to meet her. But if I reached some foreign city where, he supposed, she still kept lovers, mightn't I very well bump into her? Observe her anyway. See what she looked like now, eleven years of no photographs, and only hard words, later. She is part of *me* after all, he decided, if that's the same as my being, without choice, part of her.

'Which reminds me', his father remarked, tossing onto the fire the sticks he had just splintered in his fist, 'If this warm weather holds and spring has really sprung we should return that donk.'

The foal had stayed ten days up on the haunted farm, had hollered less frequently for her donkey over the first three days and then not at all. If she pined it was, Mark knew, only for someone to play with, to chivvy and nip. Leading her about in the grey, empty meadow behind the haunted farm she had been skittish at both ends: snapping at his arm with her teeth, hunching up and swinging her woolly rounded chestnut quarters at him. She was, as the old man had forecast, already a bit of a tartar.

She could probably have come home within a week without igniting the old urges, but Mark wanted to see Tess again the following Sunday. While Mr Salerno spent the day with the builders, Tess had not just talked to Mark, but had walked with him and the filly round and round the long meadow. It had rained in grey veils. Then she had asked him to their picnic in the car. The seat he sat in smelt so strongly of Tess that Mark could barely contain himself. Mr Salerno had been abstracted, drawn quick, clever sketches for the builders, and been in an intolerant hurry.

After the picnic the rain, as Mark had prayed, slackened from cold needles to a mist. Salerno started to dictate a long list of duties to Turpin's assistant and Tess had whispered to Mark, 'Our filly needs another walk.' Tess had led her. Mark had put his hand on top of her small fist on the rope. To reach her his arm went round her waist. She had been happy to let him. In the drizzle they had walked slowly around the meadow. Drops of rain hung on her hair and eyebrows. 'Better', she said cheerfully, 'than the most expensive shampoo. Do you know', she said, turning to this really beautiful young man with one strong arm around her, 'D'you know how much it costs –?' But she realised at once the idiocy of her question. As he shook his head, spinning the rain off it, she said, 'You're so sensible not to know', and leaned against him. Sensible? he wondered. Strange word.

The woods encompassing them were winter-quiet. The smallest wind moaned. Twigs cracked softly, muffled by the rain mist. The meadow seemed to Mark as large and private as freedom. Its great woods made a barricade against malevolence. Their feet and the filly's swished through the damp grey grasses. I love her more than anything I've ever known, Mark swore, feeling it so hard that his palms sweated with that confusion of thrill and fear he felt skating across the deep mill-pond just before the thaw, hearing the black ice crack and boom. Keep it like this. Like this, he prayed.

But coming back to the byre she had said as if she were discussing next week, 'We won't be back before the spring. Exhibitions, agents, private shows . . .' She recited a list of capital cities. Mark's expression had so slumped that she had promptly kissed him. Nearly, nearly on the mouth; he kept recapturing it. The inside of her pink nostril . . . if I'd moved a little, put my head so (tilting it), had my arm behind her. . . . Her tongue had just, he thought, touched his. A quiver.

Or had he only dreamed of it afterwards, seeing it moving in her mouth and being full of wonder how she might taste? If only he had then seized her. It was a lovely torment.

When she and Mr Salerno drove away in the great car he had slept one more night up there with the filly, conjuring up dancing images of Tess. And walked the filly home in a deluge, dejected.

'I'll take that old moke back now', he had announced brutally to his father. 'I don't want her disturbing the filly with her bloody eeaws.'

His father, cheeks mottled like mulberries, had roundly cursed him. 'That donkey saved your foal! And we're to cast her out, in winter, where those bastards left her to die on the quarry cliff with her own dead foal!' Lincoln raised his hand, but only to shake it at him like a hammer. 'You pining dog. Randy young dog. That donkey stays here till the spring. And you will care for her.'

Now softly spring was coming in. The bite was out of the air at dusk. Buds pressed out, turned sticky. The beeches at last shook off their dry brown leaves. Lime-green shoots peeped. Lincoln, smelling blandness at dawn and seeing the new grass begin with a pale green sheen through winter's yellow stems, watched for a change of wind at the full moon. It stayed southerly. 'Very well,' he said, 'you take the donkey back tomorrow while I go into the town and get seen everywhere around the market.'

The old donkey's instincts told her she was being returned from her land of plenty to that hillside of neglect. She dragged her hind-quarters as if suddenly struck with acute arthritis, stuck out her fore-legs like props, laid back her giant, foolish ears and brayed resentfully. Mark took all morning coaxing her back towards the quarry on the distant farm. There she shunned the quarry and crept along the hedge-row as if Babylon were a haunt of more pain and terror than her own.

Without a backward glance at Mark but to emphasise her new hardships she began distastefully to munch a thistle-top. Mark grinned: there was plenty of grass on the hill. Still discreetly skirting any habitations he walked cheerfully homewards. The donkey's purpose was done; she had become, like Tess's mother, only a bore. Mark felt that bounce in the balls of his feet which comes from off-loading a burden while doing a good turn. Longer gentler days were coming. Tess would soon be back again at the farm.

His father had said they would now start to break in the filly. It might be, thought Mark, breaking into a jog-trot across a greening pasture, a wonderful summer.

Old Lincoln, however, was detained in the town. Intent on flaunting himself around the market to establish his alibi while Mark returned the donkey, he had overacted his part.

15

Lincoln bobbed about the market pens like a boastful sparrow. He had brought in half a dozen bullocks and they had sold well. Usually at market he skulked behind the auctioneers' rostrum fearing a denunciation from a farmer or a snatch by the police. Today he stood upon the rostrum, all smiles and nods, sometimes impertinently touching the auctioneer's elbow to point out a new bidder between the straw-bales and the iron railings.

'Old Linky's right cocky', farmers and dealers murmured amongst themselves. 'He's be up to something.' They did not hate him, save when he stole. But he was not one of them. Their herd instinct nudged them to discard the variant. His eccentricity was shunned lest it prove contagious.

'Mad old coot!'

'Real rich he be –'

'But a miser. Oh, what a clawed-up miser.'

'Kept the woman's money as well as her girt house!'

'And let it tumble down to rack and ruin.'

'But that's to spite the flighty bitch when she pissed off.'

Lincoln was not of farming stock. He had come from the far side of the country, without even a local cousin to recommend him, to marry the landowner's only child in those strange days when great estates could still pass on within rich families.

'He's a horseman, right enough', commented one dealer fairly. He had profitably resold many of Lincoln's young horses.

'So's he should be. Weren't he a famous rider as a lad?'

'Ah, as a man, too.'

Someone sniggered. 'Ride all sorts, too, couldn' 'ee? Girls! Why girls he's had like oi've gobbled taters.'

They laughed and rubbed their noses, looking up at him.

He was, they reluctantly agreed, a great horsemaster. His advice, uneasily sought, was grudgingly given – for why should he from poverty hand out the secrets his long life had learned? That he used horses where they used tractors had first amused, then infuriated them. His unfair knowledge saved on costs in ways they could not copy. As their tractors depreciated and their fuel costs soared, his young horses appreciated in value and were sold on at profit.

Old Lincoln's skill with horses had spread to all his stock. This the farming community bitterly resented.

'Where's he get those secret mixtures, then, if he's not a bloody gypsy?'

'Gypsy he is, the bloody thief.'

'Gaw, don't he steal? The little weasel.'

Where they would borrow things from friends and neighbours, forgetting to return them, Lincoln had the gall to lift things from total strangers.

So the farmers kindly cooperated with the police whenever the

55

authorities decided it was time to have the old man put away again. The farmers feared that his son, if he ever took over that sprawling ruin, would be every whit as bad.

'They say that lad's a real wild young dog.' Two farmers and a cattle dealer from the foot-hills had buttonholed the passing sergeant of police. The slow drip of defamation of a character could bring great rewards.

The sergeant, who usually enjoyed the sounds and sights of market-day, shook his head. He didn't consider old Lincoln himself much trouble. Petty pilfering had grown so rampantly when shortages first became acute, that police policy was to overlook it and to concentrate on the gangs and looters. Remote thieves like old Lincoln were brought in every so often as gestures to soothe complaints. Living out in the wilds he couldn't bother the townspeople more than once a month. And he was a Sabbath day's journey to arrest. The sergeant said, 'No. That young Mark's been no trouble.' He savoured the disappointment in their faces. 'Decent lad', he said, booting it home.

'The pup'll learn some nasty tricks from the old whippet, though', remarked the smaller and older of the two farmers, nodding a yellow face towards the ring.

Old Lincoln was bidding flamboyantly for piglets. Not for him today the drooped eyelid or jerk of nose. He waved his catalogue like a novice. The sergeant stiffened to make a little formal space around him. His Inspector, appearing in his customary dashing clothes and dropping the butt of his small cigar, had languidly entered the market. He had seen his sergeant's uniform and was strolling across towards him when Lincoln had the pigs knocked down to him. Quite gratuitously (for the auctioneers had known him for forty years) the old man sang out like a trumpet: 'Lincoln of Mallard's Court!'

Snorts erupted round the sale-ring. 'Mallard's Court! Duckshit hovel!'

The sergeant's indifference brought the Inspector across to him in one slide. 'That's the bloody little gypsy who pinched the donkey. Went up with you to his disgustin' place last year. Smooth young son.' He liked to demonstrate that characters registered.

'You were going to let me see the Hygiene Department report', he snapped. 'And the Resettlement memo.'

'Sir', said the sergeant stolidy, 'We never found that donkey and

I've not seen the old man in town since.'

'Exactly. So now he's here, bring him in.'

So it was that Lincoln, fretting about his piglets and the balance due from the auctioneers, was now confronting the Inspector in the latter's shiny-walled and windowless interview room. Here the plastic-covered walls and floor were rounded off where they met; the more easily it was said to wash the blood away after interviewees had fallen over. Lincoln had not yet been beaten up. Pushed, yes. Jerked, shoved, and tugged here in the cells, and in the places of correction and in the labour camps, but actually punched – not yet.

The Inspector was, as his Manual of Psychological Interrogation put it, Exerting Personality. Lincoln, however, was not reacting as prescribed. The Inspector on his side, thinking of Lincoln still as 'this miserable little tinker', had miscast his victim, an error which chapter one of the Ministry's Manual was at pains to demonstrate. It recognised, which most thought strange and a few found hopeful, that personal idiosyncrasies, however reprehensible, still persisted. The Inspector had unfortunately come upon a freak, a relic from times well lost. That he could not fit Lincoln in, made the Inspector as angry as a spoilt child biting the wrong piece from a different jig-saw puzzle.

Lincoln had not read the Manual of Psychological Interrogation, but he had twelve years' practical experience on its receiving end.

The Inspector, planning a quick confrontation, admission and charge, had got nowhere. Baffled by the ways of the land, he had been frustrated to get no reply from the donkey-owner's telephone. 'Why the devil aren't they there?', he complained. To his fury he caught Lincoln attempting an exchange of glances with the sergeant. 'Don't you wretched farmers work?' he snapped.

'Terribly few telephones in the fields', Lincoln said.

Not till the agricultural dinner-hour was the telephone finally answered. Then it was by the farmer's wife. 'What donkey?' squawked the voice. 'We've lost no donkey.'

'Last autumn', explained the sergeant, raising his eyebrows and holding the ear-piece away from his head. 'You reported a donkey stolen last backend. We investigated –'

'That donkey's dead.'

'How d'you know?' inquired the sergeant reasonably.

'Because we've got the insurance money', clucked the wife with

57

modern logic. Cash made facts. The Inspector snatched the telephone and angrily demanded, 'Then why did you report the donkey missing to us?'

'So's to get the insurance money, o'corse. They don't pay else.' The police! thought the farmer's wife, dragged from her shepherds pie. They knew nothing of the workings of real life.

'So now the donkey isn't missing? Is that what you're saying?' asked the Inspector.

'Can't be, can it? I told you the insurance has paid for it being dead. So officially dead is what that donkey is.' The farmer's wife directed a long and wheezy sigh down the telephone, as if exasperated by a foolish child. That put an end to it.

Thoroughly angered by this impudent waste of his time the Inspector, to teach the tinker a lesson, was now firing his final broadside . . . 'so you see, Lincoln, modern society has no place for your sort of relic.' He paused for effect before delivering his verdict. 'You simply don't fit in.'

Lincoln nodded. 'Absolutely right, Chief Superintendent.'

The Inspector checked himself from making yet another correction of his rank. He added coldly, 'And what our society rejects, it spits out, then harries to death. We're tribal still, you know, *au fond*. More strongly than ever.'

'*Plus ça change* . . .' murmured Lincoln mildly. He inclined his head like an old time bishop, and the Inspector, intending to end on a burst of heat, clenched his fist and shouted, 'By God! We shall root you out!' He struck the desk so hard that the large calendar which he used for masking and enfilading his interrogations fell over towards Lincoln.

The old man found himself regarding a calendar print of a pleasant woodland scene. In a spring glade stood a blonde maiden with a wreath of flowers in her hair, wearing a gauze pre-Raphaelite dress. It was delectably transparent. The effect of the whole green scene, like the blue look from the girl's huge eyes, cleverly blended lyricism and eroticism. Unnecessarily it was entitled '*Primavera*'. But Lincoln's sharp eye caught the flaunting signature in the corner.

'Random Salerno!' exclaimed Lincoln quietly, oblivious of the Inspector's continuing rousting. The Inspector paused, astonished. Lincoln put his long thin dirty finger on the corner of the calendar. The signature was very plain.

58

'What about it?' demanded the inspector.

'Famous?' asked Lincoln. 'You would know, Chief Superintendent.'

This meant the Inspector shrugging modestly, revolving the picture, studying it and then murmuring, 'Ah, a new Salerno, I fancy. Famed for his girls.'

The sergeant was making a signal. The Inspector rose and joined him in the corner behind Lincoln to listen to an explanation of the artist's arrival in their backwoods. The old tinker's artistic knowledge seemed suddenly explained. 'Hah!' declared the Inspector. 'You've met your new neighbour then? Been sniffing out his new house, I dare say.' The Inspector made a sneaky movement with his hand, then made it pounce.

Lincoln shook his head. 'I've not yet had that honour', he said.

But the Inspector had found the chord on which to conclude his harangue. 'If one match, one aspirin or one dried-up baked bean goes missing from Mr Salerno's new house up there, Lincoln, we'll have you in quicker than you can fart with fear! Now eff off. I can't bear your rustic fragrance in my interview room any longer.'

Lincoln bowed courteously and pattered away to collect his thirsty piglets.

'Sub-normal,' remarked the Inspector, combing his hair with little jerks. The sergeant did not care to argue. He said instead. 'Wise of you not to hold him, sir. One time in here he screamed all night because we'd shut him up. Just like a frenzied dog-fox, he was. Next time we detained him, I pitied the old bum, so I left his cell-door open and nicked all his clothes instead. Bugger me, but he walked out stark naked and trots round and round the grounds of the railway widows' hostel making obscene gestures with their plastic gnomes.' The sergeant looked down to hide his smile.

'It's high time,' said the Inspector, studying the picture of the sylvan blonde with such relish that his tongue came out like a sliver of cold ham, '*high* time we put that thieving tinker in again. For another spot of Corrective.'

'He's sixty something', the sergeant mildly pointed out.

'Too bad.' The Inspector cleaned his comb. 'If he dies inside a work camp we can finally clean up that disgusting place of his.'

16

Lincoln crossed the cobbled yard swinging the breaking-bridle. 'Mark!' he called. He wanted to catch his son before he gave the filly her breakfast.

Mark appeared with a feed-bucket out of the dark doorway, narrowing his eyes in the flat beams of the morning sun. The snowdrop stumps, their flowers long folded, stood in bleached drifts. But the daffodils flowed like a yellow torrent flecked with specks of red and spumes of white all down the long bank at the end of the farmyard. Nothing delighted Lincoln more than the regular renewal of nature's colour without his having to lift one horny finger.

'Let's get the bit in before you feed her', said Lincoln.

'Fine.'

'We'll start off properly every day now. She'll see the bit, and she'll be rewarded later by her feed.' He touched lip and head, his shorthand for equine persuasion. He added, 'Will you find some honey?' Mark smiled, white teeth in a brown face, dark eyes opening, with wrinkles at their sides. Like the mother, thought Lincoln, when rarely she was pleased.

Mark ducked beneath the lilac trees. The buds, green and firm, were erect as candles. In two weeks they would be out. He was impatient to get on. He found a jar of clear honey from their bees, poured some into an old saucer and brought it back. He sniffed it, 'It's off the clover field', he said. 'Lucky girl.'

His father was in the filly's box, gentling her and slipping on her new, larger head collar. She had grown well over the winter. She had lost none of her quality as a yearling but was at the moment gawky like a girl of twelve. Moving, she looked a dream. Standing, the growth still in her showed in her quarters overtopping her withers. As a young girl slouches, so the filly stood as if down-hill. And, like a growing girl, she was changing visibly most weeks. Sometimes she was plain, and occasionally – twisting her head up, splay-legged, to bite the coming leaves on the wizened apple and pear trees – she was so ugly that Mark despaired of her future.

'Idiot', his father consoled him. 'There's your ugly duckling.'

And, loosed in the field each morning she would buck, twist, spring like a gazelle, swerve like an athlete and spin like a ballet-dancer. Then she had grace, and was beautiful.

The filly's first breaking-bit was a ring with three small keys which, lying on her tongue, held it down while giving her something to play with. It kept her mouth wet and therefore pliable. 'Ever kissed a dry-lipped woman?' asked Lincoln slyly.

Mark flushed: two spots on his dark cheeks. He knew his father had guessed he dreamed of Tess. 'Very gently', cautioned Lincoln again. 'This one'll have a temper if we treat her wrong.' Mark dabbled the keys liberally in the honey. Lincoln, holding the filly's head-collar said, 'Let her sniff the honey first.'

Arching her neck like a duchess, she blew at the saucer like a cook. She wrinkled up her top velvet lip showing the pink gum. Mark dipped a finger in the honey and slipped it into the side of her mouth. The filly licked cautiously, swallowed and craned forward for more. 'Loves it', said Mark delightedly, looking across at his father's face just beyond the filly's head. Lincoln was smiling lopsidedly. Mark raised an eyebrow.

'They always say', remarked Lincoln drily, 'that the man that can handle horses can handle any woman.' Mark said cheerfully, 'Good.'

Lincoln said, 'And I did pretty well with girls in my youth.'

'So I've heard.'

'So how the devil did I make such a cock-up with your mother?'

Mark frowned and was silent, jingling the bit. Lincoln began, 'With a young horse –'

– 'Prepare for all troubles!' Mark chimed in. Then he added, 'With a girl, too, I suppose.'

Both smiled. Mark clipped the ring-bit onto the offside of the filly's headcollar.

'Now gently –' Lincoln started.

'Bloody hell, father', Mark hissed, 'I've done this a hundred times.' He slipped his thumb into the same spot where he had stuck his honeyed finger, the filly opened her teeth and Mark slipped the ring between them. She set her teeth at its coldness, and started to back away. Lincoln murmured to her, held her firmly, and from his side also put a thumb into her mouth. She opened her teeth fully, the bit slid fully in over the top of her tongue and reached the corners of her lips. Lincoln had it clipped onto his side of the headcollar in a flash.

61

'That's in, my beauty,' he breathed.

Father and son stood still, watching with pleasure and affection. The filly moved her tongue beneath the honeyed keys, quickly nodding her head as if agreeing. Lincoln and Mark both laughed.

'Perfect!' cried Mark. 'Look at her arching her neck! And her mouth's wet. Oh, she'll have a lovely mouth. It'll be perfect.'

Lincoln smiled. 'Gentle and firm and we've got 'em. Just a moment more, then take the bit out while she still likes the taste. Then we'll do it again this dusk when you bring her in from the fields. She'll want it again then, you'll see.' With an extraordinary gesture he put his arm round Mark's shoulders and squeezed his son's arm high up. 'Oh, yes', he said, 'You've got to keep them wanting.'

Mark knew what he meant. 'Because otherwise . . .?'

'Otherwise they have you in their fingers. And that they never like. And will therefore drop you.' The old man let his arm fall dead. 'Deep into the mire.'

17

They were moving heifers from one of the high fields which would now be laid up for hay. It was, Mark puzzled, as if the old man wants me to see Tess, wants me to have her. It was the strangest thing that, after all the years of shunning everybody, his father wanted him to make a link with those who up in the forest would be their nearest neighbours. The only neighbours in fact which he could recall since his childhood, and the depopulation of the rural areas.

The warm spring had been too dry. The grass was backward. Lust however was in the air. The heifers, piebald lesbians, sprang upon each other grunting, staggering along six-legged. Old Lincoln pointed with the stick he waved behind them. 'No animal's all male, all female. We're all a mixture.'

In his dashing twenties Lincoln had occasionally after some victory celebration, dressed as a girl and gone to dark nightclubs with a party. It was not entirely for japes. He relished that insight into the males pressing round, of the male stirring in him, and of the female

62

quivering in him – that feminine part of him, whose sympathy with horses and with women had made him succeed for so long with both.

'Yes', said Mark, worldly-wise, but taking care to busy himself with Rip as the heifers crowded towards the gate, 'Like those two girls at school.' He roared at the dog, 'Here, Rip! Here!'

'Tell me again'. Lincoln shooed one clambering heifer so vigorously that she toppled off.

Mark had come quickly one June afternoon into the thicket of elderberry trees behind the sports field. The white elder flowers smelled like wine and there in the warm shadow he came upon the two girls entwined: the strong dark one with thick thighs; the slim blonde with bee-stings for breasts. He had checked, thinking at first they fought. Wrestling it seemed, they panted, groaned, both dipped faces scarlet. He had stared agog, heart banging, tongue between teeth. Lust rose like a poker as he watched. He heard his own breath rasp as theirs did. Both bodies were frustrated. The younger one was from his class.

When her face came up to stare at him, she didn't shriek out at being spied upon but panted all in a rush, 'Come on then! Have me! Have me now. Come on!' So he had tasted it for the first time, the big girl rolling aside to watch first, then pressing down upon his humping buttocks. But not in time, which had so maddened him. This part always amused his father. 'How could she tell the rhythm? That watcher?' Lincoln now scornfully exploded, 'What can they feel, those peepers? Nothing!'

For Mark it had felt, which astonished him, as good as anything he'd ever heard about it. The little fair girl, arching, had cried out, mouth wide, with a savage delight. But then triumphant, he had not been allowed even an instant's tenderness. The face beneath his angered in a flash. Her hands pushed up, 'Get off me!' she cried. Pulling her clothes up as if she loathed them, she seized the other girl and stalked from the thicket, arm twined in arm. Stooping beneath the last elder branches letting in the sun, the great fat girl, cheeks like purple balloons, had shouted back at him, 'You say one word, country bum, and I'll make sure that's the last girl you'll ever lay.' Her fingers had made a violent, snapping clutch like the forceps they used on the young ram lambs, and Mark had shrunk.

The heifers bottled in the gateway now burst through onto the new pasture and spurted off, tails up over the fresh grass. Liberated, they

63

separated. Their appetites now centred on their bellies.

Lincoln swung shut the rusty bedhead of a gate. He looked at his son reflectively. Mark said, still puzzled, 'I'd see those two girls together for a year till the big cow left. They'd hold hands and when they saw me they'd touch each other specially close. I saw why the big one would never look at me. But the little blonde, who'd seemed so pleased by it, she would look at me with real hate. And draw herself to the other.'

'To keep you out.'

'Yes. But she wasn't satisfied by the other's slobberings. I'd seen that.'

'That's why she hated you', said Lincoln. 'You'd shown up both. The masculine one's inadequacy. The blonde's need. And each had seen it in the other. It let in the wolf.' Old Lincoln leaned on his stick. 'But that first time you'd seen real passion, so you *felt* it. It's a tremendous thing.' He pointed upwards to the crest of the beechwoods. 'Go on up and see if that girl Tess is back yet.' He turned a half-wink into a nodding encouragement. He was sure now that if the painter Salerno found Tess tangled with Mark, he'd hate the place and move away.

He watched Mark stride up the meadow. Buttercups abounded. A cuckoo mocked. Suitable, thought Lincoln, swishing at thistles with his stick. He slid guilt aside: it'd be good for Mark to know the painter's daughter, see all that romantic life-style for a bogus act. He'd find the spoilt puss just a girl. 'Education!' he snorted, and, stooping, plucked out with anger a sprouting ragwort stump. The cattle would not touch the ragwort living with its yellow flowers. Dead they could eat its poison and die. He saw the stalks everywhere and began in a frenzy to jerk them out of the ground. 'Root out the tares!' he grunted and soon rejoiced in it, for the ground was soft enough for the roots to come smoothly, satisfyingly out.

18

Mark stepped out of the woods at the point where riding on that first winter day, he had first heard the voices of Tess and Mr Salerno. He looked anxiously at the haunted farm. Then he was delighted. A drift of smoke rose from the great chimney stack round which Salerno had built up the central turret. Below the pigeon-feather of wood smoke, Mark saw that the wide balcony was now completed. It gripped the turret like an ornate ring round a minatory finger. The house looked completed now on either side. Single storey arms thrust out to join the old farm buildings. These walls, Mark noticed with surprise as he hurried across the meadow, had been beautifully repointed. Their roofs had been freshly re-thatched with gleaming wheat straw.

They might, thought Mark with glee, be going to keep horses up there. Mr Salerno must be amazingly rich. Or perhaps the stables were now places for parties where the rich played at peasants. He had read of such things once in a magazine at the market: pictures of extraordinary lives in distant places, of a separate species. He supposed that the Salernos must belong to that different, alien race. Then Mark saw somebody moving on the balcony. He wished so hard that it might be Tess that he stopped in his track. He clenched his fingertips into his palms so that they whitened. Praying, please let it be her, he started to run.

The early summer sun was now as high as it could rise that day. The sky of pale blue was spotted only with puff-ball fine weather clouds free-wheeling across it. The sunlight fell on Tess's hair. He saw above the balcony her small head, cowslip-coloured, slowly turning. Her face was tilted up towards the sun and she was holding something which dazzled and illumined her face. He spurted forward, raising an arm. As he did so, her head disappeared behind the parapet.

His running disturbed soft clouds of butterflies and moths. Fritillaries were daubed about the grass stems in reds and browns like impressionist paintings. They flurried in front of him as he ran. When he reached the shade of the refurbished buildings, he checked. He thought, but Mr Salerno will be here too with his bloody builders. I'm an idiot (he could hear his father) racing across the meadow like a lurcher after a bitch on heat.

There was new timber on the flank of the old byre where he had slept with the foal and first spoken to Tess. It smelt wonderfully tangy as he leaned against the creosote to peep round. The place was silent. He stepped into the new courtyard. Last winter it had been a muddy square. Now it was crisp and neat in a sweep of deep gravel

65

round a mown grass circle. This embraced a large fountain, devoid of water, but awash with flowers in the basin and lapping around its base. His feet crunched alarmingly. He hesitated.

Looking across the yard he saw that the far arm of outbuildings had been renovated to make a long garage. He thought dubiously, they'll be having guests here. The prospect was menacing. But at the moment only one small car, not Mr Salerno's huge estate wagon, was parked in the shade. Through the back window he saw girls' clothes loosely cast about. He looked behind him. The old byre was now a range of fine stabling. He had seen nothing so luxurious in the countryside even for man. He walked silently along them, looking over the half doors and marvelling. The rope ties, bolts and door hinges were all made of brass. No box had yet been used. He supposed that this was how the stables were on the great studs. He thought wryly how different his filly's home now was to her place of birth.

At the end of the line a tack room had been converted where the building joined the house. Its door was locked, but he could see through the window splendid new and glossy saddlery. Never had he seen anything as rich and deep and curved as the two saddles, one large, one small, bestriding in tandem the rounded barrel of the mahogany saddle horse. Bridles, shining bright, hung on the walls. Nothing had been used. Everything had the unreality of a city shop window in a wilderness.

He heard a small click from the house and turned as if he had been caught shop-lifting. The front door at the base of the turret was still opening, but no one stood there. The grey stone wings of the strange house shone with huge plate-glass windows, but no one looked out at him.

Mark walked towards the door. It was new and made of a heavy, orange coloured wood he had never seen before. It was embossed with convoluted wrought-iron hinges, knockers and bolts. He hovered, staring inside. The floor was made of gleaming marble on which a score of dazzling scarlet and crimson carpets were flung as if in a sultan's palace. There was a lower well round the white base of the turret which rose up from the centre of the one long crescent-shaped room. The old stones of the original farmhouse chimney-stack were bold, like modern paintings. The old kitchen range had been ripped out. In its place was installed something like the port hole of a giant submarine: a fireplace, circular, and gleaming with copper rings.

66

Round the sunk area, which was as large as the four loose boxes, there extended a three-quarter circle of leather seating. It was as broad as a bed, and long enough, Mark guessed, to seat thirty people. But probably one didn't sit like that in such a place; sprawled probably; lay. He thought of Tess lying there. He went in, sniffing over the arrogance of the unwrinkled leather, to try to catch the scent of her. The cushions opposite the fireplace were still depressed. He saw a shoe and a scarf. Both smelled of her and he flung his head up, expecting to see her. Then he saw round the corner that a staircase had been built on to the outside of the turret. The shining chromium handrail spiralled upwards and disappeared.

The pull of this curve, just as Salerno had intended, drew eye and mind up it, as Mark and old Lincoln would watch the rising smoke of their open fire. But the vanishing spiral of chromium bannisters here lured the body. Mark took off his old boots and began carefully to climb the stairs, expecting them to squeak. But they were made, like the doors, of blocks of thick mahogany. They were perfectly silent.

The stairs passed into shadow where the turret's trunk blotted out the sunlight from the windows in the long room below. Mark emerged onto a circular landing, deeply carpeted. A long passage struck off towards the back. Through an open glass door was a high room bright with light. Off the circular landing close to him was an open door. He saw outside the grey rampart of the balcony, the top of distant trees, then the sweep of blue sky. This view too beckoned him on and out. He stepped softly into the sunshine and blinked.

At his feet, entirely naked on a low portable bed and dazzling in a spotlight, lay Tess. On the wall of the turret was positioned the aluminium reflector which Mark had seen flashing across the meadow. The sun's beams from overhead lapped her body in a golden light; those bouncing back from the shield dappled her flesh in silver, so that her skin rippled in gold and silver like a fish's scales through water. Over her eyes lay two pink circular pads. Her head, quite still, pointed upwards as if inhaling the sun's beams. The tip of her small nose was as red as a cherry. A few freckles showed below the flesh on her cheeks. Her lips were slightly apart – he could see the pink tip of her tongue – and so were her beautiful legs.

Mark simply stared. The first shock had been like diving through the surface smack of the cold mill-pond water on a hot August afternoon. This shock turned then into a cool stroking of his body. It was as if he drank her in from the nest of her golden hair to the tiny nails on her toes. The nails were painted, he saw with astonishment, pale pink like neat shrimps. His eyes flew up and down quicker than any bee. He could not gather up enough quickly enough. He wished he had twelve eyes with which to lap her. He felt all through him a great flush coming. He looked down and saw his damp, earth-stained bare feet, their brown arches and grimy toes and broken nails. He should tip-toe off. But he would not. He would look on and on.

'You liked the new stables then?'

Mark started at her voice. She had not moved. The pink pads over her eyes still stared blindly upwards.

'I saw you looking', she said. 'We're to have horses here. A stallion first.' Her lips smiled. 'I'm to pose with him.' A faint tremor passed through her thighs, but she did not bring them fully together. Against his will, Mark heard himself let out a sigh. He had been holding his breath.

'You like what you see, master Mark?'

He blurted out, 'How can you see me with those awful things on? How did you know it was me?' He felt the victim of a jest. 'Where's Mr Salerno then?' he asked. He expected to hear the painter's deep laughter. This new place was as strongly marked by Salerno's wide hat and cloak and smell, as was the territory of any dog fox.

'Abroad', Tess said. 'I watched you come. You ran half way across the field as soon as you saw me. Then hid behind the stables –'

'That makes me sound a thief.' Mark was angry.

'And you stole a good long view.' She pushed off her eye pads simultaneously with both hands, and looked up at him. Little beads of sweat lay on her eyelids and round her eyes. 'You did', she exclaimed 'I could *feel* your looks. So you can't deny – and anyway you're blushing.'

So he was, violently. The blush could not be stifled. She made no attempt to cover herself, but did slowly bring her legs together. Having clearly seen what was now partially hidden, Mark was by no means cooled by this gentle half-closing of a door.

'You've seen girls without clothes before though?' Tess asked. It was the same clear schoolgirl voice she had used before.

'Oh, yes.'

'Many?'

68

Mark would not answer.

She persisted, 'How many, master Mark? Several dozen?'

'No.'

'With bodies beautiful as mine?' She touched beneath her breasts, moving them up. 'These *are* good.'

'No.'

'No?' she repeated, opening her eyes fully. The silver light splashing on them made her pupils contract to pinhead dots, but she did not screw up her eyes. Their irises thus looked enormous and periwinkle blue.

'I meant I've not seen anyone as beautiful as you.'

'That I do like.'

The intonation was that of Mr Salerno. Mark said, partially to withdraw what felt like a surrender, 'There's sweat round your eyes where those awful pads were.'

'Kiss it away then.'

It was said with such a natural acceptance of his obedience that before he paused for doubt, he was kneeling down and kissing her eyelids.

'Run the tip of your tongue round my eyes. . . . That's good. . . . What does it taste like?'

'Salty.' He licked and tasted seriously. . . . 'And not quite sweet but a sort of scent of sweetness.'

'Yes, that's right. The taste of woman.'

'Elderflowers', he said. 'Their scent when we've been making wine from them.'

'Elderflowers and wine, that's lovely.'

She reached up and took his lobes in her fingers and pulled his mouth downwards onto hers. She began gently, then more strongly, then greedily to kiss him. She took in his tongue like a bee down the cone of a lily. He forgot the pain in his knees from the rough stone through his torn trousers. His right hand shot downwards over her belly. Her hand stopped it. 'No', she said, muffled, moving her mouth slightly away from his. 'Not too much too soon.'

He stood up jerkily. His head spun.

'Don't sulk', she said. 'I've wanted to kiss you since I first found you in the old stable with your foal.' She saw his smile. She added, 'But just – not too much too soon.'

'Too soon?' he repeated.

'Oh well', she said testily, 'Something like that. Don't take me literally. Don't *you* be literal, for goodness sake.' At his surprise she added, 'One says things. People swoop on them. Carry them away. Then pick them over afterwards. It always leads to trouble.'

She sat up and swung her legs towards him over the edge of the bed. She saw him looking at her breasts. 'They do grow bigger when I'm not lying down, don't they?' He nodded. 'Mark, you've not seen all those dozens of naked ladies, have you?' He shook his head. 'Well', she said with a strange face, 'You're starting with quite a good one, I suppose, if Random Salerno, popular artist, rates this body so highly.'

'He paints you?'

'But of course.' She reached under the bed and pulled out a short silk coat from the Orient and put her arms into it. Her hands came wriggling out of the sleeves. They're like delicious little mice, he thought. He wanted to grab them, to pop her whole hand into his mouth. He could easily. But he said, 'You had something there all the time.' His surprise made the statement an accusation. 'It doesn't cover . . .'

'It's only against the breeze.'

He still looked angry.

'But you don't mind, surely?' She got up. Her head was under his chin. 'I wanted you to enjoy the view. Which', moving her lips across his cheek, 'you quite did. Didn't you?'

He nodded. His face came over the top of her head. Her hair smelt like the sweetest wheat straw. He bent further, pushing his nose into it and then cupping the back of her head. It fitted into the palm of his hand as if into a nest.

'Well then', she said below him, face into his old shirt, 'Everyone's happy, or at least, reasonably so.' She mumbled, 'And anyway happier than recently.'

19

She walked into the house onto the circular landing and pushed open the first door. He saw a huge bed with dark sheets tossed off. Mirrors bewildered everywhere. There was a great window benched and curved like that in the poop of an admiral's ship-of-the-line. It opened onto a flying view of the forest's green ocean.

'I want', he began, grabbing at her arm. 'I want to –' He tugged her towards the giant raised bed. 'Please I've never felt . . . I must . . . Come. . . . I must –'

'Too many "I wants, I musts".'

'Cockteasers', he grunted out in a rage, 'we called those girls at school who showed and let us touch and never let us put it in.'

She walked into the bathroom next door, down some steps and turned on the roaring taps. She was saying something. He saw her lips moving, reflected in the glass. She did not look angry.

He followed her to the door and looked down. The bath, ridiculously large and ovoid, with golden taps and rails, was filling with a creamy foam. She was standing knee-deep in it.

'What?' he demanded. He saw beyond her in the steaming glass his shamefully grimy figure.

'I said, I'm not a girl at your little school. I said I'm far from a schoolgirl. Never was, in fact.' Half to herself and glancing down, she murmured, 'Not your sort of a school by any long chalk, anyway.' She looked up at him again. 'Don't look so bloody cross, boy.' She sat down in the bath and frowned sideways and up at him consideringly. 'Though I must say you do look marvellously fierce. Like a fox.' She made her teeth snap. 'Splendid'. He was smiling. 'Even better when you smile, horse boy. D'you like our house?'

He stepped down into the bathroom.

'There', she pointed at an antique chaise longue now covered in . deep emerald towelling. 'Sit on there. You like it?'

He said, 'It's very strange.'

She nodded and lay back in the foam. 'Strange is right.'

'I've seen nothing like it', said Mark.

'You don't like it.'

'No. It's like something pretending – pretending to have history. And it *was* old and really strange before. And it's been mucked about.'

She sat up so sharply that Mark thought he had insulted her. But she sang out: 'Pretending! Your instinct is absolutely right. Direct.' She extended her right arm, its index-finger arrowing onto a golden tap. Her breasts were wonderful. Foam fell reluctantly from their

71

upturned tips. Her back, golden against the white, was curved like a wild duck's. He could see the little vertebrae moving like an amber necklace.

She gave a long sigh as if unburdened of something, leaned back and turned into a conversational tone. 'Tell me about our lovely filly foal, then.'

Mark caught the 'our' with glee. 'She's a yearling now. . . .' he began, leaning forward, explaining her progress with his hands. And he's a boy again, thought Tess, listening. He's a sort of magic half and half creature. She was delighted with him.

'I'd love to see her now,' she said.

'I'll bring her up again', he said, dark eyes shining. 'Now that she's bitted –'

'I couldn't come to you?'

'No.'

'Just like that? "No"?'

'I'm sorry.'

'Don't be', she said. 'I like your adamantine hardness. Better than bought diamonds. Which', she added, standing up, 'sparkle only when you turn them.' She looked piercingly at him. 'When you turn them on.' She was drying herself. She said, 'I'll show you this pretending house and we'll have another picnic. But in the kitchen this time, for it's quite ready. And you will tell me what you want to about yourself, and not a sentence more.' She walked up into the bedroom and he knew that if she lay down on the bed he would rape her. She glanced back over her shoulder. 'I've tempted you far too much today. I'm really sorry. That was the real bitch part of me. I'll tell you why soon.' She pulled on trousers and a sweater.

He said in wonder, 'You knew what I was thinking without even looking at me.'

'It's not so hard. If you understand men. You, after all understand horses. I do a little. There is that one strange bond between us. That makes for understanding.'

'A horse and rider relying on each other?' It was so obvious, he had never uttered it before, and was surprised by her delight.

'Exactly', she exclaimed. 'Each can ruin the other.'

'*Make* each other', said Mark. 'They do.'

'Yes', said Tess, starting down the stairs. 'Like you and the filly, master Mark.'

72

The presence of Mr Salerno was so strong in the extraordinary living-room that Mark stopped at the foot of the spiral staircase. Tess, still going forward, called out, 'It's all right. Pop's five thousand miles away, I promise you.' She was walking over the rugs. 'He is very strong all round here though, isn't he?' She smiled from the door which led into the kitchen. 'Come on, Mark. And even if he were here', she said astonishingly, 'he'd be as afraid of you as you are of him.'

'What . . ?' Mark began. She hadn't seemed to joke. 'I don't. . . .'

But she was out of earshot in the kitchen. Mark, puzzling, shook his head once. 'Afraid?' He smiled. He could not see Mr Salerno afraid of anything in all his huge world. He began to inspect this part of it. Picking up his boots he padded across the kaleidoscope of oriental rugs. The inner walls were lined with Mr Salerno's lyrical landscapes, each wrapped like a shawl around their ladies, naked or diaphanously draped. Mark walked slowly along the line. All were smoothly executed and glowed with a natural but controlled grace. But they seemed too sweet. They were light. There was something similar too about all the bodies, though they were variously clad in the underclothes of different eras and ranged freely between blondes and raven-haired gypsies, short, curly red-haired girls and those with loose bay locks.

'My body in every one!' Tess stood behind.

Mark started.

'The faces he borrows – sketches girls wherever he is. Or sometimes I wear wigs. Like there.' She pointed at a picture of a young peasant with hair the blue-black of a rook, washing lacy clothes by a country river. She stooped in a position which temptingly displayed the white of her breasts and their vermilion nipples above a dark bodice, and the white of her thighs above dark stockings. 'That's me, too', said Tess, and laughed. 'Though you'd know that very well by now, wouldn't you, Master Peeping?'

Mark was scowling.

Tess said, 'You look ridiculously embarrassed.'

'It's like watching someone else. . . .' he hesitated, 'Want you.'

'People *wanting* me can't be bad. *That* you couldn't object to. You mean *possessing* me', said Tess.

He nodded. But it was even more than that. By switching Tess's body around, thought Mark furiously, Mr Salerno was treating her

73

like a doll. His cheeks flamed.

She asked sharply, 'You don't like that thought?'

'No, I do *not*!' He shouted.

'Good', she said, and went through into the kitchen. 'Some people like the idea . . . of me being had by others.' She said it in a low voice, leaving it to Mark to pick up if he wanted.

But he was gaping all round. 'Was this all built from absolutely nothing?' He had not understood what she meant.

She nodded from one of several splendorous cooking machines built into the pine-planked walls. They twinkled with lights and were punched with buttons like the flight-deck of an aircraft. The long room was divided by wooden walls into sections. It was grander than the only smart restaurant in the local town, The Serenade, which was the most luxurious place Mark had ever seen till now. Cupping an eye against the reflections of traffic on its glass, he had sometimes stared through its pink-tinted windows while waiting, foot-stamping and steamy-breathed, for the wintertime school bus.

Mr Salerno's artificial, palatial log-cabin was a different world. On the varnished timbers electronics buzzed and winked. Fans removed the fragrance of the sizzling bacon which, delivered from some automatic, hidden store, was now cooking beneath an auto-timed grill.

Tess from a high wooden stool observed Mark's amazement.

'You can see Pop's a theatrical designer too', she said. Her tone was curious. Mark, still staring round, could not reply.

'Do you', began Tess. 'Don't you', she amended it with surprise, 'Know what I mean?'

Mark, turning to look at her directly, shook his head.

'You've been to a play?' Tess persisted.

'I've been in one at school', Mark said.

Tess bit her lip to keep from smiling, 'But television?' she asked.

Mark said bluntly, 'No.'

Her eyebrows shot up. 'I didn't know that *anyone* – except perhaps right in the wilds –'

'We *are* in the wilds', said Mark coldly. 'We don't have electric light.' He saw with pleasure that he had further surprised her. He said in a casual way, 'My father doesn't believe in it. We manage quite well without.'

Tess, mouth so open he could watch her tongue flicker, had

thought he joked. But he was looking at her with the earnestness men use when defending a creed. She breathed out from puffed cheeks, 'Wow!'

There fell the hesitation of aliens meeting, uncertain not just of words, but of the other's basic point of value. To break it, she swivelled round briskly on the stool. 'More's to come!' she cried, and stretched across to a battery of switches. 'Morning!' she called. 'Appear!' The red glow of the rising sun stained one wall, then rose up it like a flood. 'Noon!' Tess declaimed. 'High noon in summer.' White overhead lights seethed. The room vibrated with heat. 'And of course, the quiet winter evening. . . .' Another switch curtained off all the windows with a whispering quadrophonic swoosh. On the opposite wall gleamed the descending rays of the westering sun. Above the automatic cookers appeared the flickering of a simulated log fire. 'Listen!' commanded Tess, dramatically holding up an index finger. Electronically there erupted the artificial crackling of flames.

Mark laughed. The laugh escaped from him bouyantly without a thought, as if he broke into sunlight after a deep dive into the chill of that mill-pond. The laughter gurgled up from his belly. He saw Tess's face break. She laughed. His mirth came belching out. Tears ran from his eyes. Tess ran across towards him, spluttering with merriment, and light with relief. She said, and flung her arms round around him, 'I love you.'

His laughing stopped as if he had been kicked in the groin. 'What?' To see her face, he held her off him. He looked flabbergasted.

'What's wrong?' Tess asked. 'Don't people say that to you?'

He looked at her bewildered.

'Not ever?' she asked.

He shook his head.

'Oh, Lord,' said Tess, her voice troubled. She put an arm out onto his shoulder, and stood looking at him with tenderness.

'It's all right', he said. He meant: for God's sake, no pity please. I'm not a waif. He added, for she still stared. 'We don't see anyone.' It was not a complaint. He'd heard one man at market once say, 'I don't drink'. It was a question of taste. But she repeated his words slowly in the accents of sorrow. 'You don't see anyone. You and your father. No one?'

'No one at home. Ever. Some on market-days, of course. But people don't exactly dash round the pig-pens shouting "I love you".'

75

'No?' she asked, 'I'd have thought all those bulls and things were very sexy.' She smiled. 'Aren't they?' Jollying me up thought Mark.

Tess thought, He's really beautiful. She asked, 'But girls must have said – you've had a girl, surely?'

'Oh, yes.'

A few, she thought, and probably not too good. He's been disappointed.

Mark said, 'But they don't really say I love you, do they?'

She very much liked the 'they': girls he meant, poor fellow, paid by the hour. 'Don't they?' she asked interestedly. She believed everyone must murmur something, if only out of politeness.

'Well, they grunt a bit', said Mark. He was a little sheepish. He smiled, then wondered, But did she really say it? He asked with trepidation, 'Could you say it again?'

'I love you.' She kissed his cheek.

'But why?'

'Because you laughed at all this nonsense.'

He looked round. The concerto of evening fireglow and electric flickerings and cracklings was still in full swing. 'Yes, it's nonsense!' he cried. He felt delighted, as if after being outside in the wintry forest he'd found the warmth of a barn.

Outside the May sun shone on in the early afternoon; here was mock winter.

'Nonsense', echoed Tess. 'And look – let's have. . . .' she bounded like a hare across to the switch board and studied the buttons. 'I know – let's have Storm.'

Tremendous booms immediately reverberated from the four corners of the room. It was terribly clever. The thunder was done much better than the rattling of old tin trays. If taken seriously – but suddenly the artificial lightning leapt out. Mark's face caught in a flash of it, was lit up, agog with alarm.

'You're frightened!' shouted Tess over the now thunderous uproar of Mr Salerno's personal storm. She pointed at him like a schoolgirl and began to laugh. He too started. The laughter hiccupped. Tess squeaked. They clung together, laughing chest to breast, eyes crying, shoulders galumphing like clowns.

'Oh stop it', Mark mouthed into her ear. She felt behind her. Her hand ran across the switches. Morning and evening, noon and evening and a touch more storm whizzed across, glowed, filled the kitchen and finally disappeared. The curtains swooshed open. Sunlight ran in like sparkling water released from a weir. The windows disclosed above the softness of the beech forest a sky as translucent as pale blue porcelain and with the same fragility.

'And on the seventh day. . . .' said Tess, 'Came sense again, let's sit and eat.'

20

He was gazing out of the window. 'What are you thinking?' she asked.

'Just that it's lucky that all that's still here.'

'Yes, thank God', said Tess, 'literally.' Then she asked, as if the manifestations and laughter had never occurred, 'Didn't your mother ever say she loved you?'

'No, I can't remember her saying it. And if she did, I'd have been too young. She's not dead, you know.'

'No, I gathered not. You've never mentioned her. That normally means a living bit of pain. Actually', said Tess putting her head on the side, 'the first feeling I had about her was that she mightn't be all there in the head.'

He said abruptly, 'Her head's all right, so far as I've ever known. Why'd you think that?'

'Something mysterious. And there's a special way people don't talk about relations, if there's something amiss with them.'

'Amiss' was the word Mark's father used of fillies in season when required to race. If his father only half-exaggerated, then his mother had probably been amiss most of the time. Mark did not like hearing Tess use the word, even in ignorance. She saw his scowl and said, 'We've talked a great deal about some things. We crossed a lot of chasms even that second day walking in the field round and round in the rain. I felt that she was a burden on you.' He said nothing. She tried again, 'Or a menace.'

77

He shook his head with real confidence. 'She'll never come back', he said.

Tess looked carefully at him. The mother had been a threat then.

'A problem?' She persisted.

'No problem for me. It was hard for my father, being much older than her, to bring me up on his own. But she's not a burden.' He pressed his hand down, and a new interpretation struck him. 'Except that in a certain way she is to him . . . *On* him. She does continually hover over him.' He thought of a vole in the meadow pressed to the ground beneath a kestrel hanging like death on the wind.

'He sees her?'

'Oh no.' The idea was ludicrous. 'He'd probably try to kill her again.' Mark again enjoyed Tess' shock. 'He tried several times. Even the last day, firing at her. She drove him distracted.'

'Lovers?' asked Tess brutally.

'I suppose so. Or so my father says when he speaks of her. It was her place, Mallards. Ought to have been mine. Would have been, in the old days before the new laws. Who can tell anything nowadays?' He felt exhausted. He shrugged, looked down at his dirty hands on the table and leaned his cheek on them. 'We just squat.'

'What?' Tess put her cheek, too, against the table and placed her hand on the upper side of his face.

'We live very rough. Wild really.' Their faces were very close. She raised an eyebrow. 'Well', he said wearily, for how could he explain a way of life in a sentence or two? 'We live like people used to. Off the land. So that we don't depend on anyone.' Tess did not look convinced. Mark said with force, 'On hardly anything at all, you know. So my father can feel free.' At this Tess nodded. Mark said, 'Exactly the opposite of all this.' He sat up and looked around the room. She too leaned back and looked about them. She grinned. He smiled at her. 'That's why I laughed.'

'That's why I love you.'

'Not really.'

'Oh, yes, in a way. In a way I do, Mark. People can. People do. It's not difficult. So one says so. What is the point of *not?*'

Your sort of people, perhaps, thought Mark. It was unknown to him. It added moreover to the puzzle. 'Then why on earth did you –' he jerked his head up and backwards towards the balcony – 'so tease me then, up there?'

78

'Because I wanted you, for goodness sake! And so I needed to know, did you want me?'

'Which I did.'

'Did?'

'Do.'

'Good', she said, but lightly.

'So?' He leaned across to tug her to him over the table. His arm sent the pot of hot coffee spinning into her lap. She squeaked, jumped up, seized a bright new cloth, mopped, soaked, rubbed. The moment slipped so tangibly into ordinary passing minutes that he could feel the opportunity sucked out of him, leaving a gap. She was preoccupied. He hovered. Lights on the stove flashed. Bacon grilled, and eggs ready fried, were neatly disgorged. Plates, already warmed, clicked into slots. The food was deposited. The phrase rang into his mind: Flesh to flesh Muck to muck. Cycle of farming and of life. A thing of his father's. But Mark said, 'That's all the time it's taken.'

'You mean so quick?' Tess was surprised.

'So slow', said Mark. 'It felt as if we'd been talking here for hours.'

They were both standing by the cooker's gleaming face. Its dials and time clocks waited on their commands. Mark looked at her with such yearning that Tess thought, God, he's into this too deep. She said brightly again, 'How I must have bored you then.'

'No –'

'Joke. Meant to be.' She pulled a rueful face, as if she had committed a social faux pas. Then, 'Would you watch me pose?'

'Of course.' He thought she meant then.

'Come the weekend after next then. I've to go back today. But next week the horse will be here. The stallion.' She grinned at him like a boy. He was delighted. Then she said, 'And Pop'll be back to paint me.' His joy, that light bubble, popped without a sound, leaving the fading image on the eye of those melting rainbow colours.

He shows everything in his face, she thought with pleasure. 'It'll be all right', she said. 'You'll see.'

And Mark, anxious not to overcast what remained of his time with her, declined to ask her what she meant. He wolfed the bacon. It was so crisp that amber fragments flipped across the wooden table. Licking a finger tip he picked them up on it and popped them on his tongue. He caught her watching him with an affection so glowing that he could feel her warmth. His confidence soared as if lofted by

79

one of his father's elixirs. He munched hungrily.

Tess wished, Don't let him say Pardon, or ask if that isn't the way to eat.

Mark's white teeth went on champing the bacon. 'God, these are good', he said with relish, licking a piece of egg off the corner of his mouth.

Tess watched him. I really do love him, she thought, surprised. In a quite new way. She tested the sound of 'love'. A doubt rustled. Is it because he's a hungry stray dog and I'm pleasing myself by feeding him? She asked, following this line of values, 'D'you think *these* are good, Mark?'

He looked up. She had taken a large cardboard folder from the gleaming wooden shelf. It was surprisingly worn, but it had been Salerno's first, at art-school. He was not sentimental: the old folder had become famous in the media, and thus a prop. Tess was opening it. It was full of paintings on glossy paper. 'Mr Salerno's too?' he asked. They had a shining quality which made them seem reproductions.

'Oh yes. No one else's allowed here.' She sounded sharp. He saw the end of a pout. 'No', she said, 'Sticky fingers on them would drive Pop insane. I'll turn them while you eat. I want you to say —' she broke off. She had been about to put the impossible question: 'Which are good.' She amended it. 'Say which you like.'

She flicked the sheets. He said 'They're all like the ones below. You — your body in all of them.' She nodded. The theme of the naked or flimsily draped female in country settings continued unabated. Tess turned the sheets. Cheeks and lips and eyes and breasts and thighs followed each other like expensive chocolates in frilly papers. Mark said politely, 'They're very pretty.'

She looked at him for something more. He added, 'Your body's beautiful, of course.'

'Oh, I don't mean you to say that.' She went on turning, but the flick of her wrist showed her impatience.

'Stop!' said Mark sharply. He had his mouth full again and bacon spattered. He jabbed a knife towards the painting she now held vertical. 'Is *that* his?' He was incredulous.

'Yes', said Tess.

At Mark's first glance there was no recognisable form at all. But he felt no need to peer at it, seeking a pattern. He gazed at it with pleasure. The picture contained no woman nor beast. It revealed a vibrant expanse of autumnal colours. Shapes which could have been turning leaves seemed to move in a light which shimmered from above. There was an extraordinary depth into the picture. It had caught the layers and yet the lightness of foliage. It was as if you stared upwards from a greeny ground level on a day of early autumn brightness. The more Mark looked the more he perceived. What had seemed sea-grey fountains gushing upwards through the sere and russet splotches to continue right out of the top of the paper and on for ever, were the trunks of ancient trees. They gave off alternating qualities of solidity, like the mountains, and yet of life, like spring wheat thrusting. To Mark's eye they seemed miraculous. 'You can feel those beeches', Mark said, lifting one arm, then gripping his bicep with his other hand. 'You can feel them grow. You can feel the last of the summer. You can hear those leaves rustle and the top twigs, which you can't see, must be squeaking. It's marvellous. In a way, it's more special than the real woods. Because it makes you look. And see things which I've never seen before.' His eyes shone with admiration. 'And I live here', he declared. 'Amongst these trees.'

Tess thought happily: he's right and he's so generous. She said, 'Pop can do it. He is still an artist. He can still feel. He did this that first day we came. They're the woods – they're the *feel* of the woods rather, as you'd say, out of which you walked.'

Something that first day with the filly had troubled Salerno, too. He had limped quickly to his palette and painted in fading light with so much nervous energy that sweat glistened on his forehead, and Tess could smell him. It was part of his drive, as Tess called it, one of the things she admired. Brushes darting, jabbing, fixing, overlaying. Random Salerno had set down his impression not of oncoming winter but of a time a few months earlier. 'Why?' she had asked, hugging him with praise for his picture. 'I don't know', he had said, regarding her sardonically 'It marks the beginning of an end.' He had jabbed away. 'Leaves falling, but trunks surging on, I suppose', and turned back to it greedily.

'Why aren't they all like that?' asked Mark, 'Too difficult? Would something like that take months to grow?'

'Inside him', said Tess, 'He was troubled.' She looked disconsolate herself now and added, 'Torment does make a *feeling* thing. But he won't *do* them, Mark. We've had awful arguments about it. A fight

81

really. One reason why he's away now.'

Mark was pleased. She was not then completely in his thrall. He said, 'Then the pictures of you are much easier?'

'He could do 'em without looking.'

'What a waste', said Mark, laughing. 'I'd look and look.'

Tess squeezed his hand across the table. 'Yes, but that's only because I'm a new view.' He started to protest. 'No', she said. 'The thing is these scanty pictures make him a fortune. They're commercial. That's what we argue about.'

'Why argue?'

She was scrupulously exact, because the dilemma was a malignant growth in both their lives. She put it clearly; the creator's persistent torture. The ease of compromise, the need for food, then comfort, then the unending taste for luxury, and all the while, to gain those, the deliberate snuffing out, through lack of time's oxygen, of that small flame the artist knows he has. 'Pop *needs* to paint something great!' she exclaimed, echoing Salerno's anguish from many nights. 'Or he'll die with it undone. But he needs the bloody money from these facile things which burn up all his desperate time.'

Her hand was still on Mark's and her eyes looked into his for more understanding, for another judgement, for a view in her favour. But he could see only the edge of the problem. Instead he asked. 'Really a fortune?' He could not conceive of money being earned by painting the same girl again and again.

She told him.

'For each picture?' He whistled like an owl.

Tess nodded. 'And he'll do one in a morning.'

Mark's mind could not encompass the reward. He said lamely, 'He's lucky.'

'He is not!' she snapped. Mark was startled. She demanded, 'He's on the rack, can't you see?'

'He has to sell things to be rich', said Mark mildly. 'We all sell things – even my father and me – we all give up things – to live as we want.' He looked very keenly at her, intending to say that she too was selling her beauty which was her luck, for the pictures. But he could not find words which would not offend her. He had no idea how much she benefited from being Mr Salerno's model. Under his stare, she reddened. She's very angry, he thought, and looked away from her round the enormous electronic kitchen. He moved his hand from under hers, and waved with it. 'But', he said, 'that fortune, those pictures, they bring you all this. Cars, aeroplanes. Seeing people all over the world.'

Her eyes flashed and her cheeks bloomed vermilion. 'Is that what talent's for then?' she demanded. She was seething. Her neck throbbed.

God, she's got a temper, Mark realised. She's a tartar. He looked at her amazed, but with appreciation. She spat out, 'Even you could see the one good picture.'

Mark nodded his head to one side 'Even I', he mimicked. 'Even the peasant.'

But she was not appeased. 'Well then. . . ?'

'Well then', said Mark calmly, 'I suppose his good pictures – like the one *we* think is good –' he touched the back of her hand, 'won't sell for some reason.'

'They would if he tried', Tess pressed her point. 'He won't try. He's afraid of failing again.'

'Again?'

But she was silent. She lowered her head and gripped her small fists so fiercely that the knuckles bulged. Without looking up, she said, 'Men who create things are afraid to fail, you know. They are afraid to register the limit beyond which it'll be proved they can't go.' Her tone brightened. She looked up and the clenched fists flew open and her fingers executed a skip. 'Like the high jump', she said with a sad, smiling brittleness, 'So high. That's that. No second chance. So always second-class. Bad to fail like that. That is his problem. And God, I can see it!' She raised her voice and fury grew. 'And his damned agents just promise more tons of money for another sexy nude of me for a billion bloody calendars for garagemen to goggle at and get a hard-on, dreaming of how they'll have me – this way or that, as they please, making me –'

'Stop that!' shouted Mark.

She was shocked. The flush on her cheeks retracted to two bright spots. Then, she said quietly, 'All that's true, Mark. And who the hell am I to mind? I don't even see them, let alone feel them.'

'Why say it then?'

'I'm not. I'm just saying that it's so easy for him to knock off another nude –' at that she laughed out loud; her fury was gone – 'that he simply goes on and on doing them again and again, instead of painting proper pictures. I *can't* persuade him.' Frustration was about to make her burst out again. 'He's not young. He ought to leave something good behind. Each year's one less chance, d'you see? You *must* see, for it's like a harvest – only so much, only once . . .' But it was impossible for young Mark to comprehend the artist's urgency. He did feel some other anguish between Mr Salerno and Tess: something else about succeeding or failing. He thought swiftly of his father and, determined to evade another upsetting, because incomprehensible, outburst exclaimed, 'I shall have to go back to help my father.' He looked through the window, catching the time from the sky.

'Yes', said Tess slowly. 'You don't see all the thing, do you?'

'Not the pain', he said. 'Not the burden. Not the threat.' He had a fleet thought of his mother.

Tess got up. 'One day you will.'

He was riled at the gibe at his youth, but said politely, 'Perhaps', He stood up, too. He said carefully, 'We do lead very different lives.'

'I'll put some boots on', said Tess, 'and start off with you – oh, only across this first field. Have no fear. I'll not intrude.' She's lonely, he realised. One day when things do change, she may come.

She went. Mark turned the sheets in the folder. There must be a hundred different ones, he thought, all with her breasts and thighs. His hand stopped. One unfinished picture – the landscape had not yet neatly filled the rectangle – portrayed Tess as she had been that day, thrusting out of that short Oriental coat. Her nipples stood up like loganberries. And her eyes were darting shafts of anger, as they had minutes ago. Before he knew it, he had pulled the picture out of the folder. He hesitated. Then, dropping his shabby jeans, he rolled the picture round his thigh, jerked up his belt, and was standing staring at the impressionist painting of the trees and leaves, when Tess called from the kitchen doorway, 'Come on, lightning. If our filly's as slow as you, she'll not beat a donkey down the beach.'

It did then occur to Mark to ask her if he might borrow the picture. He thought about it walking towards her up the long kitchen. But he had already declared that he didn't like the idea of Mr Salerno painting her sexily or of the million men goggling at her body. And he had the thing wrapped round his thigh already. She, like her Pop, would think him a gypsy thief. Thus he hesitated thrice and did not speak, although the instinct which he had inherited from his father presaged such doom, that he felt sweat shrink his palms. It was a flash almost of terror, as on that instant when, backing a wild young horse, he first fully bestrode it and was thus totally committed — unless he survived — to a pulverising fall.

<h1 style="text-align:center">21</h1>

Lincoln was spreading muck. The cart creaked slowly across the pasture. He stood like an ancient gondolier upon the pile of manure, forking it left and right in dark-brown lumps over the slowly pitching tail-board. One of the cart's wheels squeaked. The work-horse was old and knew her duty. She paced very slowly across the field keeping a straight line. The white feathers on her great fetlock joints kept to the diminishing unmanured green swathe of the field, and so stayed clean. Where they had passed was freckled with tiny dung hills which would next be harrowed.

Mark was running home through the wood. It was covered with deep ensnaring brambles which could snag a weary man into such a stumble that he fell among the thorns. Mark leapt the bramble banks. He was in love and felt a race horse. His father's stories of this race and that: cramming on into a final obstacle, heels driving, thighs gripping, thrust, thrust, thrust with the pelvis, then a final launch and you were soaring through the air, base earth forgotten . . . Heavenly, his father would sometimes breathe, elated by that swoop on the magic carpet of his recollections. Heavenly, he'd add if he was feeling randy, like making love well with one who ran with you.

So it was, thought Mark, running and jumping and in love with Tess. The beech trunks elephant-coloured, streaked with green, sped past. He thought of Mr Salerno's one good picture. But now was a different time of year. Summer was coming. And now, thought Mark, sucking in the loveliness all round, I've suddenly started to see . . . He ran in a pale green luminosity shed by a million leaves. He felt at the bottom of a sunlit sea. And there below him as he loped to the wood's fringe was his father, a spry speck.

The dung smelt rich. His father had seen Mark coming as his arms plunged the pitch-fork in. He had been, the pundits used to say, a graceful rider. Now he spread muck with grace. He was still athletic, Mark thought benevolently. He'll go on for years. Mark felt delighted.

Lincoln had heard long before the crashing and jumping of the boy's passage. Nothing like love, thought old Lincoln, forking a great clod of manure up and round and out for bringing that bounce to the buttocks.

'No one there then?' he asked Mark. The boy's complexion bloomed like a nectarine beneath his tan. His eyes glinted like dark stones beneath the mill race.

'Tess was. Tess was there alone.'

His father did not check the horse to speak. The old mare plodded on. Mark, half-turned, walked briskly beside the cart looking up at his father. Saying the name gives such pleasure, thought old Lincoln, like sniffing, like tasting, wine.

'Tess was sunbathing.' Mark had not meant to say so, but out it spurted. 'She'd nothing on. She's so beautiful, father. She –'

'You laid her?' enquired his father, muck fork aloft.

'No!' Shock spurted out in the word, sprung from its smear on the old man's tongue.

'Don't be so virtuous, boy.' Lincoln thrust in his fork again. 'You'd have liked to.' He speared the dung aloft and asked sharply, 'Wouldn't you?'

'Yes.'

Horse, cart, old man and youth walked on towards the tangled hedge. Mark hoped they would stop there. He wanted to sit on the bank in the sun and talk to his father. But the old mare turned, creaked the cart round, settled again to the pull of the shafts on her leather collar and plodded on. She had the incline with her now and her stride, aided by gravity pushing on the cart's shafts, lengthened over the tussocky field. Mark was jogging to keep up.

'Was the father there?' asked Lincoln.

'No.'

'Missed a good chance then, I'd say. Fathers don't mind their sons at stud, but, oh my God', cried Lincoln, 'the trouble you get with the fathers of fillies.'

Quite right too, he considered. If I'd had a daughter – if I have any (he'd slept with plenty of married women) – I'd not want 'em covered by any passing stud. Unless perhaps, glancing at Mark under his eyelids, by a good lookin' fellow like that. He asked, 'Her father – he'll be back?'

'Weekend after. I'm to go. Mr Salerno's going to paint her. I can watch.' He had no intention, though he could not analyse why, of mentioning the stallion.

'He might paint *you*', Lincoln remarked. If he could paint, he would do Mark just as he was now, tangled, looking up, as bright with hope as a fair dawn at harvest time. 'Perhaps he will.' But probably the man Salerno only drew girls: there'd be more money in his sexy calendars.

The same line of thought, coupled with the desire to boast, now impelled Mark to declare, 'I've a picture of her.'

'Where?' asked his father casually.

'Stop a minute.' Mark dropped his trousers. His father bellowed 'Who-oah' and stared down at his son. His blue eyes bulged as Mark unfurled the picture from his thigh. It was slightly crumpled. His father's hand swooped down. 'No', said Mark sharply. 'Keep your filthy hands off!'

Old Lincoln stared down. 'Lovely tits', he said. 'Love 'em when they stand upwards and outwards like that.' He swung his head left and right, lips pursed for kissing. 'Standing up proud, too. She'd have been sexed up when he painted that.' He watched Mark's scowl deepening. 'Or maybe just splashed cold water on 'em. God, she looks angry, Mark. A little spitfire.'

Mark, pleased by the turn in his father's enquiries, nodded briskly. 'Hell of a temper she's got, when roused', he said proudly.

Lincoln stuck his tongue in his cheek. 'She'll be a handful then. She'll be a tartar, too.'

Mark took the comparison, but 'Isn't she beautiful, though, father?' he demanded. He could wait no longer for praise. 'She is beautiful', Mark stated.

Old Lincoln thought of the calendar in the police office and said slowly, 'She's a model. She's sexy right enough. But she's common.'

'Common!' Mark burst out. 'Where would you find anyone like her around?'

'Round here', his father drawled, 'There'd certainly be no one. That I do grant you.'

'Well then?'

'But there'd be model girls like her, heaps of girls like her, in distant cities.' He thought as always of Mark's mother. But she had never had this common offering look. He said to Mark, 'He'd do a lot of her, I bet, the man Salerno. I saw one in the police station last time.'

'That's what you mean by common?' Gawped at, like Tess had said. He felt anger again, imagining the revolting Inspector slavering over Tess' picture.

'Yes.' He asked, 'He gave it you? Oh no, he wasn't there, was he? So she did.' Mark did not answer. Lincoln pounced. 'She *did* give it you?'

Mark shook his head.

Lincoln blazed. 'You mean you bloody nicked it?'

'Freed it, you'd say', sneered Mark, flicked on the raw of guilt.

'D'you think I'd touch a thing in that house? When we're the nearest souls to that damned place? After what the police warned? Take one baked bean, that Inspector said, and he'd have me inside again for more Correction. You're bloody well mad!' Lincoln's face was purple.

Mark weakened. 'There were hundreds of them', he said.

'But that one isn't even finished.' Lincoln pointed. Mark turned it round. It was perfectly true. Mark said, 'I'll take it back. Tess won't mind. I don't think she'll know. I only took it because –'

'Take it back?' exploded his father like a terrier. 'Tess won't mind', he mimicked. 'What about that father? Friend of authority. Famous. Won't he mind his precious picture being pinched? Crumpled? Dirty? You will *not* take it back.' The contrition on Mark's face soothed old Lincoln's squall. He thought, the boy still respects my judgement. He felt pride flicker and instantly snuffed it. 'You'll have to pray, if he's so many, that he'll not miss it.'

'He probably won't', said Mark quickly. 'It was in a huge folder of finished ones.'

Old Lincoln made a humphing noise.

To mollify him further, Mark added, 'Sorry.'

'Hum', said Lincoln, 'What you mustn't do is start to play my tricks.' He paused. 'Without my wits. See?'

Mark saw. His father slapped the reins on the mare's great bay rump, and clicked at her. She started from her reverie and plodded forward again. Once more Lincoln resumed the swing and fling of the manure.

Mark, holding the rolled up picture like a blanched and fragile baton, called after him, 'Tess asked about the filly, father. Our filly, she said. I'm to take her up there.'

'Why?'

'Tess wants to see her again, father. She asked to come here.'

Lincoln went rigid. His forking action froze. He bellowed at the cart mare. 'Whoa, damn you!' He yanked the reins. Down at Mark he spat, 'By Christ's blood, they'll not come here. They'll not come within a step –'

Mark, over-excited, flung up his arm, 'Shut up!' His father's eyes popped. Mark said, 'That's idiots' talk.' The old man could not object to his own phrase. 'I said Never', Mark declared. Lincoln blew out his lips as if ejecting a plumstone. 'That's right. Well done.' He clicked at the cart horse with tongue in cheek. 'Giddup. Giddup then.' They rocked forward. Mark stood. His father turned with the pitch-fork and shouted back. 'Well, you'll have to get a move on with the filly, won't you? To get her ready for your other filly now.'

Mark flew down the field to the stables brandishing his rolled-up painting like an assegai. His father bellowed after him across the greensward and the creaking wheel, 'Specially as it's "our filly" now.'

22

The filly lay out all night now. She grazed through most of the summer darkness, then lay down to sleep when the sun had moved the mist and warmed the grass. She ran with the herd of youngsters, eight all told, in the water-meadow by the mill-stream. The filly was not just the only thoroughbred; she was the only yearling. The others would make carthorses and cobs and all be sold at four years old.

Browns, bays and greys moved leisurely, tails swishing, against the first buzz of flies. The dapple showed like coins in their gleaming coats. Among them, marked by her different, more elegant build and aflame in her colour, the filly stood out.

The water-meadows were handy. Lincoln could catch a youngster within minutes, carry on with its breaking for half an hour, taking it one step further, and then loose it off again. There were no colts in the herd. Lincoln had never kept a colt on the place since the small stud he had been building up had collapsed on his wife's departure. Because all the horses would be used for work they had to be geldings. Lincoln castrated them himself in the spring of their first year, before the flies came to trouble the wound. He would cast them and Mark would sit upon their heads. Lincoln would pull one leg up, and away, neatly under his sharp knife, would come their testicles.

Once the youngster was on his feet again, the cut drained easily. A swelling persisted for a few days and the new gelding moved his hind-legs stiffly. But the cool green grass of spring and the gentle exercise soon reduced the swollen parts. The cut grew together. In a month it was hard to tell, even by stooping down and peering up, that the youngsters had lost the ability to reproduce and, generally, all their libido.

Lincoln had cut a thousand colts in his life. 'You must do them early', he taught Mark. 'As soon as both their balls are safely down, you want to cut them off. Leave them longer, let them be all summer, and they'll grow colty. Then, when you come to geld them, they've still the inclinations. Or a *recollection* of those inclinations. But no ability. They're like eunuchs in seraglios deliberately castrated late so that they'd be tormented all their days.

'Cut a colt before he knows. Before he "shows",' old Lincoln declared. 'And he'll never know what he's missing. The tree still grows, but the branch feels nothing.'

But Mark still wondered whether the gelded horse that walked away was not aware of what he had lost. Their instinct, his instinct reasoned, must tell them of the enormity of their change.

Sometimes a lingering desire persisted. Either the yearling had been exceptionally precocious (and some colt foals would demonstrate their masculinity, like classical kings, by leaping upon their mothers); or Lincoln had not castrated them perfectly. A testicle not fully dropped, and thus only partially removed, allowed the longings to linger.

One such, a cob from the mountains, plump as a plum, was running this summer with the herd of young stock. They called him

'Stiffy' and he looked a clown. His head was crudely white-blazed and he had that common thing in his mountain strain: one clouded blue wall-eye. But the sex that survived in him made the neck of the ugly cob bulge like a stallion's proud crest. He showed stiffly and at length every time a female in the herd came into season. Now Mark's filly was on. The cob, small, waddling like a jester at a court, followed wretchedly behind her, demonstrating the erection which could never be relieved by an ejaculation.

The filly, flirting with him, permitted his impotent pursuit only occasionally, raising her tail, backing towards him and 'winking', as Lincoln called that pink manifestation of impending consent.

The cob though two years older than the filly, was only half her height. Squat where she was lengthy, bull-necked where she was swan-like, paddling in action where she floated, he yearned after her, thick head extended on stubby neck, neighing with vain desire.

His mixed masculinity made him awkward to break. He would stand for minutes dumbly, stubbornly. 'Just like he's not with us', old Lincoln grumbled, exasperated by that rare thing, a horse with which he could not communicate. The cob would sulk. Then, whatever were the stultifying thoughts which clouded his brain and immobilised his limbs, he would suddenly stir himself into action. For the next ten minutes he would be active, obedient and normal.

Mark longed for him to go. It was not only pity for the cob. Seeing the animal's vain, ludicrous yearnings made Mark dissatisfied with his own cut-off existence. As he ran now towards the water-meadows and vaulted over the brass bedstead in the gateway, he saw the cob sniffing over his filly's quarters. Mark had a pocketful of oats and the filly's headcollar over his shoulder. He shouted 'C'm on now!' and the echo came rolling back off the ivy-clustered walls of the ruined mill. Normally he stood at the gate and called from there. The filly knew his voice and would turn her head. Sometimes she dawdled towards him, as if she sauntered along a boulevard. At other times when her mood was either more energetic or more affectionate, (and as with girls, the one sparked off the other) she would gallop at him, stopping in a swirl of hooves and mane and flying tail.

But Mark was now on fire. He ran across the water-meadow calling for her and swinging the headcollar like a lasso. It was the wild approach for which his father had beaten him as a boy. But he had forgotten rules and sense. He raced across the grass like a savage, delighting in life. Then the filly, stirred up by sex, squealed twice. He saw the cob behind her stretching forward vainly. Then her hindlegs lashed out against the poor cob's chest. The crack of hooves into flesh and bone smacked across the pasture. The cob was halted. It grunted with pain, and held on one foreleg. 'The little bitch has lamed him', swore Mark, running on again in anger.

The filly, amused by her treatment of her admirer, now pranced off at an exaggerated dressage trot. She carried her tail up like an orange fountain. Her legs shot out like a ballerina miming a giant's strides. She saw Mark, spared him a haughty glance, and trotted past him, ridiculing him too.

'Hey!' shouted Mark, angry, astonished and standing still. 'C'mon then, filly', he called too loudly, too peremptorily. She trotted on, giving him the mocking backward glances of a minx. He bit his lip to stifle his urge to bellow at her. He took a deep breath and lowered his tone and called out again, but this time quietly and cajolingly, 'Oh, c'mon now.' He held out his hand cupped with overflowing oats. He hid her headcollar in his other hand behind his back. 'C'mon', he called softly. 'C'mon, love, do.'

She turned. She came gavotting back towards him. But she did not come up to him. Three long bounds away she swung off and began a circle round him. 'Well, blast her guts', Mark cursed, 'She's bloody laughing at me.'

He was not at all amused. But she was. Her circles became ellipses. Thus she passed closer and closer to him on one side then away she glided. Now she was snorting extravagantly through her nostrils. She wheeled in again, giving Mark a look of that mockery which the fleet have always felt for the pedestrian and the knight for the serf. He launched himself at her in a fury.

Gripping the headcollar like a lasso he propelled himself in a tackle towards her neck. He got it over her shoulder, grabbed it beneath her neck and noosed it to the dangling rope. She was arrested. But she did not capitulate. Quite the reverse: astonished and angered by his onslaught, and assured of her superiority, she accelerated away. She jerked him forwards onto his face. His right shoulder was struck a sledge-hammering blow by her swinging hind hoof. A pain as violent as a red-hot branding-iron burned into his shoulder-blade. He dropped the rope and headcollar, and rolled over on the grass, letting out a moan of agony. He heard his breath grunt out and, tumbling over, tried to save his shoulder with his other arm. He thought, the bitch has bust my arm I'll never get up to Tess now next week and this rotten filly has mucked up all my life. . . . He half-sat up and felt sick and chilly. Sweat smeared his forehead and the breeze on it made it feel it froze. He was about to faint. The colours of the field were flooded out in a thick film of crimson. He thrust his head down. His head sunk through, lead-heavy, between his knees like an axe onto a chopping block. He just felt his brow bang into the turf and wondered why it did not hurt at all. There was even no crack or boom. Dying? he wondered.

The next thing of which he became aware was a return of sound. There was a distant cavernous thumping and a rasping like the bellows in his father's old forge. Then he smelled grass. He saw gigantic stems brushing his eyelids. His heart's beats and his lungs, deep gasps diminished. He felt something softly gliding over the hair at the back of his head and he groaned, Oh Tess, I was sorry, I was sorry to miss you. Tess, I'd not meant, not meant. . . . Then he felt warm breath on his ear, and he very slowly started to roll over. As his head poked cautiously round, he saw the filly's muzzle just off his back. She was standing over him, one knee in that long leg bent to allow her to stretch her head right down to his. The genuflection seemed an attempted attitude of human contrition.

Gingerly he sat up facing her. She regarded him steadily. He would have liked to see in her large amber eyes a long look of regret. He certainly saw wonder and affection. 'Silly thing. . . .' he murmured. His voice came out fondly. He tried to move his right arm, but it hurt impossibly. Letting it hang, he got clumsily to his feet. He would limp home and let his father feel for the break.

Then he saw the headcollar and rope lying a long way off. The filly must have carried it on at full gallop for a hundred flying strides, after she had shaken him off. He walked very slowly towards it, holding his body steady so that his shoulder was not jolted as his feet progressed through the thick grass. She came back to find me, he realised. She walked a long way back to me. He wondered how long he had been concussed. He felt warmth behind him and now instinctively ducked. Pain lanced him again. Windy, he chided himself. But it was the filly. She was walking sedately behind him, solicitous as a nurse. I do believe she's trying to rest her head on my shoulder, Mark thought. Walking on, he put his left hand out behind his back, and she licked it. Well, I really am damned, he thought, she honestly is saying she's sorry.

And when he stooped to pick up the headcollar, she stood still, waiting. 'Very well', said Mark, 'God knows if I can get this thing on you left-handed, let alone lead you, let alone open that bloody ruin of a gate. . . .' He had the headcollar over her lowered head. She had almost slipped her muzzle into it herself. 'But I s'pose I'll have to try.' His left hand was inefficient and he did up the buckle with a struggle, holding the tag end in his teeth. 'Seeing', he grunted, 'how much you seem to want it.'

23

The sun sizzled on the flaking terrace. The flagstones, blistered by centuries of weather and pimpled with amber mosses, had absorbed the morning's heat. Now even the shadow breathed it out again like an oven wall. The square files of weeds sprouting between the cracks had begun to wither. Mark, with his right arm in a sling torn from one of Lincoln's tattered handkerchiefs, sat on the stone balustrade. He swayed a little and his eyes looked moist and vacant.

'God, father,' he said, swinging his tin mug, 'This shtuff's shtron'.'

Lincoln was keeping him well dosed with a blend of dandelion wine and a herbal extraction which in his experience proved, like time, a great healer of torn ligaments.

The more painful part of Mark's treatment entailed vigorous massaging of shoulder-blade with a stenching unguent. It contained a mild blister. If Mark covered up his skin over the fresh rubbed embrocation, it felt as if he was grilling in oil.

Thus he sat, bare from his waist up, on what had been the balustrade along the formal terrace. That façade above its famous falling gardens had been the one most painted by artists in the past. On the terrace Mark's ancestors had posed in velvet coats, with shooting dogs, or beneath plumed hats and parasols, with children like fresh washed dolls, smiling over hoops and hobby-horses.

Lincoln, squatting cross-legged on the flagstones like a tailor, was restitching a broken rein. He was relieved that Mark's arm had not been snapped. The haymaking and harvest would have been impossible without him.

'Mind you', said Lincoln mumbling round his cobbler's thread, 'I was race-riding three weeks after a broken forearm. And I won on that good mare –'

'Rubbish, father, three weeks after a collarbone, you mean. And Brave Diana was after you bust that wrist.' He nodded down at it. 'Or so you've always said.'

Old Lincoln grimaced up at him like an organ-grinder's monkey.

'I dare say', Lincoln was huffish. 'Can't remember every bloody accident, can I?' To demonstrate he pulled open his torn, blue shirt.

He never worked uncovered even on the hottest days so his body was the white of putty. From this sprouted arms brown as a chimpanzee from his biceps down, and a mahogany, wrinkled neck. On his pale frame the wounds, blows, fractures compound and ordinary, the ugly overlaps of bad collar-bone links, the cracked ribs joined like bamboo shoots, all hideously stood out. It resembled the body of an old prisoner from a concentration camp. In committing his body to that career in his pursuit of glory Lincoln had willingly exposed it to a life of punishment. Women, holding it to them, had gasped at the wounds, had stroked the broken bones and kissed his scars. He supposed this met their need both to admire and to care. He thought very little of them himself. 'Honourable scars', an antique dealer had once said, stroking the centuries-blemished surface of the huge dining-room table, before taking it away to sell. Lincoln had liked the phrase. His body would not again be on offer before his death.

Mark could look at it now without revulsion and without condemning the mad price his father had paid for fame and a sort of glamour. But the sight of his father's battered frame sparked in him not only anger against those hosts of uncaring spectators but affection for the old man. His father had intended to produce the latter. The former was of no importance; to Lincoln's mind most of the human race were merely watchers from the stands.

'D'you reckon you could lead the filly up one-armed to see the Salerno's?' Lincoln enquired.

Mark nodded. 'You said Salerno's!'

'Their name, isn't it?' His father looked amused.

'But you've always said "The Haunted Farm" or "your modern

friends".

'Getting used to 'em'. Lincoln bit off the cobblers thread. 'The idea of them, I mean, of course.' He regraded Mark drolly. 'I've not yet been asked to call.'

'We should ask them really. That is,' Mark added quickly, 'if we ever ask anyone.' The appearance of the great house, though disintegrating on close inspection, gave off a distant air of such authority, elegance and fame that Mark longed to show it to Tess. He left the notion like a fly on the pool for his father to snap at.

But Lincoln was speaking of the filly. He praised her at last with real warmth. Lincoln had never heard of such extraordinary behaviour after the accident. As if she had been his daughter whom he was defending against an accusation of vice, Lincoln could not contemplate that the filly had meant even to kick out at Mark. It had been Mark's fault, charging in there, over excited by thoughts of the Salerno girl. Mark had virtually attacked the filly. 'And she depends on you', old Lincoln said again. 'She's linked to you. From that first finding. For your saving her.' He considered this as he sewed, then said gruffly, 'Though this loving might make her soft, you know. And what good would that be in our racehorse? We want her character to be steely.' He snaked his left arm forward. 'Like a rapier,' he said.

Mark, flushed with the wine, boasted, 'She'd let me lunge her left-handed.'

Lincoln considered, 'She might.'

'I'll show you.'

The filly came to his call. Lincoln watched, eyes narrowed to suppress emotion, as the filly again bent her head to receive the headcollar from his son. At Mark's fumbling with the buckle, Lincoln reached out.

'No', said Mark sharply. '*We* will do it. Together.'

He means the filly and him, thought Lincoln and blinked. He had taken too much wine under a noon sun. He was growing maudlin, he told himself. But that instant, as briefly passed and yet as final as the verdict at a winning post, had marked his transition into old age and his son's into manhood. I *will* help them, he insisted, furiously rubbing away a pathetic tear in the corner of his left eye. I must move now. But he delayed. The verdict was unchallenged. Mark's back was turned against him. He was coping. To the headcollar Mark left-handedly fixed the jingling bit. From its rings led the long lungeing rein. He looped the slack round his left forearm, frustrated by his impotent right hand.

'I'll lead her on the offside', said Mark shortly, going round her head.

'It's wrong', Lincoln grunted. '*And* you should have the cavesson.'

'Not if I've only one working arm', Mark retorted. 'Anyway, it's good for her. To be done differently.'

Thus demurely and from a strange side the filly let Mark lead her down to the level sward where she did her lungeing. It had been the bowling green field in the days when the demesne workers rolled bowls on summer evenings and smoked clay pipes. The grass was still smooth. No other horse was allowed to use it. The hopes of Lincoln and his son lay in the filly's fragile legs: they would not risk her turning tightly on rough ground.

'I'll start her off', Lincoln stepped eagerly forward onto the green.

'No!' Mark saw his father's disappointment. 'But it's so much better if I keep on at it myself.'

'Very well', said Lincoln. He suggested, 'Will you try her on the left rein first?'

Mark nodded. It was the way she went best. But his right arm was not available to urge her forward or to prevent her coming in towards him.

'I'll keep her out for you with the lungeing whip.' His father tapped it gently.

Mark said, less confidently, 'I *think* she'll do it by word of mouth.' He was leading her to the centre of the bowling green. 'Particularly if she starts on her old track.'

Stepping into its centre, and gradually playing out the lungeing rein, Mark called out firmly, 'Walk on.' The filly started to walk out on the beaten path. Mark, falling back so that he was level with her hindquarters, continued to play out the line. The gap, a man's length, between his left hand and her head quietly doubled.

'Look', he breathed, 'She's doing it.'

As the filly moved round Mark walked backwards to the ring's centre. The filly was now at the fullest extent of the lungeing rein. If she played up there was now no slack left to take the strain. If she plunged away all her weight would jerk on Mark's left hand and arm and pull him to the ground.

'Steady', murmured Lincoln from the perimeter. He was tense.

97

'Walk on', called Mark boldly. He could feel her docility and obedience through the tension on the long rein. His hand and her lips played with one another on this slim connection. His hand was firm but gentle. Her mouth was receptive and responsive. The thing was working. They were in accord. The filly, arching her neck to perfection, playing with the bit and looking boldly forwards, lengthened her stride round the large circle. As she came round and Mark turned, Lincoln saw the glow of triumph in his son's dark face.

'Well done.' Lincoln said it quietly.

Mark flushed. 'Trot on', he called to the filly.

'No!', shouted Lincoln, 'She'll be off.'

'Trot *on*! Trot *on*!' called Mark, ignoring him and clicking his tongue to the filly. She hesitated for two strides then trotted forward. Lincoln bit his lip. From this pace she could hit full gallop in four strides and smash Mark onto the ground.

Mark felt the increased tug on the rein as a sailor feels the wind's strength grow in the sheet in his hand. 'Steady', he cooed across the grass. 'Steadeee . . . .' The tension dropped. The filly, losing concentration as she listened to his voice, slowed her pace and half-turned her head inwards enquiringly towards her master.

'Look at her eye!' called Mark. 'She's beautiful. How she uses herself!'

'She moves well', Lincoln conceded. 'But better when she doesn't gawp at you.'

Mark had only to click, to make a little hunch with his right shoulder, and a flutter with his slung right arm, and the filly again looked about her business and quickened.

'That's enough', called Lincoln after twenty circuits. 'She'll get bored.'

'Two more', said Mark firmly out of the side of his mouth.

His father said, 'Your shoulder's hurting.'

'A bit.'

'She's very good.'

'She's marvellous', said Mark. His face was pale and sweat drips stood on his lip and brow, but his eyes shone with satisfaction. He would take her up next week and show her off to Tess.

24

Mr Salerno shaded his eyes with his long dark hand. 'That boy is bringing another horse', he called back irritably from the balcony.

'I'm changing Pop', Tess' voice was muffled from her bedroom.

'The short white smock', reminded Random Salerno, turning sharply on his artificial leg.

'Yes.' Tess appeared behind him on the balcony. 'Ça va?'

Mr Salerno, tall under his wide brimmed hat, looked down at her. She was barefoot. The smock, as he called it, was made of the thinnest diaphanous cotton. It concealed nothing and ended only halfway down her thighs. 'Delectable, edible,' murmured Mr Salerno, licking his lips and making vulpine pouncing movements with his hands. 'You're like those delicious golden pêches glacées we had last week.'

'On that island with the coconuts', said Tess, making her breasts bounce beneath the shift.

'Coconuts', Mr Salerno repeated distastefully, 'you insult yourself, my dear.' He disapproved of jollity at all times, but never more fiercely than when he was fanning up his mood for an erotic painting. 'Nothing', he said, 'so withers passion as a joke.' He half turned away from her, his wide mouth pulled out sideways.

Tess pouted. Friction still stalked between them. They walked delicately. She asked, 'What about the boy?'

Salerno pointed across the meadow, now expensively fenced with stout posts and rails to become a paddock for the new stallion. But a gate at its far end opened onto the woods through which Mark had led the filly. Still using only his left hand, and with his right arm slung in a scarlet scarf, he was coming towards them over the grass. The filly was on her toes. She moved like a smouldering flame.

'That's not "another horse", Pop. That's the filly. How she's come on.' She leaned over the balcony waving at Mark. 'She'll be nearly two now.'

'The boy does not respond', Mr Salerno commented drily.

'He's only got one arm!' Tess exclaimed.

Mr Salerno had made a frame of his two thumbs and forefingers. Holding this square to his eye, he framed Mark moving across the meadow. He murmured, 'That scarlet sling has a dramatic touch.'

99

Tess shouted out, 'What's up? What's wrong, Mark?' Quite anxious, thought Mr Salerno, but he did not turn to look at her. He was, as he liked to put it, composing. Mark's reply, blown sideways by the breeze into the depths of the forest, was unintelligible. He humped his right shoulder and turned his head to nod at it.

'He sounds cheerful anyway', said Tess.

'We'll have him in the picture', Salerno decided. 'Holding Sultan for you. Bare-waisted. A sort of slave.'

Tess shrugged. 'Very well. Better than that awful man.' To care for the stallion Mr Salerno had engaged the squat groom who had imported the horse. The man and his fat wife, refugees from overseas, were now installed in the cottage converted from the byre where Mark and the filly had slept. The woman, who smelled of haddock, was intended to help around the house.

'I'd never considered having that peasant baboon in the picture', said Salerno, turning to enter the house and descend the stairs. He had no pity for ugliness and used it only for contrast. His voice contained the rustle of anger. Tess asked crossly, 'Did you think Sultan would have stood for me? Without anyone to hold him?'

'Why not?' Salerno was limping down the stairs. His metal foot squeaked on the solid mahogany treads. The sound which mocked him always put him in a rage. 'You've managed him perfectly all this week riding round the paddock.'

Tess did not argue that riding a stallion round was a great deal easier than compelling him to keep a pose. Salerno called back, 'And why has that gypsy boy brought his wretched horse? Am I to stable it yet again? I should be in the business of liveries.' His foreign intonation made Tess smile. She went inside and leaned over the spiral staircase.

'D'you want hat or not hat?' She called down to him. 'What about the straw with flowers?'

Salerno had reached the silence of the rugs in the long living room. He turned and smiled. 'Exactly right.' His deep voice went dreamy. 'A ladylike confection topping the smock . . . all that above the negroid sheen of the stallion. . . . It's colour is so right. Damson hue beneath the ebony. . . .' Then he ordered crisply, 'But get some scarlet poppies, Tess. Drape them in your hat. They should droop, opiates, as if they slept. As if they and you had passed a long hot day adventuring.' He could keep colours in his head and match them across continents without a pattern. 'The poppies behind the black barn will be perfection with the boy's sling. And their small black hearts. . . .' His voice lilted, as if he sang of love. 'Eminently suitable', he concluded in his business tone.

Mark met Tess as he rounded the corner of the barn. The filly checked and cocked her ears. Mark stared. His mouth opened. His cheeks reddened. She had one hairy bitter-tasting poppy stalk sucked between her lips. She was threading another through the brim of the straw hat in her lap. Its falling head joined a fringe of others which, too heavy for their stalks, hung over the hat's brim like girls over the side of a punt.

'What's the matter with your arm then?' she asked round the stalk and looking up at him with her head still bent over the hat. Haltingly, for he was on fire from gazing at her, Mark related the accident.

'Bitch', said Tess. Mark had barely any mind with which to defend the filly. The throbbing in his body also boomed in his brain. Then Tess caught the blast of heat from his eyes. She too blushed. Unable to move with one hand holding the filly and the other pinned up by the scarlet sling, Mark's eyes simply moved all over her. They darkly caressed her face, her visible breasts, the curling shadow beneath the roundness of her small belly where her legs so plainly joined.

'I know', said Tess at last, and nodded at Mark's jeans. 'I see, too.'

'Oh', he glanced down, rigidly embarrassed. With both hands thus encumbered and inept, the picture of the vainly besotted cob leapt into his brain. Tess saw his discomfort, rose from the ground and swung the hat onto the back of her head.

'That's a compliment', Tess said. She walked up to him, hat flopping on the fall of golden hair. The filly watched it warily. Mark stepped forward. Very quietly Tess put an arm round Mark's neck. They pressed together. 'A great compliment,' murmured Tess into his ear.

'Don't think I can bear this', he muttered into her neck. 'Couldn't control if — I could eat you. Every piece.' He opened his mouth wide against her skin. His teeth moved up and down. Between them his tongue wriggled.

'Just what Pop said.'

Mark withdrew and looked at her. 'What?'

'That I was delectably edible.' She let her hand drift slowly down over his belly.

'When?' he asked. 'Please when?'

'I don't know.' Her shoulders shrugged. 'I do want you.'

'Well then?' He lunged his head at her.

She said 'You're to be in the picture with me.'

'Oh, I can't. Like this. How can I? He'll see it.'

'He'll like it.'

'Like it . . .?' Mark stared. 'Is he –?'

'Does he like boys, you mean? Even delicious boys of the woods like you – no. Not yet, I think. But the picture' – she dropped into a lecturing voice – 'is all about desire, you see. For his new series. So when you show it –' her hand again brushed him. Without the cursed filly he could have leapt on her.

Mr Salerno's voice shouted, 'Tess, I'm all set up. Trapchek! Get the stallion out will you please. . . . No', (impatiently) 'of course, no saddle.' One of his heavy histrionic sighs could be heard round the corner of the barn, followed by unintelligible grunting from the groom. The stallion suddenly neighed.

'Come on', said Tess, leading Mark and the filly into sight onto the raked gravel sweep.

'Not that bloody horse', shouted Mr Salerno flinging up an arm at them and looking enormously tall. He had two cameras, one still, one ciné, both mounted on shining tripods like two machine guns. But he stooped over them again like a magician. To one side stood his easel supporting a stiff glossy board. By its side was a wheeled table bearing his palette and a fanned out display of brushes. The artist knew that everything had its place.

'I'm sorry, Mr Salerno', Mark began, stepping forward from behind Tess. Salerno looked sharply at him, across to Tess and smiled crookedly: 'Whoever ordered *two* stallions?' Before she could utter, he addressed Mark in a warm, apparently friendly voice, 'Put that creature in that box. It might upset the other stallion!'

'She's not in season', Mark started. 'I'd never have brought her up if –'

'Season! Season! Shove her in that stable, boy, please. And no speeches. I want you simply to hold Sultan for Tess. Can you get your shirt off for it?'

Mark looked uncertain. 'I'll help,' Tess said.

'I don't want a bloody explosion', said Mr Salerno and began to laugh. 'Not yet.' His laughter rumbled deeply. Mark led the filly quickly into the loose box and looked back perplexed at the artist. The tall man's shoulders were hunching up and down rather strangely. Mark could still hear him laughing from the stable, as he stripped the headcollar and cavesson off the filly. He whispered to Tess, 'Is he a bit odd?'

'Um.' Tess undid Mark's shirt and pulled it gently off him. But her fingers did not caress this time. They were crisp now. She was in a hurry, and on duty.

Mark rushed out, 'Truly I can't stop myself I am just mad for you Tess Tess I must have you.' His voice crackled like the deep straw in which they stood. The filly behind them pawed at it, snuffling.

Sultan's hooves scrunched on the gravel. Salerno boomed, 'Come on with you. I shall lose the high light. Trapchek!' He spoke slowly and clearly as if to an idiot. 'Give Sultan now to the boy. *Sultan!*' screamed Mr Salerno. 'The black horse you have, my God!'

The black stallion was enormous. He towered over the groom like a panther over a frog. Mark came across uncertainly. He was, as he would say of a young horse, on the boil. Energy foamed in him, but he kept himself bridled. He could not look at Mr Salerno. The groom Trapchek handed him the reins. 'Quiet?' asked Mark. 'Bite or kick?' 'Ver' good, OK', grunted the groom. His breath was rank with garlic. He waited at Mark's side, ogling Tess. Most of his stubby teeth were steel-capped.

'Off please, Trapchek', Mr Salerno waved an imperious arm. 'Right away. Out of camera, Trapchek.'

The groom reluctantly stumped back to his cottage, but could be seen hovering in the doorway. Tess stepped towards Salerno. 'Pop', she asked gently, 'Will Mark hold him? With that arm?'

Salerno was crouched behind the ciné-camera's view-finder. 'First shots on the ground', he called. 'Arms round his neck, Tess, please.'

'Mine?' Mark called back. A combination of nerves and arrogance, uncertainty and lust made him bold.

'The horse's', retorted Mr Salerno fiercely, emitting another exasperated sigh. 'As we discussed, Tess. You slightly beneath, *curved* backwards' . . . He made the verb linger.

'Supplicating?' Tess asked.

Salerno did not reply, but crossed with a crunch to the other camera tripod and adjusted the focus on the lens' snout. 'The horse's marks are *there!*' he shouted at Mark impatiently.

'Where he's to stand', murmured Tess.

'But where?' Mark whispered.

'Have you never done this before?' bellowed Mr Salerno, standing up so abruptly that his broad hat lifted backwards off his head. His grey hair sprang outwards, but he did not notice it.

Mark shook his head. He was now hard put not to laugh out loud. He felt Tess tremble. 'How on earth could he, Pop?' she asked, nudging Mark. She pointed to a cross marked in the gravel. 'Horse's hoof-spot', she said, her face so puckered with laughter that she put her head down. 'Dead professional.'

Thus primed, Mark without much difficulty moved the stallion forward a pace and a half and posed him so that he stood forefeet as together as a soldier's but with one hind-foot slightly forward of the other. It was the stance his father had taught him, which best displayed the conformation of their horses for sale. 'Fine, Sultan, fine', Mark murmured, looking round towards the artist for approval. The stallion's muzzle was just above Mark's bare shoulder and Mark could feel his breath. The horse half-opened his jaw showing a flash of yellowed teeth and Mark, always conscious now of the pain in his shoulder, involuntarily shrank away.

'Under his neck, now, Tess.' called Mr Salerno. 'Your breast very white against that fine bold curve. More. Show more. Slip the smock off your right shoulder. . . . Completely. . . . So. Hold that. Now caress his neck. . . . Perfect, you don't obscure your breast with your arm. You're clever. Tess. Now, *woo* that horse. . . .' The ciné-camera began to whirr and Salerno left it. He limped across to start clicking the shutter of the still camera. Tess was bent backwards under the stallion's neck. Mark held the reins behind her head. The ends of her hair stirred against his palm. He saw the pinkness of her parting where the straw hat slipped back. She smelled as sweet as white elderberry flowers. He saw the tension firm in the line of her breast and a faint shiver down her backbone. He longed to be her support.

Tess, without looking at Salerno or altering the arch of her back said, 'I can't hold this much longer.'

'You must!' Salerno was at his palette frenziedly mixing colours in squirts. He shot a look at her. 'You *must*, Tess. The horse – he's randy for you now.'

'God!' Tess exclaimed, but without alarm, 'He'll not rape me, will he?'

'Look at him!' called Salerno, jabbing a paint brush forward. It was daubed in pinky-white magnolia to match her breast. Salerno's eyes were flashing behind his glasses. He had a high colour in his long face.

Sultan was fretting hard. Mark accelerated the jangling of the bit in his mouth. He was so agitated himself that he could feel his loins pulsing. Unconsciously his buttocks were starting to squeeze.

'Put her up!' ordered Mr Salerno. 'Quick.'

'But – ' Mark began. He meant to explain that his right arm was incapable of hoisting Tess up onto the stallion's high back.

'Quick!' shrieked Salerno. 'Put her up, I say.'

'You must', Tess commanded. 'I'll spring.' She turned away from him, pressing both her breasts against the stallion's dark shoulder. She bent one knee. 'One flick', she said urgently. Sultan feeling her body leaning against his and smelling her excitement, started to tremble violently, to arch his great neck and to rumba his thrusting quarters from side to side, like a negro boxer limbering up. Mark had him still by his left hand. He stooped down. His left cheek brushed against her round neat buttocks. He loosed his right arm from its sling and placed his hand boldly beneath her bent left knee and thigh. 'One two three up!' he breathed. Though she had sprung up lightly as a thrush his ripped shoulder muscles tore as he lifted her upwards. The pain which darted through him made him gasp with delight because she caused it. His head came forward against her knee as she bestrode the black horse bareback. The smock had run up round her waist. To grip the stallion her thighs were splayed.

'Perfection!' cried Salerno. He had the still camera in his hand and now ran in with it stooping from a low angle, shooting and clicking for three-quarter frontal shots. From its fixed position the ciné continued to whirr. Mark's face, turned away from the artist, remained pressed against her knee which now began to squeeze and move. He opened his mouth and began to lick her skin. He yearned up towards her. But Tess, eyes rolled up to the skies, moved to and fro on the stallion's back. Her cheeks and neck flushed. Her breasts rocked. Her eyes became half-closed. She rode upon the stallion, quicker and quicker and quicker, yet with longer strokes.

Salerno pushed Mark aside and reached up at her. Her bent knee jabbed past Mark's face. Without looking down at him, she commanded: 'Take the horse away', and, lifting her right leg forwards over the stallion's neck, sat sideways on his back. 'Catch me, Pop', she half-slid, half-jumped at Salerno. He caught her, twisted her and together, he hopping, she pulling him, they ran into the house.

The front door swung shut with a bang. The stallion sprang aside, tugging on his bridle and Mark's left arm. Mark's right shoulder, as if by magic, had lost its pain. Turning Sultan he made it move. He swung his right arm, still it did not hurt. She's cured it, he thought wildly, for miracles at her hands seemed possible. Where's that groom? he cursed, leading the stallion back to his box. His right arm moved easily. My idiot father, he thought, urging Sultan impatiently forwards to get him off his hands. My bloody shoulder was just out of joint. He and his unguents. The leap of Tess against his hand had jerked it back. She's a goddess, he breathed, slamming the great bolts on the stallion's door, as the groom appeared, picking cheese from his capped teeth.

'Here! Take him', ordered Mark and began to run towards the house. She's divine, he thought, jumping through the front door frame.

He thought: Mr Salerno's beating her up. He heard cracks and groans. Then long rasps of breath. Then he saw over the back of the great sunk sofa Mr Salerno's long clothed back hunched up, and rutting. His metal leg stuck up behind at a grotesque angle. It flicked out backwards like a silvery whip. And beneath Salerno's head Mark saw half the scarlet face of Tess. One eye, all white, was rolled backwards. He sprang forward. The lunatic was killing her. Her eye rolled down and looked directly at Mark. She moved her face a little from under Salerno. Her bare legs did not cease to move in rhythm with the artist's thrusts. Her hands, Mark saw, gripped the long grizzled locks at the back of Salerno's head. But not in anger. Nor in defence. Her eyes looked straight at Mark and she motioned with her face towards the door. It was a gesture of tacit, but urgent dismissal. Then, because Mark still stood there aghast, her lips which were wet, mouthed at him 'Away. *Go away.*' Even before he had turned to stumble out, she had stopped looking at him, casually trusting him to depart, and was half-sunk again beneath the mounting frenzy of her lover.

25

Mark was running with the filly through the woods. His breath too rasped in and out, each gasp reminding him of the obscene sounds on the leather seat. He had got to the stable door before he knew it, had groped for the filly's headcollar and had spun choking into the door-hinges, slamming his head. He had vomited. 'OK? OK?' The squat groom loomed. 'Arm is hurt?'

Arm, he thought, retching again. What's an arm? He stood giddily in a red fog. Through it the filly reappeared. She was watching him. He got her headcollared. Trapchek, regarding him curiously, handed over the cavesson, and said with a glottal wheeze, 'Plenty fick-fick.' He made an oval of his muck-stained thumb and forefinger and thrust the other horny index finger with its black nail to and fro inside the orifice. 'Hot-tail bitch', he grunted and elbowed Mark. 'Good poke.' Mark turned, kicked and punched him simultaneously, spat at the groom's falling face, and was gone with the filly.

Then he was racing across the long meadow, now turned paddock. He wrestled with the gate locks. He could not see properly. Tears coursed from his eyes. But no relief, no great sobs broke from his lungs. There was only the ache and creak of running which hammered home the grotesque copulation of Mr Salerno and that girl.

The filly at his side had occasionally to canter so hard was Mark running in his despair. Coming upon a thicket of those gripping briars, she leaped them, taking the slack out of Mark's hand in a burning run across the palm. She waited as he crashed through behind her. His thoughts went to the filly for the first time since he had seen the girl's one white eye turned up. In terror, he'd thought at first, then seen it was delight. He realised that the filly, unattended, had kept steadily with him all those miles, running beside him with no trouble, with no attempt to linger or to break away.

'Oh you are good', he sighed aloud and clasped her neck. On the word 'good' a huge sob at last burst out of him. His eyes flooded. Shaking, he began to cry. And the filly, standing patiently, put her head over his shoulder and pressed her muzzle to his bare back. 'I've no shirt, no sling', he realised over his crying 'And I'll never go back there. I'll never see Tess again. Never see you again', he cried out, clasping the filly. Sobs, like surf around a little craft, completely engulfed him.

26

Old Lincoln glowered like a turkey cock over the hearth. Smoke gusted down the chimney. The wind had veered south-westerly, bringing a sharp rain. Drops rattled against those panes remaining in the drawing room and through the hundreds of empty gaps, spattering on the broken boarded floor.

Lincoln spat. His gob struck the sulky fire and sizzled. 'Disgusting', he said. 'Bitch.'

Mark was calm again. But he felt extraordinarily tired. His bones were chilled. He was lying on his blanket propped on one elbow by the fire. Little of dusk's light came in from the overgrown garden. Outside, the rain swirled. Bitch was what the girl had called the filly. Wrong about that, too. And bitch was rightly what the groom had called the girl.

'. . . . moderns for you', his father was continuing his tirade. 'Daughters laid by peg-legged fathers. Ugh!' He tried again to spit, but his throat had gone dry. He looked down at Mark who wearily realised that another reply was expected.

'Wouldn't be the first time', he said dully.

Lincoln pounced, wanting to stir hatred out of his son against the vile, interloping Salerno's. No profit would come out of this numbed acceptance. And there was a lesson to come from the pain: the modern world, all strangers, were a menace. Lincoln kept goading, 'At it all this time, I'll bet', he spat. 'Soon as you'd been up there the first time when she was so lovey dovey with the filly, why I bet they were only waiting then for another bout of slippery incest.'

Mark winced, but he said quietly, 'I didn't mean them. You used to tell me about in the slums. Cold, crammed together, fathers with daughters . . .' He flicked his hand, trying to dispose of Tess with all those faceless figures in city tenements where urban poverty made human beasts.

His shoulder had remained cured. Even that dismissive gesture of his hand conjured up instantly the feel of her small knee, the curve of her behind. I gloried in the pain she gave me, he reviled himself. She needed me and that was beautiful. She used me, and so. . . . He was too tired to think it through. 'Is it so vile to be used?' he asked. 'To serve?'

But his father was slanting away on the tack of incest. 'But in the slums they were poor. Real poverty smashes you into beasts', his father expostulated, giving the broken wainscot another kick and precipitating a fall of crumbling timber. 'These Salernos stink with riches. And then with that stallion —' Lincoln caricatured a bobbing, bestraddling motion.

'No', Mark spoke out sharply. He would never forget the sight of the effervescent bliss in her face. 'That's quite another thing'. His father was about to argue. Mark said, 'Leave that alone please.'

Lincoln shrugged. 'Do you', he hesitated to find a tactful word, 'desire her still?' he asked.

Mark nodded immediately. 'Oh yes', he said. It was a matter of fact.

'Do you?' Lincoln was so astonished that he stooped to look into Mark's face. 'After all that?'

'I can't see, father', Mark got up stiffly, 'how *desiring* people — as you put it — has got the faintest thing to do with what they're *like*, as characters.' He pointed at the stained picture of his mother's ancestors over their belching fire. 'Wanting a woman isn't liking her.' He looked levelly at his father. 'As you do know.'

Lincoln thought about Mark's mother and about himself. He thought about his son's face, white, runnelled with tears, coming out of the wood. He realised, I'm over sixty, I've done wrongs, but I've never till this day felt deep pain in someone else, and longed to help, and been enraged by what they've suffered. By what Mark has suffered, for no fault of his own. His birth he couldn't help, but his upbringing here, this clinging to the old, this delusion of dreams — all this is my fault, Lincoln realised. He understood simultaneously that these wrongs could never now be righted, and that he had directed his son on a dreadful course.

A freak of the wind above precipitated a sudden fall of rain down the great chimney. Their fading fire hissed and dwindled. Lincoln seized the coach-horn and began in a fever to poke the logs, to stir up heat, to recreate a hearth. 'Burn, you sods', he cried, striking the ashy logs.

'Oh, leave it, father'. There was an awful acceptance in Mark's tone.

'I will not.'

He glared fiercely at his son, but his eyes blinked twice. He crouched and blew and a flame rekindled. 'Well', said old Lincoln gruffly, 'We've got one hell of a lot to do with our filly. If we're going to race her next year.'

'Oddly enough', said Mark, resting his hand lightly on his father's shoulder, 'I was just going down to see her before night falls. I really gave her a terrible time today.'

27

The rain and wind had not abated by dusk, but neither could be heard in Mr Salerno's overheated living room. All the big windows though still uncurtained, were double-glazed. The fire burned brightly within its strange brass cylinder. Constructed to consume not wasteful ash-producing wood, but neat nuggets of artificial fuel, it glowed with chemically-blue flares inside the crimson inferno.

It was so hot that Tess, after bathing, had come downstairs again in only the light dressing gown she took for their flights to the tropics. Even in this she simmered, curled upon the sofa. It had now fallen open and the fire made pink patches on her knees and belly. 'Pouf', she said restlessly. She had timed the automatic cooker to deliver their suppers an hour hence, and would have liked now to speed its process. Food, mastication, the movement of forks and knives, mouths opening again, might ease the silent failure brooding over all.

Mr Salerno did not move from his hunched position in the corner of the banquette. He had hardly moved all day since the events of the bright morning. The coupling of his metal leg had become twisted during his endeavours with Tess. It hurt the stump of his thigh exceedingly, and the buckled metal joint squealed whenever he put his great weight on it. The next day he would fly to the specialist to have it readjusted. He had an hour between his publishers and the paint corporation which was courting his franchise. Soon he should be out of pain, on a course of new injections, and his abominable metal extension should once again perform efficiently.

His other disability could not be so swiftly cured. Never now, he thought. A pall fell over his spirit like a hangman's hood. Contemplating his cold predicament in that hot room he let out the start of a groan. His long hand pushed his locks back again and again from his forehead. It was his reflex when defeated.

Tess watched him sympathetically. 'Aren't you too hot, Pop?' Even that question, like almost every phrase she used after these débâcles, carried an unintended barb upon which he would impale himself, flinching, and so turn to rend her.

'Can't be too hot for me.' He did not look up. It was true. He needed heat. 'As you well know', he said. Here it would come, she knew from his shade of tone. 'And then again, I am not hot enough.' This time he half-turned one huge dark eye and lugubriously regarded her. She crawled on hands and knees like a puppy down the long leather seat and squatted neatly against him. His body was set very stiffly. He looked not only forlorn, but very old. She glimpsed in her mind again Mark's appalled look, his body sideways to that morning's sun, crumpled as if smitten by a boulder, and in that instant a shocking doubt struck her.

Random Salerno said, looking at his rugs, 'It wasn't at all good. It was no better. No, not at all.'

She said gently, for brightness only maddened him, 'It doesn't matter.'

There was a long complete silence. Then Salerno said with a return of eagerness, 'Yet I've never seen you quite so –' he frothed his arms up and down – 'as on that horse.'

'True', she said.

'It was a good idea of mine, the stallion, anyway.'

She nodded firmly. 'It'll make good pictures.' She asked 'You'd got enough stuff before. . . ?'

'Good *commercial* pictures', said Salerno drily. 'Great erotic calendars.' He gave her his first wisp of a smile since the morning. Under the self-mockery he had escaped into thoughts of his work. She would not be drawn into that argument now. To keep his mind bent upon his painting she enquired. 'When will you start?'

'What happened to that boy?' Salerno asked. 'I'd quite forgotten

III

him. And his wretched horse.'

The change in his tone emboldened her to say, 'He looked in.' She had only to nod from the sofa towards the door to explain it. It was part of her great pleasure in him that his mind moved like lightning, so that they could communicate in nods and semi-phrases.

'Did he?' Salerno swung round. 'Early or late?'

She said truthfully, though she would have lied then to save his pride, 'Early.'

'Aah.' He was relieved. 'That's all right then.'

But Tess, revisualising Mark's horror, reacted. She answered hotly, 'It wasn't all right for him.'

'Eh? He lusts after you. I saw him with the horse. He was transported with you. In time with you. So for him to watch you giving a full *exhibition* – what, it could be fantastic for him!'

'He didn't watch', she said. 'He turned and ran.' Salerno shrugged his shoulders. 'Ran from it', Tess insisted. The shadow of Salerno's slouched head leaped on the blank windows. Tess said simply, in a small voice, 'He loves me.'

She said it with such conviction that Salerno, imagining Tess beneath him and, the boy observing him, felt his frail libido thus again aroused. He stared at her. 'What?' He exclaimed. 'That gypsy youth?' He was full of scorn. '"Love!" That horse boy *loving* you! He's only just left school'.

She said tensely, 'He may seem a boy to you. But he is only seven years younger than me.' Her eyes had started to smoulder. Catching that look in them Salerno swivelled right round and grabbed at her arm. 'Has that peasant had you?' he bellowed.

'Would you mind?' asked Tess, flinching from the pain.

'By all hell I'd mind! As you know!' He was screaming. 'And kill you for it. Has he? Those days when the dirty tramp sneaked up here?' Then he muttered, 'After we quarrelled last time probably. That would be the time. . . .' he burst out, 'Did he?' Salerno's fingers ground into the flesh of her arm. Tess yelped.

'No', she said. 'And do you know why that poor creature so loathed catching you at your clamberings?' She waited. 'At your miserable clamberings?' But he did not, as she had expected and at least half-hoped, raise his arm to strike her. 'D'you know why?' she repeated. She would make him ask. If he did so, he would be to blame. He glowered at her. 'I've just realised it', Tess said. 'But I'd not tell you –'

112

'Why not?'

'It'll hurt.'

'No more than failing with you over again.'

Tess said, 'He must believe you're my father.'

There was a silence. The sound-proofed room, the sealed fire excluded outside noises. When Salerno rose the squeal of his metal leg seemed deafening. Both he and Tess, for different reasons, winced. But the sound and the physical pain reminding Salerno of his double incapacity, also stressed a new weakness in his position. He was skilled in the balancing of relationships. Thus while he thought how best to accept this further threat, he wrinkled his brow as if all his pain came from his amputated limb. Then he asked carefully, 'Why should he? I realise the difference in our ages . . .' His deep voice ended in a cough, making it a query. He added warmly, to reestablish the vibrant sophisticated life which he and Tess enjoyed and from which the boy was excluded, 'But he'll know of men and young mistresses, of course.'

Tess declared, 'He knows *nothing* of anything like that.'

Her admiration so blazed that Salerno looked at her sharply again, 'How d'you know?'

'We talk. I know him. His is a very strange life. Quite cut away.'

'Cut off.' Salerno corrected her.

'No, I mean cut *away*. He might believe our life is cut off from *them*. Who's to say which way it is?'

'Ridiculous', said Random Salerno. 'Those people have just been left behind by time.' He was ill-disposed to paying them even the compliment of referring to them, 'I can't imagine, though, why I should have to evaluate their miserable life-styles.'

No, thought Tess, you would not. In those spheres you have no doubts; fortunate, established man.

'And what's this father thing that you think upset him?' asked Salerno. 'How did the youth grab that wrong stick? Apart from our coming from different vintages?'

'He hears me call you Pop.'

'I suppose he does', Salerno nodded. The matter now seemed of little consequence. 'Stupid name. Only let you start it because I thought of you as a child. In that strange cold studio, when I was doing those rather kinky rubber ads.'

'There you are', said Tess angrily. 'Just think how, believing that

113

must have absolutely riven him.'

Salerno did pause to contemplate Mark's pain. The prospect rather warmed him. But he said, 'I don't see why. You're not his. You're something –' he flung his arm out – 'right outside his life. He's no more right to desire you than any peasant goggling at my pictures of your body in some hot corrugated iron hut. That boy has no *right* to think himself involved with you. Let alone be hurt.'

'He does love me, Pop.' He grimaced at the name.

She declared, 'I know it. I'd be the first great love of his life.'

'He'll have to get over it.'

She did not reply. Salerno swung round with another squeal of metal and said furiously 'Well, won't he? Part of growing up. Silly little gypsy.'

'"Getting over" is no more part of growing up than of growing old.'

Now he will strike me, she was sure. Indeed, Salerno swooped over her like a vulture and flung up his painting arm into the air like a talon. 'D'you fancy him then?'

'Yes', she said, 'He's beautiful. And natural.'

'Beautiful', Salerno sneered. 'Like a girl?'

'Well, that he's not. As you saw.' Still the blow did not fall.

'Do you want him as a lover?'

'I would already', she began, 'If I were –' He lunged at her. She scrambled to one side and he pitched forward onto the leather. 'If I were free', she continued coldly, 'I was going to add.'

'He'll not want you now', Salerno's voice was muffled against the back of the seat. He was in pain again from his leg. 'Certainly not', he said bitterly, 'as he believes you get laid by your father.'

'I shall tell him that's not true.' Tess stood up out of range.

'Leave that alone.' Salerno, after contortions, scrambled again to his foot. His face was twisted. 'Leave that boy alone.'

'Not till I've told him you're not – mercifully – my father.'

He seized on this double rejection. 'Leave him alone!' screamed Random Salerno. Sweat glistened on his brow and lip from physical and emotional pain. His ebbing colour left his cheeks with the pallor of cheese. 'That is a command, Tess. Or out you'll go.' He paused, panting, 'And leave all this. For ever.'

She hesitated. Then she said softly, 'If you thought of him desiring me while you – if you thought of him even having me while you were in fact possessing me. . . . ? Would that not help you?'

As she spoke there sprang up into her mind the sight, the start of the feel, too, of Mark making his love to her while Salerno waited, watching from the shadows. In the sunshine, those poppies, Mark's chest, feeling him. . . . Salerno's hat shrouding his face behind the barn and waiting. The vision made her cheeks flush. She repeated 'Mightn't that help?'

Random Salerno's great eyes had re-awoken. He flung up both his arms like an ancient prophet. 'That's how the picture will be, Tess, Clever, Tess, clever. He will be the poor slave as I'd first thought, desperately, but vainly, desiring you. And you, up there, in a heaven of your own, will be riding on over his poor yearning head. The picture will show what we all feel: hopeless, consuming, longing for something afar.'

He brought Tess to him in a bear hug. He was more than confident; he now was aloft. 'I can't wait to start, my beauty,' he exclaimed.

28

Tess waited in the great bed until she heard Salerno's estate-car grind away down the track through the woods. He would be gone a week.

He had delayed his departure to complete his picture of Desire. Zeal had submerged the pain of his stump, the squeak of his limb, and his last failure with Tess. By the afternoon, while she fretted, he was crooning the folk songs from the sun baked soil of his forefathers: the ciné-film and the stills out of his dark room were even more erotic than he had dreamed.

Then, separated from her by his absorption he painted with a desperate energy which tired her to watch. The muscles in his neck bulged with tension. He faintly sweated. The pictures came off bolder than ever before. Her abandon, Mark's longing, the stallion's lust, blazed from the sheets. 'Wow', she said gazing at them. She could feel the horse's back between her legs. She took Salerno's

115

beautiful hand and put it there. She looked into his long, sallow face: it was exhausted. She looked at Mark's face in the picture aflame for her. Salerno had painted Mark's body bent like a cross bow arrowing at hers. She longed to see him.

She sat naked for Salerno straddling the leather back of the sofa while he recaptured her colours. But there was no passion. Restlessly she rode Sultan each afternoon while he toiled. 'Don't go near that boy', Salerno said just once, but with lasting menace. So she cantered in looping figures-of-eight around the paddock, keeping within sight and sound of her master, and champing to slip away.

Now he had gone. She jumped up, pulled on a sweater and the chaps she liked for riding and told Trapchek to get Sultan saddled immediately.

She followed the tracks Mark had made with the filly crashing homewards through the woods. She only knew the rough direction of the croft in which she imagined him living with his father. There seemed no way to reach it by any road. She supposed that she would recognise it by traces of pigs and a cow, and the filly.

Sultan moved easily beneath her. She enjoyed the spring and flow of his paces coolly. There was no lust in her now. Riding was as aesthetic a pleasure as the sights of the forest. Tess knew she rode well. To ride had been one of several accomplishments on which her mother had insisted: 'Ridin', Skiin', – that way you'll meet the right sort.' She had been blessed not only with beauty but with balance, with sympathy for animals and with courage. So she had shone, been spotted early by the famed Random Salerno, plucked out of the ruck of starting models, and made famous by him. Or my body has been, she corrected herself, glancing down at her thighs rising and falling at the trot and thinking for the first time that day of the frantic libido her nakedness had ignited nine days before on the stallion's bare black spine. She bent low beneath a branch, catching a whiff of Sultan's hot neck. She visualised herself as Mark had watched her. She felt shame, then anger spurt. It is entirely Pop's fault, she decided. I'm young, normal and I need loving. He arouses me for his pictures. He is satisfied by his pictures. But I yearn. She wished not only to be fully entered again, but to be embraced. 'I only want to be held', she heard her voice murmur pathetically and immediately laughed at herself. The low branches and stroking twigs of the beeches swept over her back. She could not see where she was being carried through this thick belt of the woods.

When she could sit up straight again the trees had thinned on a downward slope. At their edge a fringe of deep bracken started above a long meadow already high with hay. And there in the valley set about with ornamental trees and a royal expanse of parkland, stood an immense house. Tess squeezed Sultan into a quicker trot. The grey beech trunks flickered past. She snatched between their branches glimpses of the golden stoned façade of a wonderful mansion, standing behind its parapeted terraces, and gazing down with grand security over its own demesne. Tess had never in all her world travels seen such a house in such a setting. She was so struck that she grabbed at Sultan's reins and yanked him to a stop so that she might continue staring on and on. She was entirely bewildered.

The crash of Sultan's hooves through the briars and rustling drifts of beech mast had excluded all other sounds. Now on this still midsummer morning the noises, the gentle music of the countryside, came flooding in. Tess saw to her far left the glitter of a river, willows, a mill, herds of horses and of cattle. Some cows lowed. From what seemed a small lake set about with thick trees below the house, duck arose whirring, necks straining into the sky. Distantly flocks of geese honked in the other long arm of woods behind the mansion and its sprawl of barns and stables and farm buildings.

Then much nearer to her from somewhere in the meadow, she heard the swish of a scythe through grass. It paused. She caught the scrape of a whet-stone sharpening a long blade. It could be Mark, she thought, squeezing Sultan forward.

She emerged from the trees and paused on the edge of the bracken. It seemed deep like a treacherous green sea, and she saw that it lapped the remnants of some wall that must once have held back the woods.

The whet-stone's scraping ceased. Yet the sound of the scythe was not resumed. She thought she caught the low growl of a large dog. Sultan's ears flicked back and forth. He swung his head towards the wavy tops of the bracken and stared. The tips of the fronds moved as if by some animal under water. Tess glanced across the valley: but the pillar of grey blue smoke rose vertically from the house in the windless air. No breeze. So something was stealthily approaching her under the bracken. The dog that had growled? And they would need guard-dogs around such a palace. She had not known that such places could still exist.

The setting of the house remained as its master builder had intended. The colour of its stones still glowed across the valley in the sunlight, like a topaz in a setting of cabochon emeralds. Tess's distant view lent more than enchantment. At this range, the mansion seemed unaltered from its heyday. Oh, what a perfect place to live, she thought, feasting her eyes upon it. To spend one's life in this secret valley.

'Out!' screamed a voice. The bracken erupted. Out burst a flash of brindle coat and bared white fangs. A huge dog sprang. Sultan leapt sideways. As he whirled, the dog hurled itself past his quarters and crashed into the briars. From the tail of her eye Tess, twirling round, glimpsed the flash of long steel in sunlight. 'Out!' screamed an old bent man, brandishing a wicked scythe. His face was purple. His eyes, bright blue, bulged. He spat, and his wrinkled neck gobbled like a turkey's. Tess turned Sultan towards him.

The black horse towered over the small man at the foot of the bank, but the stallion trembled before the fury of the human body. Without Tess' legs firmly gripping him he would have whipped round and fled. The old man crawled steadily forward up the bank dwarfed by the great scythe.

Then the lurcher leaped again at Sultan's hind-leg, snarling with red mouth agape, for the hamstring above the horse's hock. This if severed, as by humble soldiery against knights' chargers, would paralyse the horse and immobilise its rider for summary execution. Sultan swung round so quickly that he half flung Tess off. She felt him lash out, heard a crack and the dog's high yelp. Then she was round again, one foot lost from a stirrup iron, and desperately grabbing for it. The lurcher limped to the bracken's edge, head down, tail low, dragging a hind leg.

'Whore!' screamed the old man, struggling over the lip of the bank to get at her. His scythe was drawn back over his back but its silver bright beak was swaying forward above his head. 'I'll slash –' he burst into a fit of coughing, 'I'll slash your wicked . . . face . . . into . . . long . . . bleeding ribbons.'

He had checked to cough. He brought forward the scythe, but only to lean upon it. His head was down. He was heaving. The dog, whining, looked anxiously across at him.

Tess was white. She heard her voice come out squeakily. 'I wanted to tell Mark. . . . I want to see Mark to tell him something. . . .' She hesitated. The old man was still bent over his scythe like a frail serf. She could explain nothing to this creature. His breath kept catching. Another bout of coughing racked him and he spat horribly over his boots. Tess said quietly, 'I must tell Mark something very important. If you'll tell me —'

Old Lincoln revived. 'I tell you: Out!' He glared up at her, seeing her with Mark's eyes coupling with her father. 'Hot-tailed perverted bitch. Leave my son. Never see him.'

Lincoln heard a faint roaring in his ears. The light seemed to have leaked out of the scene as from an under-exposed photograph. The sky, tree trunks, this whore on its horse, had all darkened to the colour of old blood. Lincoln peered up and clutched the scythe to sustain him. He whispered 'No more harm. Ever.'

'I've done *none*', began Tess angrily now. 'I want to *explain*.' Her frustration lent the last word a whine which exactly echoed his ex-wife's voice each time he'd caught her with another lover. Lincoln felt, through the blur of his vision and the mounting thrum in his eardrums, as if a garotte was being tightened around the middle of his chest. Mark's mother and Mark's girl merged. The old man swung back the scythe and lunged at the shadow rider in the dark. He felt its sharpened point pierce, then snag, then tear on downwards as he tumbled forwards. The floor of the forest rose very slowly, silently and squeezed itself into his face.

The stallion, seeing the sickle flash, had whipped aside. The scythe's point caught Tess' leather chaps, pierced them and ran down her calf. In the instant that Sultan swerved, the dog sprang forward. Tess, crouched on the stallion's back, booted him with her heels. She felt hot blood ooze, looked down and saw the left leg of her chaps ripped apart. Her calf was a scarlet mess beneath it. She felt no fear, but only a soaring anger with the old maniac. She glanced behind her as Sultan galloped on. There was no sign nor sound of the pursuing dog. But she did not slacken her pace. She thought vividly, it'll be bad if my leg is scarred. The horse pounded on. The beech-trunks flashed past. She felt slightly giddy as the sun dazzled and darkened overhead. She thought, but my body and face are still all right. And the conviction burst up: I'll not fail, even if the worst happens.

29

Mark heard the lurcher howling. Even in the hot stillness of noon the wailing made his back hairs rise. His father had been scything the first swathe round the hay meadow. Mark knew from the sound that Rip's howls sprang from terror for his master, as the banshee shrieks before a death in the family to which she is attached.

He was in the bowling green field driving the filly under saddle with a rein each side of her now. Since he had rushed from the Salerno's coupling Mark had poured his heart into the breaking of the filly. Daily and all day he had worked on her. Yesterday had been the final stage before backing. A potato sack had been gently placed on her saddle. She had shrunk down, then turned to sniff it. Old Lincoln had tied it on with binder twine. 'She'll buck now', the old man had chortled, loosing her head. Three quick leaps she had let fly in a row, her back arched, her tail up, her head shaking. 'What a girl!' Lincoln had cried.

The bowling green field lay equidistantly between the forest's edge and the stables. At Rip's howl Mark hesitated only while the filly completed six strides of her circular canter round him. Then, directing her head towards the haymeadow, he ran behind her.

They trotted up the slope following the apple-pale swathe. The dog had ceased to howl. But Mark drove the filly on up, convinced that his father must have fallen upon his scythe, and was now bleeding to death. Fear literally choked him. The swathe ended. He pulled the filly's reins. She stopped. There was no sign of his father's body.

'Father!' he shouted. 'Father!'

The agitation in his mind was transmitted by his hands to the filly's mouth. She trembled.

His call echoed in the forest. A flock of wood-pigeons rose applauding with a clapping of wings. The distant geese honked furiously.

'Father!' bellowed Mark. He was out of breath, and for that reason too, his heart was thumping. The filly uneasily moved forward. 'Stop', Mark hissed, realising even in his alarm the danger of upsetting her. He was in a quandary. He would not be able to urge the filly safely through the deep belt of bracken. Nor could he leave her loose to gallop away across the open hay-meadow.

Then Rip limped out of the bracken whimpering. The dog turned his head back to the edge of the forest and began to slink back. 'Wait' ordered Mark, but Rip crept back into the depths of the bracken again.

Mark dropped the filly's offside rein. Holding the other, he swiftly cut the twine holding the heavy sack onto the filly's saddle, and laid it quietly on the mown grass. She turned to stare at it, affecting alarm. He loosed the offside rein quickly from the bit and, as he did so, heard from beyond the bracken a faint moan. 'Father' he cried. He was now in dread.

Some answer, a sort of strangled 'I . . . I . . . .I . . .' came back. Mark's fingers fumblingly unthreaded the long near-side rein from the stirrup iron through which it ran. He took it past the filly's anxious head and, paying it out slowly, began to push his way backwards through the waist-high bracken. He kept his eyes fixed commandingly upon the filly. She followed him to the very start of the big fronds. 'Stay!' he commanded, as if she were a dog. 'Stay!'. With one arm raised and palm flattened, he gestured towards her urgently to stand still. She hesitated, then stood staring at his peculiar departure.

He had still an arm's length of slack canvas rein but no more, as he backed at last out of the clinging bracken sea and saw his father cast up like jetsam on the bank. Mark called Rip to him, put the loop of the lungeing rein round his collar, and swore softly at him: 'Sit. Sit. Sit!' The dog crouched. Mark saw blood on his haunch. He scrambled up the bank and reached his father. The old man was still breathing. It was quite loud, but burbled noisily. Mark started to turn him face upwards, but Lincoln's fist clutched fiercely at the handle of the long scythe before him. 'Father. Let go.' Mark whispered. 'It's me.'

'No, she'll not,' babbled his father. 'Slash wicked face . . . something to say . . . bleeding ribbons.' As Lincoln's face turned up, Mark saw that its left side was curiously set. It looked as if pinned back by internal claws. The left eye drooped, the cheek was stretched, the left corner of the lip was drawn back as if he snarled. In the sagging pouch of his mouth, spittle had collected which moved and shrank as he gasped in and out.

'Oh God', prayed Mark, 'Let him live.' He felt, to his shame, primarily terror at his own immediate predicament and guideless future. He was positive that if he now took one false step he would lose

121

his father. He prised Lincoln's fingers from the handle of the scythe. The blade moved and he saw the tip of it was stained by blood. 'What?' He put his mouth to his father's ear as if the physical contact of lips to mouth could stem the leak between life and speeding death. 'Father, what happened?'

'Bitch came to get you.' It was mumbled but quite comprehensible. Mark supposed that the girl, totally unashamed, left alone again and needing sex, or the need to have him strain for her, had come to find him. Even in that instant he pictured her jerking body and lusted for it.

Mark looked into the wood. 'Have you killed her?'

'Slash her. Ran away', said Lincoln, with satisfaction.

'But are *you* cut?'

Lincoln waggled his head. 'Bit of black-out.' His eyes closed and he suddenly sagged. Mark attempted smoothly to scoop him up. But to his astonishment his father's small frame weighed ominously heavy. He recalled old Lincoln's voice, 'I always rode heavier than I looked.'

Mark heaved and, for the first time in his life, held his father briefly in his arms. Then he twisted and with a grunt got him laid across his shoulders. Mark knew what he must now try. It would be a wild risk, but he could see no other way. Listening for the continuance of his father's breathing against his shoulder, Mark whistled to Rip. 'Heel', he ordered. The dog, still attached to the lungeing rein, followed him back through the depths of the bracken. The filly, seeing this apparition of the double man swaying towards her over the bracken's surface, took fright, and started to back away. The end of the rein and Rip were still invisible. 'Whoa', called Mark pleadingly. 'Whoa, girl, whoa. . . .'

And his father, head down, by reflex repeated 'Whoa, girl, whoa.' The filly backed off twenty paces, then stood alarmed, snorting at Mark's approach. Rip emerged. Mark, staggering with his burden, stooped and took up the rein again. Then he carried his father very slowly along the rein up to the filly's head. He turned to let her sniff his father. 'There's a great girl then', blabbered old Lincoln. His voice was amazing. It might have come from an upside-down doll.

'She'll carry you home', said Mark. He hoped his voice sounded strong with conviction. Unless the filly proved really exceptional there was the fearful probability that she would go wild and cast Lincoln's poor crumpled body to the ground. The macabre humour touched Mark. What circumstances were theirs in which a thorough-bred filly would first be backed by a semi-conscious and perhaps dying man. But there was no other way he could get his father home. He could not tell whether his father had any notion where he was. There was a long silence. Then Lincoln said firmly, 'Just lay me on her. Gently, so,' and sighed.

Holding the filly's rein close to the ring of the bit, Mark manoeuvred her crabwise so that at last she was penned against the wall of bracken. His body ached and he was sweating. Then he started gradually to transfer his father's sagging weight from his shoulders to the filly's back. She went rigid. At any moment she could leap forward or plunge backwards and his father would crash head first onto the ground. 'Father', grunted Mark hoarsely, 'Talk to her, for God's sake. Talk softly to her. As you always do.'

Old Lincoln surfaced from semi-consciousness and began to croon. The tension melted out of the filly like ice. She turned her head to look at the old man who now carefully stroked her off-side shoulder. He began to help Mark by slithering across the saddle until his belly lay upon it. He was now precariously balanced, but in the position he always used when first backing a youngster: head down off-side; legs down near-side.

'Ready?' murmured Mark. 'We'll try to move. . . .'

It would be impossible for Lincoln to remain as completely immobile as the trussed sack. The filly, feeling for the first time another living creature upon her, might panic. In Lincoln's weak body there was neither the balance to coordinate his limbs nor the strength to flip himself off onto the safety of the ground. Mark was convinced now that he had taken a lunatic risk with the only two creatures he loved. His palms sweated coldly. There was still time to haul his father off. But if I do, how will I ever get him home? Mark coaxed the filly into taking one step to test whether she would accept her burden.

She took three uncertain paces forward, trying to adjust her bearing to the weight. Then she stopped. Uncertainty flickered in her eye. 'Come on', wheedled Mark. 'Come on then. All's well, filly. All's well.'

Then his father's voice came firmly from the other side in her accustomed command, 'Walk on!' The filly's ears flicked back and forth like a rabbit's. Then she stepped boldly forwards and made her way back along the cut swathe of the meadow. She walked as fearlessly as if she had been ridden for years. But Mark was sure she stepped more carefully.

At the bottom of the slope, where the dark yew trees lined the glade, old Lincoln let out a groan. Mark stopped the filly. 'Whoa girl . . . Father? You all right still?'

'Have to get up. Head burstin'.'

'I'll carry you.'

'You can't. I'll get *up*, I said.'

God, he means to sit up on her legs down either side she'll go mad, Mark thought in a rush.

'Hurry', his father grunted. 'Hoist me up.'

So Mark crept round to the filly's off-side and saw his father's purple twisted face and gently levered him back and upwards. 'How will you swing your leg over?' he asked.

'I will', old Lincoln declared with clarity as well as firmness. 'Stand to her head.'

'But can you cope?' Mark went to the filly's head and held both rings of her bridle.

'Always had to. Always *got* to cope.' Lincoln started to wriggle back. 'Watch', grunted the old man, and with a heave and a jerk of his right leg and a twist forward of his body and a long sigh, he was suddenly but smoothly sitting in the saddle. Triumph flashed from his eyes as he sat there. 'Well, go on then', he called to Mark. 'Lead her on in. She's backed, isn't she? I'll ride her home.'

30

But Lincoln's exultation was that of a wounded commander who had driven off an enemy attack and then achieved more speedily than anyone had hoped, the conquest of an objective. The aftermath of victory was relapse. As physical and emotional reaction ran out like the tide, Lincoln was left desperately tired. His face was still puckered by the stroke he had suffered. His left arm and hand barely functioned. He uttered for the first time that first admission of the steeply inclining slope towards the grave: 'I'm getting old.'

The confession chilled Mark. He continually wondered as he toiled from dawn to dusk around the place how on earth he could carry on without his father. He worried what he could do to help his father. He had no notion of what a stroke portended. He decided that his father's eyes must be kept looking forward to some not impossible goal this side of death. The filly provided it. Mark's initial work on her, kindly called by Lincoln, 'the nine day wonder', followed by her enforced, early backing by the old man himself, had advanced her programme by several months.

Her physique was now undoubtedly that of a flat-racer, and an early-maturing one at that. It was feasible to plan that she should run in a race the following summer at some small country meeting. Towards this end Lincoln carefully laid down the steps of her programme. 'So she must be galloping on properly by the spring, and in good strong canters before Christmas.' The old man blocked in the stages of her preparation with shaky chalk marks on the cracked panels of their room. Where tapestries, then silken wall coverings and those beautiful pictures had once hung like jewels, now ran the dusty hieroglyphics with which old Lincoln plotted the filly's progress.

Mark saw the project as tangled with snags as a blackthorn hedge. What horse could work with the filly? Where was the old racehorse who would teach her to gallop? How would they ever know how fast she was? He kept these doubts private, lest he discourage his father. But there remained one monumental nonsense: Lincoln was dreaming of riding the filly himself.

When he had first let this fall, Mark's incredulous laughter burst out. Then, catching the whipped look in his father's eyes, he had converted it to a bout of coughing. 'Fire smoking like hell', he had spluttered. He did not laugh again, but let Lincoln run on, talking of the filly's first easy race in which he'd try her, let her run sweetly outside the crowd (Lincoln's hands, his left one flopping, moved up the filly's imagined neck), making a little progress just to test how good she was . . .

In the meantime, Mark rode the filly every summer dawn, before he harnessed the work horses to finish cutting the hay. Lincoln sat in the sun on the terrace ensuring from his vantage point that Mark was cutting no corners, leaving no wasted headlands.

At last the big hay meadow on the slope to the wood was cut, turned and dried. On his own, save for the limping Rip, Mark forked the hay onto the rows of little haycocks. They patterned the apple-green field like neat trees in an orchard.

They made inviting rows down which to make the filly canter, weaving in and out, right rein and left rein bearing and turning. She moved with such balance and grace, marking the dew in a long serpent of her hoof-marks, that Mark whistled in the dawn in time with her floating strides and dreamed of the day when he would win upon her.

Rip sat by a haycock watching her cantering in the first long beams of the sun. The dog would not approach the wooded top of the field, where the stallion had wounded him, and where his master had lain gurgling on the bank. Mark, too, kept the filly towards the bottom of the meadow. The image of Tess was seeping out of his thoughts. He had no wish to reinforce it by approaching that spot, so close to home, where she had done the last of her damage.

Cantering across the slope, he saw ahead of him Rip suddenly rise and point towards the wood's edge, one paw raised, long tail low and extended. It was the attitude he adopted to indicate game for the pot. But Mark saw that the hackles along the dog's back were bristling. The dog stared into the wood. The picket-lines of trees lay in deep shadow behind the horizontal shafts of the rising sun. Mark pulled the filly up, and took one hand gently from her reins to shield his eyes and peer. Rip, on his belly and emitting low growls, began to crawl through the damp grass towards the spot where Lincoln had fallen.

Mark had not seen his father awake since the previous evening. He had left him covered in his blankets by the crumbling ashes of the old fire. It occurred to Mark with a clutch of cold hands down his spine, that his father had finally died in his sleep and that his ghost was up there at the point where it had so nearly left his body before. He turned the filly's head towards the wood, still dazzled by the sun's beams across his front, and made her walk towards the trees.

'The filly's marvellous.' The voice of Tess called from the wood's edge. Mark's body jumped, as if convulsed. The filly with a snort shied sideways. The lurcher froze and crouched. Mark's heart boomed. He got one hand out to stroke the filly's neck. He saw to his disgust that his fingers were quivering. He scowled. The dog Rip, growling, quickened his forward crawl again. Mark could see nothing in the dark shade and the filly, moving her head about to

126

listen, showed that she too could not see the girl.

When the voice came again Mark could smell the poppies in her hat and the scent of her skin. Another shiver went through him. 'Can I explain something?' called Tess politely in the little girl tone which had so surprised him when they had first met in the byre.

His shivering passed. Drawing himself right up he shouted into the quiet wood the words she had used to him beneath Salerno's rutting back. 'Go away!' shouted Mark. 'Go away!' And all the trees around the green slope set the echoes ringing, 'Away . . . away. . . .'

Mark flung his arm forward as if casting a stone at a wolf, called Rip loudly and turned dismissively away. As the echoes ceased reverberating he heard her call again, temper sharpening her tone. 'Your mad old father tried to kill me, do you know? He cut my leg —'

Giving his back a histrionic hunch and without even turning, Mark shouted to the sky, 'Go away. Curse you.'

Again the woods rustled back like witches, 'Curse you. . . . Curse you. . . .' and he heard Sultan's hoof-falls galloping away through the forest. And that, he thought, but biting his lower lip so sharply that tears started in his eyes, will be the end of all that.

31

Physical hardship sent the days wheeling past. It was another hot summer. The harvest came ready quickly, and old Lincoln was still incapable. Mark slaved. By early August he had so sweated his weight away that he was all wrinkled skin and weary bones. His eyes glowered from his gaunt face. The nights were the worst times, for dreams of Tess kept coming. When the cocks crowed Mark could barely rise from fatigue. In the harvest fields his legs and body and arms maintained the steady motion of a slave chained to a galley oar. His brain, too, fell into a sullen rhythm.

Lincoln could just feed some stock. He found small repairs which he believed necessitated a morning's tapping with a hammer like a child. Weariness came over him too soon. He began to think of Mark's future alone. He was increasingly agitated by the conviction that he had perpetuated his hermit's existence out of lunatic pride and from fear of the world, and that he had wantonly saddled Mark with all the liabilities of this folly. Thus tormented, he hardly slept but twitched before the hearth like a fretting terrier. Guilt badgered him in the grey nights. Sleep took its toll from him at noon.

He watched Mark toiling. He thought first: he has grown into a man; and then within a month he thought: but he ages a year each week; he is becoming a skeleton.

Each worried about the other, but neither could discuss the future, except so far as the filly was concerned. Round her all their conversation rolled. Plans for her kept both their minds up from the dust at their feet.

As if she knew how much her two men now depended upon her who had originally so depended on them, the filly behaved with sweet decorum. She learned quickly. She would joke, but not wickedly, pretending at fear, but giving sporting notice that she was about to shy, and showing her good humour by small strings of running bucks while cantering. Mark several times was nearly unseated, but, where one swerve and dip of her shoulder would have sent him flying, the filly always gallantly refrained. Mark saw humour and compassion in the eye she turned back towards him. She never sulked.

Mark grew each day to love the filly more. She began to fill half the wound where Tess had lain. She had a future where his father had none. With her Mark had a partnership of purpose; he could not believe his father would be long with him.

There were a few setbacks. The filly acquired an overreach the first time Mark let her stride out in a gallop. Lincoln blamed Mark for not keeping her hind toes better trimmed. Mark said, 'Farriery is still your department.' His father found he could no longer lift up her hind legs. Being healthy, the filly healed quickly. She took a summer cough which, irritated by the wheat dust, had swept through the work horses, and for several weeks could only walk quietly. But she soon shook it off.

As Mark nodded over their evening soup Lincoln would recite the bends and gradients of little country courses. He recalled races he had ridden round them and pontificated about those which would suit the filly. Most of the courses he described had been, for years, defunct. Lincoln spoke no more of riding himself. One night he let fall, 'You must lie handy coming to the last bend', and thus accepted that another curtain had fallen on another act. Sorrow for his father's final surrender swamped Mark's elation: the filly would make her start, if all continued well, next spring. 'And I'll not let myself die before then', said old Lincoln fiercely, jabbing the embers of the fire with blackthorn stick and copper coach horn. Mark heaved his eyelids up and gave his father's drooping left hand a squeeze.

Mr Salerno and his Tess, though thought about at first with hatred, then with distaste, were never discussed. They were far out of sight, on the opposite side of the world, and had been abroad for four months completing a luxurious global tour at the expense of an airline. Random Salerno had been commissioned, for a vast fee, to create a series of paintings depicting the airline's most exotic ports of call. Each picture would feature the body and face of Tess, differently dressed for each location.

Her shape would thus be identified with the corporation. 'Personifying speed with comfort, beauty with joie-de-vivre, Tess will become the company's new image', its head of public relations had enthused. He had left unspoken the innuendoes that her body offered for sprightly executives flying alone. For an enormous supplement, in which Tess had been asking vainly that she should share, the airline had bought exclusive rights over her body for one calendar year.

Confirmation of this arrangement reached Salerno fortuitously when they were on an island halfway round their flying girdle, and at the maximum distance from home. The cost of her return was the prime restraint upon Tess walking out on Random Salerno there and then. 'But it is my body!' she raged. 'My work', returned Salerno, cold towards her as always when plunged into his painting. 'They pay me'.

'But to paint me!' stamping her foot on the beach verandah, while he reclined with his pencil.

'I made you.'

'I'm not your creature.'

'But you precisely are.'

Against this she so rebelled that she raised a naked arm to strike him. He never flinched. 'Flashing your beauty glows when hot aroused', he remarked in his quoting voice and started to sketch her attitude on an envelope. 'Hold that threat. It'll please our masochistic fans, who dream, I dare say, of being sweetly whipped by you.' Then he murmured, 'But you are being handsomely rewarded —' he waved his pencil round the complex of that ocean's most luxurious hotel – 'for your arduous tasks, my dearest Tess. I'll want you displayed against the balcony in that silk shawl for at least thirty minutes this morning. If you can spare the time.'

She lost that battle, but was determined not to let slip the principle on which she had fought it. She had ceased to accept her exploitation from the time they had arrived at their farm in the woods. Her relationship with Salerno had slightly improved away from the place. Their leaps around the world provided, in addition to dramatic views and exotic entertainments, a quickly changing series of hotel beds, so that neither could be too long reminded of Salerno's uncompleted sexual efforts. He had, too, sufficient excuses not to begin: the long 'plane flight, jet-lag, his early work start, the wearying long-distance calls with his agents. The picture named 'Desire' was rushing into the best-seller league. A song based upon it (from which Random Salerno drew royalties) had sold half a million copies in one continent already.

Mr Salerno spared no thought for the horse boy who had held the stallion. Tess, however, and to her chagrin, found herself thinking of Mark more and more. She had been convinced that she could dismiss him from her mind. Nor were her feelings – and this astonished her – simply those of physical desire aroused and denied.

As they moved from one palatial suite in the tropics to another, Tess conjured up the woods and him and the golden filly cantering among the haycocks in that soft green valley.

The cut on her calf had healed within weeks. So far from disliking the mad old father she found now that she respected his defence. 'If I were him', she murmured to herself lying alone one morning on the silver sand and reminded by the green surf of that bracken sea through which he had crawled to attack her, 'If I were Mark's Dad I'd kill me to keep me off him!' She smiled at the thought. And a young man passing by caught her eye and smiled back. His lithe, dark and burning look flung up in her the keenest remembrance of Mark.

The man, staying at the same hotel, was foreign, spoke little, but desired her. That evening there had been dancing to the native drummers and he had approached, bowing, gesturing romantically without speaking, to ask her. From habit she had refused, glancing at Salerno for his usual approval. She danced so seldom she had ceased to miss it, and hated anyway to see Salerno sitting immobilised and feeling pain. But he said surprisingly, 'Go ahead.' He felt victorious. Having won his financial fight with her, he could be kind to her. He had ensured the future of the airline series, as well as her continued life with him. For her to dance with a stranger under his eye, Salerno thought, might be exciting. He thus let her out on leash.

The young man immediately pressed himself to her. The clothes both wore in the hot night were silken thin. She felt him immediately. Embarrassed in front of Salerno and wary of his reaction, she glanced round to see his expression. But he was sketching her on a menu. She pressed back against the man and he began to move against her. Over his shoulder Tess looked again at Salerno. He was continuing his drawing, but his eyes were glittering behind his glasses. On an impulse, Tess steered the young man closer towards him. Salerno rose. 'No', said Tess to the man, 'I must stop.' She left him with his mouth open, yearning after her with such lust that Tess felt he might spring on her back like a puma and rape her.

Salerno stalked peg-legged to their bungalow under the palms. When she was through the door he tore her dress off, fell upon her, entered her fully and after a delay first satisfying, but then fraught and hesitant, finally consummated their coupling. He lay triumphant, panting on his back. Tess was delighted. 'It was seeing that young man', she said.

Salerno, still gasping, had his eyes closed. He nodded, 'Crazy for you, poor bastard.' He smiled contentedly.

She thought, this way something can be worked out. Salerno murmured, 'Looked a little like that gypsy. That poor lovesick fellow in the woods.'

Tess asked carefully, 'D'you think, when we go back there – if you saw him with me – that it might help you again?'

He did not immediately answer nor open his eyes. But Tess saw from the tick of his eyelid and the idiosyncratic twitch of his eyebrow, that he was urgently calculating. He was weighing the risk of that boy's constant availability in the woods against the sexual capability he might again achieve, if similarly ignited.

'We could try it', he said at last. 'I take pleasure in the idea', he said sensuously and stroked his long fingers over the curve of her small, very warm belly. As he did so, Tess desired Mark so intensely that she could not believe that Salerno did not feel it. He must guess, too, she thought, where these steps might lead them. His mind was always as he boasted, those two springs ahead of hers. If so he would know that by this route she could take Mark for a lover. She took Salerno's fingers and placed them. 'There', she said, 'exactly there, please.' She sighed with pleasure. It might now be possible, she thought, to obtain the best of both her worlds. Allowing Salerno's artistic fingers to gratify her while she imagined Mark, her responses quickened, and she cried out sharply, like a gull against the surf-sound, with passing delight.

Her pleasure was transitory. As they began to fly home her tension increased and with it his cold reserve. He was painting against the sound of the winged chariot and was exhausted by the pressure. Worse, he was dissatisfied with some of his work. He dreaded that he might at last be losing his Midas touch. The airline, having staked so much, particularly pestered him.

Because there had been no more passing strangers with whom Tess danced, there had been no more satisfactory aftermaths. It had been, as Tess unkindly jested, 'the flash in the pan.' So she longed more each day to see Mark and that lovely settled and enduring house of his again. Her impatience grated on Salerno. His work suffered again, their schedule became delayed, she grew more restless still, and he fretted with nerves like an old bare wintry tree unhappily rattling against its neighbour.

As she could not speak about his sexual failures without reaping a whirlwind she again brought up the question of his 'proper' painting.

'Surely you've made enough now', she persisted two stops from home, 'to let the commercial pictures rest for a while and do some more of those beautiful impressions.'

Salerno grunted. 'I've got to finish this accursed commission.'

'But after then', Tess pleaded, 'when there's no pressure. You could do more – when you felt like it – of those wonderful things in the woods.'

'They'll think I've lost my touch', Salerno said. 'And my urge', he threw at her. She ignored the gauntlet. 'They'll think you've found yourself', said Tess. She was convinced of it, though she recognised her other motive: to link Salerno's work to Mark's woods. She wished to join, not to sever (she maintained), for the greater good of all, her two worlds.

'Ordinary people wouldn't understand them', Salerno said with a sting of scorn. But doubt for the first time fluttered. The exclusive airline contract did after all bar him for a year for producing further erotic paintings of Tess. . . . He would talk again with his agent. Provided he was reassured that his name and earning capabilities would not be damaged he could paint three or four impressionist landscapes. They would be a relief from this wretchedly extended series.

Tess watched him. She thought, how clever you are, a wonderful brain. And a real talent. But wasted so far. She said firmly, 'Ordinary people would love them.'

Salerno shrugged. 'Who can tell? No one's seen them, foolish girl.'

Tess heard herself blurt out, 'Mark loved that one of the woods.'

Salerno lanced her with the steeliest of looks. She felt herself blushing. 'Really?' he demanded. 'Did you spend much time then, showing that grimy peasant my – er – etchings?'

'No.' She hid her confusion behind anger. 'And if he is a peasant, well – he liked that one painting. Which proves –'

'Which is all he saw?'

'Yes, that first day he came back.'

'When he saw all of you naked on the balcony?'

Tess nodded, pink-cheeked. 'That day.'

'I think he had you then', said Salerno. His voice was very low and on one bass note. 'I thought so before.'

'He did not!' shouted Tess.' I swore to you and you believed me.'

'That was before I knew', said Salerno savagely, 'that you had shared with him the intimacy of examining – of probing about in – of exposing my pictures.' He glared at her. She realised that he was more hurt, more revengeful and therefore more dangerous than she had ever seen him. She felt suddenly afraid of him. Then there came a flush of pleasure that she should. His revulsion was as if she and Mark had raped him. 'Probing about', she repeated and muttered, 'Your mind's like a serpent.'

He was relieved that she had shown fear. He asked less hostilely, 'Why didn't you tell me?'

'I told you how he didn't like the pictures of me.'

'But that was negative criticism. Personal too, as we saw later. Why didn't you tell me about the woods one?'

'I knew you'd be angry.'

'Why?'

'Well, you are. You're violated that we examined your private work, aren't you?' He nodded. Tess added, 'And I knew you'd be

133

particularly angry that Mark agreed with me.'

That was nearly true, he considered. But it was not quite anger, more a response to a threat. He looked very grave and tired. 'Nothing else?' he asked, 'Promise?'

'Promise', she said giving him that direct look of truth which had first ensnared him.

They flew homewards towards autumn.

32

Random Salerno did not forget his doubts about his painting of the woods. Something important, his powerful artistic, feminine instinct assured him, was connected with the damned picture. He recalled the mood of impermanence in which he had painted it that chill day when the boy had been found in the ruined farm with his filly.

Salerno landed, would not delay on any business in the city, but returned directly to the farm with Tess. He was secretly agitated, and showed it in anger with the groom Trapchek and his wife. The baboon had not comprehended the heating and airconditioning controls. He had upset the delicate balance of the thermostats. The living room was baking like an oven. To cool it Trapchek had opened the front door to the cold grey autumn day. Expensive heat gushed out. The heating boilers rumbled like furies to replace it.

'D'you think I pay to heat the arses of the sparrows, cretin?' screamed Mr Salerno.

Nor had Trapchek's thick wife succeeded in leaving well alone in the bizarre kitchen. She had fused the automatic cooking apparatus by repeatedly manually over-riding it to brew up humble broths. She had moreover contrived that the special effect controls were locked permanently on Winter Evening. Salerno, cursing and striding out on his single leg, passed from real grey noon into a shuttered, redlit glow.

'Stupid bitch!' he shouted at Mrs Trapchek. 'How dare you cook your pig's mess in here?' The Trapcheks retired gibbering to their cottage. Salerno was blanched by anger. He snapped at Tess, 'See those two orang-utans depart before the month is out.'

'But what about Sultan?'

'Sultan?'

'The horse, Pop! The stallion, for God's sake!' Without the horse Tess would be cut off from Mark, isolated in the woods.

'He can go', said Salerno. He stepped directly to the shelf to find the stiff cardboard folder of paintings and sketches. He was riffling through them. He muttered, 'Where's the one of you looking furious? I need to match it with the sketch I did of you threatening me on that verandah. The island with palms.'

'What d'you mean?' demanded Tess. '"He can go?"'

'I've finished the stallion picture, have I not?' Salerno turned the pictures more briskly. '"*Desire*", d'you recall? The money-spinning record, sung by apes for robots? It has been a frantic success, earned us great money and kept you in the luxury you now require. We now move on.' He turned the sheets back and forth. 'Where *is* that one?' He was peering down. Evening Light made it very hard to see properly.

'But what can I ride?' asked Tess.

'Me, if you please.' Salerno shot her an evil look under his arm.

'That won't –' She closed her lips.

'Won't satisfy you?' Salerno finished for her. 'So you will ride my stallion out from my stables at my house here to be satisfied by your miserable adolescent wood-serf? No, you will not. The horse will go with those abominable Clapsticks.'

She hesitated. 'But when we were away, Pop, and I suggested that letting . . .' (She would not mention Mark's name) 'letting the boy see me might help you –' He jerked his shoulder, goaded. She added, 'You thought it would help. You liked the idea.'

'The idea, yes.' He tapped his forehead. 'I like the idea in here.'

'Well, then?' She was too eager. 'Now the real thing –'

'Because, you little idiot, ideas are mine. I can control them. Make them come when I call them up. Make them vanish, when I've sucked them. That's why I paint, have talent. But', he mimicked her with a sneer, '"The real thing"', I cannot always control. Not absolutely always.'

'You do me', she burst out.

'Because you love your chains', he said, turning back to the folder.

He reached the woodland impression, drew it out with a flourish

135

and held it up. 'The work of genius of which an ignorant girl and creeping stable lad, my expert hanging committee, so cordially approve.' He stood back as if studying it.

'But what shall I do up here', Tess demanded, 'If I can't ride?'

'Not come', said Salerno.

'What?'

'Not come', he repeated and with his pelvis made an obscene jerking motion. 'Not come in either sense of the word.' He laughed very deeply. She raised her arm and something glittered in it.

'Put that knife down, Tess', he commanded. He was quite calm.

She held the thin ham-knife up, out to one side, unsure how one used a rapier as a weapon. Salerno cocked his head. 'That's the pose I want.' He turned away from her, back to the pictures again. 'Now where *is* that angry one of you in the Oriental tunic?'

She flung the knife. Ill-thrown, it hit the closed shutters handle-first, and clattered down on the wood bench where she had sat facing Mark and laid her cheek against his on the table-top. 'Rot the picture of me! I'm here alive!' she shouted. 'I'm me. Not your work.'

She leaned against the wooden edge of the table. Her shoulders slumped. She clasped her hands together between her knees and pressed them together.

He had his back to her. 'Are you crying yet?'

She gave a fierce sniff. 'No.'

'Then would you mind helping me find the picture I want? You recall it?'

'Yes. You hadn't finished it.'

'Exactly. Now here's the index. All in order. We come to 42, "*Woods Impression*", then 43, "*Anger* (unfinished)". But where *is* it, Tess?' He turned round and had the long knife in his hand. 'With this', he said, 'I could so mark you, as I learned from the street-gangs in those slums of my childhood – I could so mark your face and body that never would you earn a living from your looks again. You understand me absolutely?'

She had sprung back against the tall wooden back of the bench. She watched the tip of the knife, then Salerno's eyes. 'D'you think I've stolen it?' she asked. She had been holding her breath, so the words came rushing out.

'No. I think you gave it to the wood boy.'

'I certainly did not. He didn't like those pictures, so –'

Salerno waved the knife to interrupt her. 'You stole it for him to drivel over in his hovel. Unfinished, so unwanted, you believed. And you thought –' he broke into a mimicry of her childhood accent, 'You thought the sight of my tits and pussy will keep Master Marky on the rut for me while I'm away. Not so?'

'No!' She was furious.

'Well, then, the tinker simply pinched it.' Salerno put down the knife. 'Probably while you were perched upon the bidet', he added savagely. He limped to the intercom. 'Cleaning up', he spat back at her and buzzed the button.

She remained silent. Salerno finally obtained a reply from the wall-machine and shouted into it for Trapchek to present himself.

Tess went to the folder and began carefully to check through the pictures. Her fingers quivered. She had indeed been frightened by this second glimpse of a maimed future in which even she might not survive. The fragility of the luck which had so far combined her life with Random Salerno's was perilous. Her fame was sustained by an illusion; by the delusions of millions. Without her, the pictures of her body would still sell and sell. But she could starve.

33

Mark was autumn-ploughing on the slopes furthest from the house. The crunch of his horses' great hooves on the flinty bank, the creak of leather trappings, the clank of iron chains, the squeak and break of the turned earth and the tramp of his own boots across the stubble drowned even the cacophony of the warning geese-flocks.

Reaching one headland, he heard their honking, scrambled up a hedgerow tree to scout, and saw the back of the police vehicle turning round the corner of the distant house. He would take at least half an hour running all the way down, along the brookside and then up to the house. He hesitated up in the boughs of the sycamore. What could the police want? The old man had not been off the place for all the months since he had been struck down. He could have stolen nothing. Mark ran through his mind his own muddled transactions in the market: could he in anyway have contravened some new regulation?

The days were too short anyway, single-handed as he was, without losing an hour's work on a fair day. Cursing, he dropped out of the sycamore, hitched the plough-horses to its lowest branch and set off for the house at a steady lope, grumbling as he ran.

One chapter in the Inspector's Manual of Psychological Interrogation detailed the virtues of snatching suspects out of sleep. Questions shafted then met the weakest, most befuddled, resistance. So the Inspector found it helpful in his windowless interview room to let the criminal nod off for ten minutes, have the wall-clock whirled forward by five hours and then rouse the confused wretch from slumber with fearful cries. Without physical hurt villains could be convinced by these stops and starts that they had passed days and nights in the Inspector's clutches. They became lost without the comforting milestones of time, and disturbed by the apparently crazy malfunctioning of their biological needs.

So the Inspector was delighted to swoop upon Lincoln in a noontide doze in a warm corner of the terrace.

'Right then! Where is it, you old thief?' he bellowed, stooping, into Lincoln's ear. He was dressed in a new broad-checked overcoat, and sported an unlikely green velour hat with the sawn-off stump of a drake's feather in its band.

Lincoln, jerked from a reverie of his childhood, believed he saw, towering over him, some comic character from a pantomine of sixty years ago. He blinked and recognised with a chilly shock the face of his tormentor. The Inspector's face, even after the summer's sun (of which he did not approve), retained the pallor and consistency of the fat of hams.

Lincoln gathered his wits together like an old crone tidying its knitting. 'Good morning, Chief Superintendent', he said politely. 'A glass of elderberry wine?' He made a crabwise move towards the broken windows of the old drawing-room. The Inspector grabbed him. 'You stay here, tramp.' He motioned to the hovering sergeant. 'Well, get inside this morgue and start searching.' His gesture released from his clothing a puff of that smell with which Lincoln associated him: small cigars, after-shave and the stuffy well-used seats of tightly-closed cars. Lincoln wrinkled his nose. 'Can I tell you where to find anything?' he enquired.

'You bloody can!' The Inspector shook him and old Lincoln

winced. The Inspector examined him as if he were an elderly turkey only fit for stewing. 'You've lost weight,' he said. 'Face twisted. Look old. Very old. Had a stroke?'

'A shock', muttered Lincoln uneasily.

'How was that? Where? Who shocked you? When?'

Lincoln could hear the sergeant knocking holes in the wainscoting and cocked his head. The Inspector did not shake him again: old bugger might well snuff right there. 'Well, what shock?' he repeated. 'Nearly caught nicking something? So where?'

'Doing too much in the fields', said Lincoln.

'Too much round Mr Salerno's grand new place, you mean.' The Inspector saw the old man's blue eyes widen at the name, and knew he had struck home. 'Right', he said. 'We're there.' He stared at Lincoln. He shouted to the Sergeant, 'Keep knocking all those rotten panels in, till the creature tells us where it is, or where he's flogged it.'

Then Lincoln realised they were after Mark's picture of that bitch. And she, he supposed, still unsatisfied with all her damage done, now wanted vengeance for the fright he'd given her before this dreadful, dragging summer. Oh God, he groaned, hadn't he warned Mark?

'So', said the Inspector, giving one of his luxuriant side-boards a contented stroke while pincering Lincoln's small shoulder with the other hand. 'We know where we're at, Lincoln, don't we? And you will recall our little chat last year in my interview room. I said if you nicked one thing from Mr Salerno, I'd run you in, didn't I?'

'One aspirin, you said, sir, or one baked bean . . .' The Inspector preened himself, gratified by the impression he had made even on this time-lost, backwoods idiot. The Inspector waited. Lincoln's mind whirled round in a blur of autumn leaves. He could not believe that Mark had still kept the cursed picture nor, if he had, where it might be. And he knew that if Mark were arrested the whole place would collapse. The realisation, never having entered his calculations before, now struck him with the force of the kick of a horse in his belly.

'Have me in quicker than I could fart, you said, Chief Superintendent', mumbled Lincoln, freeing a moment's more thinking time in which to decide whether to sacrifice himself as an offering for the continuance of this place.

'And so I will', said the Inspector comfortably, with victory in sight. This odious relic of the lax past would now be dispatched for another, longer spell of Corrective Training. Probably prove lethal, considered the Inspector studying the twisted half of the old man's face and his drooping side. It was unlikely, with Lincoln's record and his own recommendations, that the court would be lenient towards this misfit.

'You said I'd be spat out and harried to death', said Lincoln, making up his mind, and thereby finding it, by some divine grace, suddenly clarified. 'I'm sorry about the picture, Chief Superintendant. But I'd admired Mr Salerno's work so much on that calendar in your nice interview room. . . .' He shrugged. He was now only in dread that Mark, warned by the honking of the sentinel geese, would be hurrying back and might get caught. Speed was vital. 'You'll take me in?' he asked, with a touch too much eagerness.

The Inspector looked carefully at the old man's expression, sniffing at least the passage of a rat behind the arras. Maybe he likes the discipline of the Correctives, he considered. Some of these old thieves were subconscious masochists. 'Plead guilty, then? Breaking, entering, stealing an original masterpiece?'

'I'm afraid so.'

'Right! Sergeant!' shouted the Inspector, 'The old weasel's confessed. Handcuffs. Formal charge and off we go from this ruin.' He clapped his fat white hands together. 'And the evidence?' he asked Lincoln.

'Evidence?'

'Mr Salerno's beautiful picture, Lincoln: Nude, isn't it, comme d'habitude? His famous model, Miss Tess, is it not? Droolin' over it, you've been, eh?' The Inspector half closed his hand and jerked it up and down as if hammering. 'Dirty old goat', added the Inspector gratuitously. 'Your days of poke are done.'

Lincoln saw behind the Inspector's pantomine velour hat the figure of Mark running across the bowling green field. His son couldn't have wanted to keep that picture. He began, 'Feeling guilty of my crime, sir, I disposed of the painting.'

'You what?' stormed the Inspector. 'By God, you're for it now! Destroying the original work of one of the great masters of our time and state! It'll be the Solitaries for you.'

'No', begged Lincoln, loathing himself for cringing.

'Ah', breathed the Inspector with a dreadful smile, 'I'd forgotten. . . . You go mad shut up, don't you, my little old bird of the woods? Oh yes, you do. My sergeant told me. Beat your tiny wings to death in one of our windowless cages, won't you?'

Lincoln, for all his old will, could not now control his trembling. He knew he would not survive a week in the Solitaries. But if the picture was still about, only Mark could say. Lincoln's mind darted back and forth, already like a trapped sparrow. Yet if Mark arrived, he'd confess and be arrested.

The Sergeant's voice called from the ruined room. 'Think I've got it, sir.' He came out with the roll of stiff cartridge paper and unfurled it. 'In a smashed cupboard by the left of that smoky great fire.'

Lincoln sighed. But it was a respite, not a relief. He thought: Mark kept it all these months. He's hooked on that bitch still. So he'll be lost, too, then. In the end.

The Inspector scrutinised the painting, 'Lovely pair of tits.' He stuck his thick tongue out. It was stained with nicotine. He grunted. 'I really would relish that,' he pronounced. 'Though one shouldn't say so, I s'pose, about a lady of such pulchritude and fame.' He brought his mind back to business. 'Concealing it were you? Denying its presence? Two more charges, sergeant. You heard him.'

'Sir.' The sergeant too considered Tess' body. He said, 'It's very crumpled. D'you think he's ruined it?'

The Inspector peered. The picture had been well-thumbed. 'Disgusting!' he spat at Lincoln. Another thought occurred.

'Was this all you stole?'

Lincoln nodded.

'But why?' persisted the Inspector. 'Must have been valuables to hand!' Lincoln shrugged. 'But you just nicked this. And kept it!' The Inspector's eyebrows hooped incredulously. 'Why?'

Old Lincoln drew himself up and made his declaration. 'Let us say that the girl in the picture reminded me forcibly of my former wife.' A quiver of a smile crossed the unparalysed half of his face. 'That's all', he said and looked aside.

Mark appeared over the edge of the balustrade and hovered, trying to grasp what was happening.

'I think it's the son', said the sergeant doubtfully, staring at the gaunt waiting man. 'Mark, isn't it?'

Mark came forward cautiously. When he saw the picture he stopped abruptly. His hand flew up to his mouth. 'What are you doing with that?'

'Returning it', said the Inspector briskly. 'Your father's confessed in full detail.' He supposed that the son might start fussing now about his father's age and health, so he ordered his sergeant. 'Quick, cuffs and away.' The sergeant clicked on the handcuffs. Lincoln looked with such meaning at Mark that his blue eyes goggled.

'No!' shouted Mark. 'He didn't steal that. He's far too ill and old. I –'

'Silence, Mark!' spat old Lincoln with more force than Mark had heard in his voice for a year. 'Get on with the work here. There is already far too much –' He broke off into a bout of coughing. Mark came up to him and stroked his bent, heaving back. Lincoln whispered out of the side of his mouth, 'Better so. Not a word.' He choked again. 'Promise?'

Mark nodded, patting his back.

'And I'll expect you', said his father more firmly, 'to get the filly ready.'

The Inspector, mistaking his meaning, shot old Lincoln a crafty glance. 'Filly?' he demanded. 'What girl you going on about then?'

'Private', said Lincoln. 'Between the two of us. Horses.' His eyelid drooped in his son's direction. 'As for the other one,' he said savagely, 'keep out of her heels. She'll kick you to death. You'll never break her.'

The sergeant urged, 'Come on now, ole feller,' and placed a not unfriendly hand behind Lincoln's protruding shoulder-blades. He said to Mark, 'Good try, lad. You're a good son. But', he shrugged, 'It's a disease with some folk, isn't it?'

The Inspector flashed his watch. 'Time for my dinner', he said and let his cold eyes run derisively over the cracked façade of the mansion. He pushed old Lincoln up into the back of the police vehicle and took the wheel. He spoke down to Mark, 'When winter comes and you're starving, I could maybe get you into the Welfare.'

Mark looked away from his father. The old man sat huddled in the back of the truck like one of those swallows which every year were caught by the first fatal storms of autumn. They cowered under the eaves of the old barn, too late to migrate and waiting only to die. After the great flocks had flown south to the sun, they were left. There were no flies in the chilly air. The cold rains beat upon them. Their claws unfurled and they fell dying to the ground.

Mark spoke. 'Sir, I took that picture. I'll swear it in the court.'

'Don't waste my time', said the Inspector. 'Your old man's got a record longer than this bloody ruin.'

'Is that just why you came here today?' asked Mark.

'Mr Random Salerno', the Inspector said, 'creator and owner of the work of art, laid certain information to me this morning.' He slammed the window shut and drove away rapidly. The bouncing of the police truck over the ruts made old Lincoln's body flutter up and down like a heap of feathers.

34

Mark had not decided that he was going to kill Mr Salerno, for he had not considered how he would commit such an act. He was carrying no weapon, bar that of the spur of vengeance, as he pushed the filly forward through the wood. He had resolved, as soon as he heard the Inspector, to confront Salerno before he could leave again on one of his world tours. He would shout at him, shake him, frighten him, and hurt him. He would make the artist, the foreigner, the rich invader from the city, suffer, too.

Mark literally ground his teeth. His chin jutted. His elbows worked and he savagely kicked the filly onwards up the slope of the forest. The leaves were turning. Matching his mood the light in the woods was a blur of browns and reds. The filly was in season. Her burning sex-urge made her behave minxishly, resenting, then loving his legs beating against her flanks. Sometimes she dwelt for extra squeezing, and sometimes sprang forward with a quiver which he could feel all through his knees and thighs. She was coquettish, affecting to be afraid of the bramble thickets, dawdling, when what he wanted from her was speed, more speed to reach Salerno.

'Suffer,' he breathed out, 'Yes, I'll make him suffer.' The ground, crackling with leaves, levelled out and he found the track which led to the vast paddock this side of the Salernos' farm. He would put Salerno to pain.

Mark's right hand flew from the filly's reins, grabbing forward at the air and squeezing. 'I'll strangle him', he swore. 'I'll . . .' he lashed out – 'I'll teach him such a lesson he'll never trouble us again.'

Mark was panting, not only from the physical effort of keeping the filly going forward fast, but from spurts of his emotional rage. Guilt goaded him. Should he not have flung himself on the Inspector, admitting every detail about the picture, to save his father? His mind swirled with uncertainties. Vengeance, needing destructive action, sprang out of these fogs. So he galloped forward like a fury, seeing Mr Salerno in the eye of his mind's storm: first, big-hatted, then stooped over his clicking, whirring cameras: then hunched upon Tess with that tin leg jerking like a whip. I could have smashed him then, he thought, bursting out of the woods by the gate to the paddock. I should have smashed him then, as he lay rutting on his daughter. He felt the joy which such a blow would have given him, a blow like water over the weir swirling away the scum. 'Ugh!' he spat like his father. He leaned down the filly's wet, steaming neck to unlatch the gate – 'Stand still, you crazy bitch!' he swore, flung the gate open, looked up, and saw Tess on the black stallion galloping straight down the field towards him.

He stared. He thought he dreamt. Or had gone mad. With all his rage focussed upon Salerno he had directed no thought to the girl. His self-preserving instincts had excluded her image. He did not recognise this. He had simply felt she would never figure in his life again. But here she was thundering towards him, waving. The crazy girl was galloping the stallion bareback. Her blonde hair blew out behind her in waves. Her short skirt billowed outwards and upwards, too, like spume off a flooded river, showing the rise and fall of her golden legs.

As Mark hesitated, the filly trembled between his legs, flung up her head, stared excitedly at the onrushing stallion and let out a small squeal.

'Mark!' shouted Tess. 'Thank God!' Her voice sounded less of a little girl's. It was hoarser. She was in some panic and nature showed. He thought, with one cool element of his mind, I like it better. She reached him, pulling Sultan up in a swerve. Her face was scarlet. Her eyes flashed. She was, he saw with dread, even more beautiful than the girl whose image he had been erasing. He stared and felt his heart scurry. That picture which he had tried so hard not to look at and which now lay in the Inspector's hands was a cheap parody of her beauty.

She gasped out, 'The bastard's sent the police after you . . .' She too, was panting from her need to hurry. She saw his look of bemusement. 'Salerno's told them that you stole a picture of me. Did you?' She leaned forward, turning towards him.

'I did.'

Her face which had been so tense now dissolved. It glowed with delight. 'I thought you had.' She tried to urge Sultan closer, but the stallion, scenting the filly's heat, was sidling restlessly, trying to get behind her. 'Stand still,' snapped Tess tugging at his reins. Then to Mark, 'I've finished with him. I've come to warn you about the police. I'll look after you both.'

He could not grasp even the outline of what she meant. Catching at the start and the end of her extraordinary statement, he repeated, 'Finished? Look after?' He scowled. He shook his head like old Rip beset by bees, and the filly beneath him minced a little closer towards Sultan. One thing he did understand though. He said bluntly, 'You're too late about the police. They took my father away this morning.'

'Your father?' Tess now was perplexed.

'The man who nearly died fending you off our place', said Mark bitterly.

'I can't – your *father*. . . .? I've no idea what you even mean.' Her head was aslant, her brow furrowed. Wrinkles rose vertically between her eyebrows.

'He collapsed that day', Mark said.

'When? When he came at me with the scythe? He was trying to kill me. I told you that – I tried to tell you that next time. You turned and rode away. You shouted at me, at the sky, "Go away"'.

'He had a stroke. It half-finished him. And now –' He moved his arm as if smoothing something away, and as he did so felt a gulp of sorrow rise in him. The filly, loosely held, stuck out her muzzle towards the stallion's.

Tess began a noise of sympathy, and she, too, dropped a rein to stretch her hand out towards Mark's. She had nearly touched his hand when the horses' muzzles came together and their breath entwined. The filly suddenly whirled round and backed in towards the stallion. Mark drummed his heels vainly into the filly's flanks to stop her retreat. He looked behind him. The stallion's mouth, just behind and above him, was open. His yellow teeth grimaced. The great eyes

145

in his black head glowed like orbs. His nostrils were flared open, deep red inside their pink, softly curved lips. Mark felt on his neck and cheek the twin jets of the black horse's breath. He raised an arm to fend him off.

Mark saw Tess pulling. She was hauling back on Sultan's reins, but she had no saddle to give her purchase. Her thighs slipped on the stallion's hot black skin.

The stallion came slowly deliberately forward like a panther stalking, ready to spring. Lust made him rise upon his hoof-toes. He looked enormous. His head was higher than Mark's, and Tess behind that crested neck sat upon the stallion's swaying back, higher than Mark's shoulders. Her skirt had run up to her waist. The smell of horse-sweat steamed sweetly. Through its faint mist Mark saw the stallion gathering itself. Its black back was so slippery with sweat that Tess frantically squeezed her thighs inwards to hold herself there. Mark saw the paler gold at the very join of her thighs as she began to slip backwards. 'Hold his mane!' he bellowed.

'Mark! For God's sake!' screamed Tess. 'Look out!' He flung himself off sideways.

The stallion leapt. His great black forelegs flashed. The filly, buckling under his weight, took steps to balance him. The stallion's two hind feet stamped upon the ground to fix their footing so that he could fire in his seed. The air thundered with their breathing.

The stallion, not yet fully home into the filly, was still clambering his way forward along her back. His great mouth gnawed with passion at her neck and his forelegs scrabbled for better purchase on her shoulders. She felt their crush and caress. She felt his teeth bite her neck. She squealed with delight and stood hind-legs splayed, tail swirled sideways, waiting for the stallion, as if she had been copulating for years. The stallion's great organ, seeking its entry, jerked like a striking snake. It touched the filly and she screamed.

On the stallion's black back rode Tess ten feet above the ground. She flew up there, a golden girl on a heaving dark monster asteam with sweat. She leaned forward along the stallion's clambering back, gripping his mane in her small hands. She was beginning to move in rhythm with the stallion, as she felt his great thrust begin beneath her. She looked down from her soaring height, and saw Mark upon the ground. She saw his eyes open, watching. She looked down into them and started to smile. For she felt beneath her now, between her own legs bestriding the stallion, the horse's desperate urgency to complete his coupling. So she began to urge him on, with her face against his huge bent neck and her hands clasping that neck and caressing it. His great mass was an extension of her, doing her will, pleasuring Mark's filly. . . .

Then, with a great groan, the stallion shot forth his sperm into the filly. He gave her one more bite into her neck. Then he slipped sideways off her. He stumbled, heaving, onto one knee, and Tess rolled from his back onto the ground. She turned over on the turf towards Mark who rose to meet her. She was on her back, knees still widely splayed. She raised her buttocks up and down. She stretched out both her arms to him, stiffly, as if she were praying, and cried out, 'Oh, Mark, come.' He launched himself between her arms and her spread thighs. As he pierced her, she let out a great shout of joy and, gripping him with a wild ferocity, worked herself up and down beneath him, as if galvanised by an electrical storm. She clutched his back with crossed hands, bit at his neck, and held him to her, as if she would die if prised off him. Her back arched like a horse leaping beneath him. She cried out once again, and he too was spent, speeding into her like leaps into a crimson night.

They lay still linked. She laid her hand behind the nape of his neck. Her eyes softly watched him. He asked, 'What about your father?' He asked gently and now without repugnance, for he felt that he had vanquished Salerno.

'He's not my father.'

'What?' He shot himself off her on to his elbow but, before he could speak again, she said, 'Just because I called him Pop? Because he's older? I told you early on that I was his mistress.'

'No', he said.

'I know I must have. That first day. When we were going away. And surely you must have known.'

Pictures of her and Salerno in these new roles shuffled through his mind.

'In fact', said Tess, 'I never knew my father.'

He thought of his, then. 'Nor I, my mother.'

'No', she said, gently stroking the side of his nose. 'It must have been hideous for you thinking that when you saw him on me.' He nodded. She said, 'Your face went white. Appalled, it was. You blundered out. But', she added with a rueful smile, 'I could hardly stop and explain.' He scowled. She said, 'That is after all, the duty of a mistress: to try to make her man happy, didn't you know? That's the *deal.*'

He asked. 'But are you not his mistress now?'

'I told you.' She was impatient, 'I've left him. I was coming to warn you.' He enfolded her. He kissed her eyes. 'I love you as if I'm dying' he murmured. 'You are magic.'

'You are', she said, 'I knew that from the very start.' They clung together. Then Tess asked, 'But what about your poor father?'

Mark told her. She declared, 'But it was *you* Pop wanted to be rid of!'

Rejoicing, he wanted to hear her voice say why.

She said, 'Because he's afraid of you. Always was afraid from the first. Because he knows I love you. I told him I desired you when we went away. And *that* I did tell you. On our very second day walking round this meadow in the rain I told you I loved you.' She kissed him. 'Didn't I?'

'Yes. But I didn't believe you.'

'I'll prove it again.' She raised herself and looked across to where Sultan and the filly were grazing side by side. 'They're content now', she said. 'But we —'

He had quite forgotten the filly. Dread struck him. 'She's only two. If he's got her in foal she'll be ruined.'

'Me, too,' said Tess wickedly.

He rose instantly. Alarm increased in his face. She said, 'Don't fret. I'll not conceive. I'm taken care of — needlessly really. And surely the filly won't take with just one covering.'

'It was a tremendous one', said Mark.

Tess reached down and held him. 'If she has, it's too late for worries now', she said, and with a steady concentration, knelt, turned and took hold of him. Time whirled like clouds, dappling, darkening, opening bright golden gaps. 'Now', she would say. 'Put your tongue exactly there . . . perfect . . . and here . . . Now I'll do — *this*! . . . And then *this*!'

He thought at times that he flew among the clouds. When she did certain things to please him his body emptied and he felt air in his veins and he groaned with rapture. Then, beneath her, he felt like the root of a tree along the turf, and she the trunk growing out of him. Thoughts of Salerno coupling with her came and went in spasms between his bursts of joy.

Then the sun slipped behind the russet tops of the enormous beech woods. In that second, autumnal cold slid across the grass and they felt to their astonishment the starting of the dew. The horses, too, had moved far away. An hour had passed. They grazed in a slight wash of pearly ground mist at the distant end of the field. No lights showed from Mr Salerno's tower. 'Has he gone?' Mark asked.

'After he had called on the police', she said.

'Did he know you would leave?'

'I told him. He probably won't believe it. I've said it before', she said honestly.

Mark asked, 'Did Salerno do these things? Do you . . . could you do them for him?'

'No.' She thought: how fortunate that that is true. I wouldn't want to lie, but I wouldn't want to hurt.

'Promise?'

Oh, she thought, how men are obsessed with what is past. First him, now Mark. But 'I promise', she said, being both forthright and simultaneously tender which she knew would delight him.

'Oh Tess', cried Mark, 'I love you utterly.'

'And for some time, too, I hope', she said, getting up and busying herself with buttons and brushing-off the stalks of grass. He too stood, but watched her uneasily. She looked at him. 'I'm coming home with you. To look after you.' She looped her arms around his neck.

'Now?' he asked. 'Exactly now?'

'Of course. You're alone. You love me and need me. I love you. And how I need you. So we'll ride down. Exactly now.' She let out a long whistle for Sultan who came obediently trotting towards them.

'Oh, it's marvellous', Mark shouted. 'It's untrue. It's − Oh, it'll be −,' he began to laugh and to squeeze her, to kiss her mouth and hands. He was jumping about in the misty field. 'Look at the filly!' He pointed. The filly had overtaken the stallion and was flirting with him.

'Never satisfied − fillies', said Tess. 'I shall wear you out.'

He fumbled for the right words. 'It'll be a pleasure for you to try, madam.'

She looked at him delightedly. 'We *are* gall*ant*.' She gathered Sultan's reins and turned her back to Mark and raised one knee as she had done the day of the painting. 'Give me a leg up', she said.

'In a moment', Mark said, turning her round to him, and dexterously opening her legs again with his knee. 'I died wanting to do this that day with him. Now I will have you.' And as they stood, her back to the stallion's shoulder, he thrust into her again. 'Ah', she sighed, 'And he never achieved me then. And hardly –' she moved her pelvis lower and gripped him – 'hardly ever', she breathed.

'No?' cried Mark the victor. 'How I pity him!'

35

As the mist seeped through the trees, the trunks began to gleam and it grew colder. Tess shivered. Mark passed her his old torn jacket. 'You're mad', he said, 'coming out in just that skirt.'

'I didn't exactly have time to pack.' Her teeth chattered slightly and she huddled down into his coat. 'He locked me in, you know.'

'You never said that.' Mark was troubled. It was not the happy runaway as he had first understood.

'Well, he locked his stupid doors. I climbed down from the tower balcony with the proverbial sheet. Wouldn't have been so easy with suitcases', she added a little huffily.

'He doesn't want to lose you then', Mark pursued his point. The threat of Mr Salerno, only just banished, now loomed again. It would mean another police raid. Then his detention for an offence, like luring away the girl. He glanced at Tess, who was looking about fifteen. His unease led him to grumble, 'I hope to God the filly's all right. That she's not been hurt by that black brute. She doesn't feel the same to me.'

'She's not, is she?' Tess grinned. 'I wasn't when I was deflowered.' Only part of Mark urged him to enquire. 'On my seventeenth birthday', said Tess. 'A disappointing little present, as it turned out. But my ambitious mother thought it was the right time for me to offer it to a rich man.'

Mark scowled. He asked crossly, 'How did you get that horse out?'

'Sultan is mine.'

'Properly?'

'As much as anything is', said Tess as confidently as she could. 'He'll be useful training the filly, won't he?' She shivered again, and caught him looking at her with real concern. 'It'll be all right when we get into your house.'

Mark did not answer.

'Well, won't it?'

'I don't know', said Mark. 'It's very cold and draughty.'

But, as they neared the edge of the wood, it did not look it. The westering autumn sun washed the whole flank of the mansion. The splintered edges of the panes fiercely reflected the rays. 'It looks as if it's on fire', said Tess. 'It's so lovely.'

Mark, in mounting anxiety, knuckled his brow.

They rode into the hay meadow past the point where old Lincoln had collapsed, but Tess was feasting her eyes on the house beyond the valley. Mark's apprehension grew. She called across, 'Are you worried about your father?'

'Of course.' He was abrupt. The filly stumbled over the remnants of a haycock. He jabbed her mouth crossly.

'What'll happen?'

'They'll hold him for trial. Sentence him. Then', said Mark bitterly, 'if he's lucky he'll get Corrective Detention.' He blurted out, 'He'll die if they give him the Solitaries.'

'But why should he get sentenced at all?'

'He's got a long record.'

'For *stealing*?' Tess was incredulous. Perhaps the old man was mad in other ways, too.

Mark was angered by having to defend him. 'He borrows things and forgets.' He saw Tess's astonished face. 'He calls it "freeing" things,' he explained and let out a short laugh. It sounded ludicrous. Tess did not join in. Mark added dejectedly, 'And the authorities do just want us out of here. They've been trying to flush us out for bloody years.'

Tess rode up closer to him, 'We'll stop them', she said confidently. 'And help your father.' He did not reply, but turned his head away. When he looked up again she saw that his eyes were wet. He cleared his throat and said gruffly, 'It's too late. For my father. I'm afraid. As for our place –' he nodded at its great bulk now plunged into the long blue shadows of the woods – 'God knows how it'll survive.' Indeed as the sun dimmed, the house was accelerating its disappearance among the encircling trees.

'I'll help.' Tess was as firm as she could be. 'I will, you know. I'm strong.'

'It's stood here for two hundred and fifty years,' he said defiantly.

Did he mean, she wondered, that like every principality and power, its end was therefore due? Or that having survived so much it would still endure? They entered the darkness of the yew tree alley which ran towards the bowling green field. It was very cold in the dark-green shade. Tess was staring all around her with rising doubt, then with sharp alarm. She saw on all sides the unfolding desolation of the great garden run wild for years.

There had been no resistance. Nature, cut back nearly three centuries ago and regulated by countless civilising hands, had, by its infinite majority, seized control again. The effect on Tess was appalling. As they rode forward over what had once been the lower lawn, now run to a seedy meadow studded with thorn bushes and elder suckers, she could no longer fend off the truth.

'What happened?' she asked in a small voice.

They had reached the tangled circular wilderness of the formal hedged garden and the ornamental pond. Mark could not answer her. Instead, ducking her meaning, he explained, 'That's where the filly got stuck in the bog as a foal. She nearly died. I nursed her for weeks. A bottle –'

'But what happened to all this place?' Tess asked firmly.

Mark looked around in the gloaming, seeing for the first time through someone else's eyes the ruin of all the demesne. It exploded with the speed of a nightmare. Where he could imagine the gravel paths, borders and flower beds, grouped shrubs, pruned roses and elegant statues was all, to a stranger's eyes, nothing but jungle. How could he make Tess see it as his father had contrived to believe that it continued? Desperately wanting her just to understand his love for it, he stared at the awful undergrowth. And as he did so, the images of those lost times started to slip from reality like a mist which had been obscuring a ruin. Against his most fierce will, he saw the place as she saw it. He felt suddenly cold, stripped of all hope.

He looked at her expression and round the desolation and back at her again. From their horses' nostrils puffs of steam issued like dragons' breaths. The sentinel geese erupted into their cacophanous alarums. The thickets creaked, snapped and groaned. He asked gently, 'Are you very frightened?'

'No', she said immediately. Then, 'Well, it is very strange.'

The last evening light had left the façade of the house. It ran grim and battered as a fortress along its embankment. The flocks of starlings, retiring for the night, flew in whirring clouds right through its long lines of shattered windows. Tess said directly, 'It's a ruin, isn't it?'

'Yes.'

Their horses' hooves crunched across the forecourt's broken slabs. The filly, sighting her stable at last after her long and violent day, quickened her stride so that Mark was carried in front of Tess. He could not see her face. He thought: she will turn round in four strides and go home and leave me forever. But the horses' feet paced on across the gravel. He thought: If I can bustle her into the house, warm her by the hearth, give her home-made wine to drink. . . .

And then the farm animals in their collapsing buildings heard them coming. Untended since the morning, they set up a bedlam of shrieking cries for food and water. Bullocks bellowed, calves lowed, chickens shrieked, pigs squealed, geese honked and Rip came barking. The noise expanded till it deafened. Mark cursed them. Their cries, as of a hesitant revolution, were checked.

'My!' said Tess. 'What a lovely menagerie!'

At last he turned to face her. She held her head up. Her face was a pale heart in the dusk. Dew damped her hair. He asked very hesitantly, 'You . . . don't . . . mind. . . ?'

She could not answer. She said instead, 'Look. I'll help. All these creatures are starving.'

'But –' Mark flung out his arm over the scene. 'Can you bear it?'

'Who knows?' asked Tess dreadfully. 'But I've got to try, haven't I?'

Now he had no reply. He sat upon the filly staring at Tess, and she beneath him gave a restless quiver and nickered. One of the workhorses whinneyed back. The stallion neighed assertively and the expulsion of air from his lungs made him tremble between Tess' cold thighs. Tess said busily, 'The first thing must be to separate the lovers.'

'What?' But he dismounted. It was something to do.

'Oh, not us. Not poor us. We've got to cling together. I mean', said

153

Tess, 'Sultan and the filly. Then feed all the rest of your dependent hordes. At least it may get me warm.'

36

The fire at last burned bright. It had been old Lincoln's task to gather the dry kindling which, of an evening, would reignite the thick, smouldering logs. That morning Mark had put it off until too late. Tess sat crouched like a savage under one of his old blankets. She held her hands and face out towards the blaze. The catalogue of omissions and deprivations had been unending as evening bustled into night: the no light, the no running water, the no bedrooms nor bathroom nor kitchen, had all progressively multiplied until she could herself say, attempting a brave face, 'And no loo naturally?' And Mark had replied that he and his father always used the gardens: 'What used to be the gardens', he had now perforce to correct himself. 'Quite big once-upon-a-time gardens, anyway', he said, attempting a joke.

At least there was no wind that night to thrust through the window sockets. And he had warned her about the great white owl, Ozymandias, before it swept out of the vaulted roof of the hall like a ghost, so she was not scared of it. She, too, thought the owl a spirit. 'Clinging to this poor corpse of house', she said. 'Brave, idiotic thing.'

Those were the only blessings he could count. And when he did not think of her predicament, he thought about his father caged by the police in illness and terror, and he thought about his own impotence to keep the place alive.

They had been cold, even after feeding all the animals. They were still hungry. The broth in the blackened billy-can tasted only faintly of the partridge that had stewed in it for two days. The broth left a scum of grease on Tess' lips and had burned her pink tongue. But she had gulped it down, holding the pot in her hands. She sat, looking steadfastly into the fire's heart. 'Well, that was hot. And the fire's marvellous.'

He said it at last. 'You'll have to go back.'

'How can I?' The words flashed out quick as the double crack of a huntsman's thong. She had been waiting for them. 'Impossible. I've burned those boats.'

'I didn't ask you.'

'I'm not blaming you. I'm not complaining. But I can't duck back, you know.'

'Would you have come if you'd known it was all like this?'

'How can one ever tell with "ifs"? You decide on what you *believe*. On what your mood is *then*. I'd made the first decision: to warn you. And the other: to leave him. Then you needed help. So I came. Because you do need help.'

'So. . . .' he asked gently, lest he fracture her tenderness. 'Will you stay a little, anyway? To see if you can bear it?'

But Tess was angered by his tolerance of the situation. 'We must make the *best* of it!' She turned fiercely towards him, one cheek blazing, one eye glittering in the fireglow, the other half of her face sliced off by the chilly darkness of the room. 'And that's what you and your father have never done, so far as I can see. You've just *existed* here.' There was so much fury in her voice that it trembled.

'We didn't want to change', said Mark.

'Why not?'

'My father didn't like new things. Why should he? There's no rule that new is good and that you must like it. He had fame – of a sort – in the old days. And this place was something of my mother's which she couldn't take away.'

'He loved her?' Tess was surprised.

Mark shrugged. 'He never stopped thinking about her.'

Tess asked 'After all those years? It's crazy.'

'Is it?' asked Mark, looking at her to fix her image more firmly in the developing pan of his memory. He was convinced that he would never, all his days, be able to forget Tess. She was aware of his thought and, unflattered by the comparison, bit her lip. 'But why did you, why do you, love this place?' she asked.

'I feel it right in me. In my blood, in my body. All those years. Two centuries. Our past. We don't want to change', he repeated. 'We want things as they have been.'

'But they're not!' she shouted, 'Can't you bloody see? By doing nothing, by this dreary drifting, *you* may not change, but life is changing all around you. You're like a log miles and miles and miles on downstream. The country's different now, haven't you noticed? From your dream? In a ruin? What's the *point* of it, Mark?'

'It was the way of our life that we grew from those days.'

She shrugged, but noted the past tense. She said, 'You were pretending.'

'Father didn't like what's *happening* in the modern world.' Again the past.

'But modern isn't a thing you like', she said. 'Modern is simply happening, like it or not. It's living, however horrible. All this is dead.' She flung her arm round. 'Cold as a robbed grave, too.' She was relaxing though. 'And ghosts. . . .!'

'You get –' He corrected himself, 'We got used to it.'

'Ah yes', she said gently, holding out that arm to him, 'You got used to the decay. You really noticed nothing. Not just because you didn't want to, but because your eyes and outlook were all falling inwards – gummed up with that dreadful ivy like these jokes of windows. Who named your owl Ozymandias?'

'My mother.'

'Well, that sonnet goes, you know, "Round the decay of that colossal wreck . . ."' She laughed. 'True. And Ozymandias says "Look on my works, ye Mighty, and *despair*!" Don't you know it?' He shook his head. He knew nothing of poetry or the arts. Tess declared, sharp as a trumpet, 'Well, I'm not going to despair. There are things we can do.'

There were, as it turned out, only things they tried to do. After a few days they rode back to the haunted farm to try to collect all her clothes and bedding, some drink and some provisions. All the lower windows had been boarded over. The Trapcheks had gone. In their place a uniformed security guard with two Alsatians was patrolling. He drove them away with threats of violence and prosecutions. He had a radio, he said chewing his gum, in direct link with the town police force.

They went into the town: Mark to argue again with the farmers' cooperative about his harvest grain; Tess to sound out Mr Salerno's bank. The buyer at the cooperative, pleased by the aberrant Lincoln's incarceration, was particularly tough with his son. Pressure now, the buyer considered, could bring the lad into line with the rest of them.

Lincoln was still in the town cells. Mark applied to see him. The old man was very frail and his blue eyes were fever-bright. He fussed about delays to the filly's training: 'She must run next summer!' Mark let fall that Tess and Sultan could now gallop with her. 'Get her off the place!' shrieked old Lincoln, rising behind the iron grille to strike at Mark. The guards removed him, spluttering, back to his cell.

And Tess, at the local branch of the international bank which handled Random Salerno's earnings, found their joint account already closed.

'Hadn't you any money of your own?' Mark asked Tess.

She shook her head impatiently. It was the point on which her mother had always nagged her. She repeated what she always sardonically replied: 'He likes to keep me that way.' But Mark did not see the pun.

Tess said, 'I didn't ask if *you* had any money.'

'No', said Mark more cheerfully, 'But we always knew we hadn't. Father just traded.'

'That's as foolish as me', Tess said. 'As my mother always bloody well griped, "What you got to show for it when he's done with you then?"'

'We've got the place', Mark said, looking firmly at her. Her lips parted to comment cruelly. But she did not. She said instead, 'And if we're very lucky and hard-working and I don't die of pneumonia or exhaustion we might just feed ourselves – on peasant broth.' She added lightly, 'What a nonsense it all is. That mother of mine would *know* now I was insane!'

Thus pressed, Mark accepted the low price he had been bid for his wheat and Tess blamed him for not holding out. With his advance he bought her from the market a pair of leathers and a sheepskin coat stitched crudely together in the detention centre by the political prisoners. They rode home silently but as quickly as Mark could force the pace. They had lost half a day's work and to lose even one hour now of the swiftly shrinking daylight made their tasks Augean.

Tess worked at a frenzied pace. She darted from byre to midden like a wren. Mark cajoled her to relax into the gentle rustic rhythm. She would try for several minutes. Then the mocking evidence all round her of what would take till doomsday to be done spurred her wildly forward once again.

They conversed only in the early night, lying together under their blankets. 'D'you know', said Tess, 'there's not even a pencil here?'

'There's chalk by the barn', said Mark. 'We use it to tally up the wheat on the black planks. Why? D'you want to write a letter?'

'Who to?' Tess demanded. 'No, I wanted to make a list of just some essentials. Some clean blankets', she began, 'a new kettle and stewing pot, some oil-lanterns for in here, planks, nails, boards, so that you close up some of these smashed windows –'

'The money from the harvest', said Mark coldly, 'must go for animal feeds and the seed corn.'

She did not argue. She said merely, 'Just because Mr Salerno has quite cut off both my retreat and my money, I'm not merely going to grow like you and get to lump it. I shall try to improve things.' They held each other tightly, but physical exhaustion sucked them both into sleep before they could do more than lay their hands upon each other.

When the cocks crowed Mark stirred from habit. He began gently to try to arouse her under the old blankets by the ashy fire. She said after a while, 'I'm truly sorry. Even this sexy body of mine seems quite drained. Unusual – like this life. But I expect I'll grow used to it. Soul and body.'

But she did not. Nor did she 'get to lump it.' Each early morning, as they blundered about in the mid-winter sluicing rains and first slippery snow falls, she would make suggestions for cutting costs and corners. But even those ideas which were sound tasted unpalatable to Mark. He doesn't know *how* to change, Tess thought, watching him with gnawing frustration as, in a storm of hail, he went the old long way round taking the turnips to feed the shivering calves.

There had been no time at all to train the filly as they had planned. Tess rode her a few days a week while Mark ploughed on and cleared the jammed ditches. But the filly was moody. She was becoming awkward. She would not canter when Tess wanted her. She propped and dug her toes in. Tess hit her. The filly squealed and stood rigid, her forelegs braced out, sulking. It happened again. Mark from his ditch saw Tess leading her home, squelching across the still untilled great spread of stubble. Tess had a face of fury in the driving rain.

'She's a bloody bitch!' Swore Tess. 'You've spoilt her.'

'Come. I'll try.' Dripping in the rain, his legs shining with black mud from the blocked ditch, Mark came up to the filly and began to coax her – 'There', said Tess. 'Spoiling.'

'Wait and see. At least I know her.'

158

'Knew.'

Mark climbed up. The filly walked off for home. 'There!' shouted Mark triumphant.

'But I was trying to canter away from home', Tess called. 'Turn her round. If you can, Mr Centaur.'

'Very well.' Mark lowered his voice and began to croon to the filly, as his father always had. He would aim to glide her round in a large and gentle circle one leg caressing her off-side with firmness, the off-side rein just stroking her wet neck, while the near rein not so much pulled at her head, as nibbled at her left lip. All the time he would exert a firm, coaxing pressure on her with his pelvis. She did begin to move away from home across the slope of stubble, but as he asked her like a yacht to come up into the wind, its force, full of the quills of rain, dashed into her eyes and ears. She checked and swung away. He exerted more pressure. His seat bones ground onto the saddle. His right leg squeezed harder, then booted her flank. The filly hunched herself up and napped. She would not move up hill again away from home. Tess stood with her arms akimbo and a smile on her face. 'There, you've spoilt her!' She mocked. 'Fillies need firmness. You've got to master us!' she shouted, and stamped her boots on the sharp stubble.

'I did.' He was raging. 'You've spoiled her. She never did this till you rode her!' The rain whipped across the stubble in grey shrouds. They bellowed at each other through it. 'She doesn't like you', shouted Mark.

'Why should she? I've nicked her lover, haven't I?'

Mark hit the filly then. She leapt and reared up, head and neck stretching to the pewter skies, forelegs pawing and her hind hooves staggering beneath her. She slipped, whipped round to catch her balance and he crashed sideways off her. Tess came running. 'Oh, God, are you all right?'

Mark rose with care, feeling himself tenderly, particularly the shoulder he had once damaged. 'Yes', he said. 'Pride hurt though.' Tess put her arm around his sodden mud-caked back. 'We're both losing a lot of pride every day', she said. The filly, back to the wind, tail tucked between her legs, regarded them balefully. She consented to be led home.

It was thus easier for Mark to make the decision which he knew was already overdue. He could not prepare the filly to run in any race next summer. He decided to rough her off and turn her out in the fields. He had not only lost the most formative year of her life, if she were ever to be a racehorse, but the distant beacon, which had kept his father and himself going forward with some flickering of purpose, had now sunk out of sight. Temporarily, he told himself. The enforced delay could help the filly develop better, he assured himself. It was not, he affirmed, the major defeat it seemed.

He did not report this surrender to his father, now removed to Corrective Detention. Mark continued to post fortnightly accounts of the gallops she should by then have accomplished. His father's replies in the post office contained many recollections about racecourses in distant lands, interspersed with advice about reteaching old steeplechasers to jump or dealing with mares and foals. Each letter concluded, 'I trust you have kept the hot bitch off the place.'

Since his father asked no question, Mark did not have to lie. He simply ignored old Lincoln's assumption. He ignored it, in his replies; but the regular reminders of his father's view of Tess, repeated word for word, did begin, like the rain padding through their roof, to have some final effect on the ground floor of his mind.

Because market-days were the only outings of her week, Tess contrived always to find something to sell and buy. She laboured in the firelight making muffs and caps from the fur of hares, but got little money for her trouble. She quickly discovered, however, that she could get as many free drinks and snacks as she pleased from the crowded bar in the market's seedy hotel. The squalor in which she was now living had in no way diminished her beauty. Her attraction was even increased. Hungry and unkempt, and having knowingly erred, she needed more than in all her life the oxygen of admiration. So she was determined to please the merchants, farmers, officials, street traders and soldiers who frequented the place on market day.

She saw boots and clothes to keep out the wet, but had no money to buy them. She announced to Mark, 'I will sell Sultan.' He did not make a protest, but because she had expected one, she went on, 'The filly won't race, so what's the point of him? He eats your corn. He takes my time. Will you sell him for me?'

But the horse-dealers in the market were wary. 'Bain't that the great artist's horse? He that knows the p'lice like they be his dogs. That'd be too dangerous a nag to touch.' And one plum-cheeked old coper, who knew Lincoln, plucked Mark aside and breathed gin

fumes round his ear, 'Don' you start a-nickin' thin's, man, like ole
Linky. You leave his thievin' antics well alone.'

Mark found Tess perched radiantly upon a bar stool, surrounded
by four men, two merchants, a farmer and a man in a city suit beneath his fur-collared overcoat. He pushed his way through the press
to reach her. The city man had his hand on her thigh, and did not
move it on Mark's arrival. Tess was not pleased to be disturbed, for
the sallow man in the furry coat was asking her to share a chicken
with him and a bottle of wine.

Mark interrupted, 'There's a farmer out in the country that'll take
Sultan.' He was brusque. He glared at the man from the city, who put
a cigar into his mouth and with a curious intimate look into Tess'
eyes, rolled the cigar along his full lower lip with the end of his
tongue. She smiled at him, then turned her shoulder round to Mark.

'Good', she said. 'Well done', she added.

'But they'll cut him', Mark said.

'What?' Tess looked round again, and the man's hand took the
chance to creep a little closer up towards the warm conjuction of her
legs.

'They'll have his balls off', snapped Mark, raging. 'Turn him into
a gelding. So he can run out in the fields.'

Tess hesitated. But the group of her admirers were laughing. 'Balls
off!' One of the merchants leered. 'No good to you, eh, love?'

Mark pushed himself forward glowering. 'Well?' he demanded.
'It's your decision.'

He was determined to make her respond to him. She, feeling his
tension, started to slip off her bar stool to come with him. The man
with the cigar swayed it's red end in her way like a warning lantern.
'Our meal is waitin'. . . .' he murmured.

'Yes.' Tess was harassed. Mark touched her arm.

'Oh, sell him', she sighed and turned away.

Mark burst out, 'But you love him.'

'Love?' Her head jerked back. She sounded incredulous.

Some of the group surrounding her mumbled to one another.
'Who's she love then?' Mark said to her angrily, 'Yes, like I love the
filly. I've seen you on him.' Again the strangers murmured. The city
man smiled widely. There came the sniggers which wipe away the
dropping of a dirty jest. Tess, embarrassed, said in a firm, low voice to
Mark, '*You do* love the filly. Sultan sexes me up. Can't you see the

difference?'

'Yes I can', said Mark bitterly.

He turned to go.

Tess touched his arm and said, 'Sell him best you can. I'm sorry. But we've got to. And he had a last good go on top of your filly, didn't he?' Mark, angrily pushed his way against the tide of men. He went out into the late winter afternoon to ride Sultan through the cold countryside to find the outlying farmer.

The man, having Mark far from home and late in the day, drove a cruel bargain. Then he asked, 'You're a horseman plainly. Will you hold him while I cut his balls off right away?'

'I will not!' Mark swore. 'And may he kick you to hell.' He slammed the door and carrying Tess's saddle and bridle started the long walk back into town. A frost was starting. His feet crackled on the puddles. The sound triggered in him a sense of urgency. He started to run.

The bar was even more crowded. He took several minutes to squeeze and push himself through the throng, cursing the impeding saddle and being damned by those he bumped. When he reached the bar there was no sign of Tess or of any of her circle of men. It took several more minutes for Mark to attract the barmaid to ask where Tess might be.

'She's in the club, o'course', the aging barmaid snapped. 'You orderin'?'

'The club?'

The woman, painted and powdered over a face lined with discontent, jerked her henna'd hair towards the corner door. Then, sneering over Mark's torn wet clothes she added, 'There's only members let in that place.'

Mark went through the door into a draughty tunnel which opened at one end onto the now empty pens and stalls of the market-place. The animals had all left for other lives or death. No one now stood around peering and poking at their flesh, to carp at their shape, or put a value on their bodies. But from the other end of the alley came the soft beat of music. A red sign glowed over a door. He hurried towards it. He felt sick with dread. The club lay beneath the hotel in which travellers and merchants hired women by the half-hour. He saw that city man's hand, soft as a snake out of it's white cuff, creeping up Tess' thigh, fingers ready to mesmerise and slide home. In the dank alley he felt sweat start on his brow and palms.

He pushed open the door to the club. He was in a small warm vestible lit by orange lights. Through crimson curtains hanging across an oval door surged the louder beat of music. A girl looked up behind the desk on which she was reading a pornographic magazine. A huge man in a frayed scarlet tunic strode across, barring the way. 'Get out. You're not a member here, tinker.'

Mark started to explain.

'Knows one of the girls, eh?' The doorman repeated to the ticket girl. 'Not very likely. Ours aren't that cheap.'

'He might', said the girl, buffing her nails crossly. 'Amateur competition night, innit?' It was uttered with professional distrust.

'Still?' asked the doorman.

'They've got the new one who won, doin' it all again', said the girl. 'Hark at 'em. Perhaps his', she said, looking at Mark again. 'You're a good looking feller', allowing him a view of her breasts. 'But have you got any money?'

He swallowed and nodded. He held out a note. 'Go on in quick', she said. 'It's ending soon, by the music.' She smiled at him. 'As for the other stuff afterwards, *that* you couldn't afford, I *am* sure. But come and see me after, luv, if you like.'

'You leave that kit here', ordered the doorman, angered by the glimpse of the money from Sultan's sale in Mark's rough hand. He threw the black horse's saddle and bridle behind the rickety gilt couch, and several photographs of the strip-teasers quivered on the board wall.

Mark pushed aside the curtain. He saw, as he had known he would, Tess on the bright stage, naked above the heads of fifty steaming men. Smoke swirled. Some men writhed. Some standing at the back and sides had relieving hands stuck in their pockets. Several on the lip of the stage leaned on it, looking up and into her, but they were kept back by two strands of electric wire, guarded by a negro costumed as a eunuch.

Tess was gyrating to the beat of old crackling tapes. She crossed her arms to caress her breasts from underneath. She oscillated backwards to sway at the foot of a low bed covered in plastic tiger-skin. She placed her legs even wider apart. She jerked her pelvis at her audience at each quickening beat of the drums. As the tempo was increasing, so was her energy and abandon. At each thrust she flashed more of herself forwards, by leaning further backwards. Her blonde body was bent back like a hoop as it had been beneath the stallion. Her face was half-hidden now behind her two white breasts from which, stimulated by her fingers and the mass lust from fifty men, her pink nipples stood up firmly, quivering as her body jerked. Thus curved, she fell back upon the bed, her legs still splayed and bent. The soles of her feet were dusty. The stage lights snapped off. A wail of fury, grief, frustration, desire roared from the audience. Then, as if the prayers of a foaming congregation were being suddenly granted by a deity, one bright white spotlight sprang from the roof, directed exactly at that one pulsing part of her which they all craved. All else lay in a dark stillness. The audience let out a corporate sign and groan of satisfaction, as if they had been transported by her performance into feeling her conclusion with her.

The light cut out. A sound of curtains whirred from the stage. The dim red house lights in the cramped room went up on a dozen men clambering onto the apron stage, and the negro beating them back behind the wire with smacks of his baton. The rest of the audience pushed their way out past Mark. Their eyes glinted, faces were purple, all sweated. They spoke of Tess with wet lips and thick tongues. 'She's no amateur . . . cor! What a performance . . . won by a bloody street . . . Ah, real pro that . . .' Their breaths, bitter with beer and the wafts of their drying clothes, steamed past Mark's face. 'How much'd she cost, d'you think? . . . Not in your league, cock . . . Give a week's pay, I would, for just one great deep screw . . . A week? She'd cost a year of *your* money. . . .'

Mark was picking up the saddle as the last of the audience, the group who had tried to storm the stage, were bustled out by the negro stage-guard and the door man. They were still demanding access to her. 'She's private, darlings, I told you', said the negro blowing out a kiss while pushing them on and smiling cozily at the door man. 'You'll have to ask Mr Ali in the bar.' He caught sight of Mark and his saddle, and his eyes rolled whitely. 'You want to ride 'em that way, pretty boy? Or me? Or I ride you? Now that's real wild . . .'

'It's over', said the doorman. 'Out you go.' He then asked curiously, 'Was she ever yours then, the last hot cat who won?' Mark could not answer. Carrying the saddle he went back down the cold alley to the bar. To the beat of his feet and the squeak of leather he heard repeating in his head: 'Was she ever yours?'

He spent another note on half a tumbler of fierce spirits. Over the next three minutes he looked thirteen times at his father's old watch. Was she ever mine? To his disgust he was as much on fire for Tess as any of that band of strangers now gloating over her tantalisations.

She arrived hidden in sheepskins and aglow, ushered in by Mr Ali in the city suit. Seeing Mark waiting by the bar, she turned to the man, and murmured something at which he nodded and then left. The hood of the sheepskin concealed her face from the crowd, which still talking of her, turned as she pressed against them, smelling her fragrance and the heat of her excitement.

'Sorry', she said to Mark and kissed him on his lips. 'Sorry, I'm late', she expanded. Then, 'You're drinking!' Her breath too smelt of wine. 'May I?' she asked mock-politely. Then, 'How about poor old Sultan?'

Mark silently took from his hip pocket the wad of crumpled notes and put them by her hand on the wet bar top. She riffled the notes briefly and made a moue. 'It's not much for that poor horse . . . Perhaps I was wrong.' But her eyes were brilliant. As they always were, thought Mark, when she's sexually on fire. He could have laid her in that instant, and, in one thrust, exploded. She saw that look and took a great stack of new notes from her sheepskin jacket pocket and put them on the bar. Her pile was twice the height of Sultan's sale.

Mark uttered for the first time. 'Did you get that', he spat, 'for being screwed?'

'Certainly not!' She went livid. 'It's a prize.' She stared at him. He waited for her. She whispered, so close to his face that his tongue could have reached in and touched hers. 'All that for just taking my clothes off. When Mr Ali — he gave me lunch — told me about his contest, I had to do it. The rest were local girls — things from shops, a few gauche secretaries, plump, clumsy wives. I knew I must win. Look', she picked up her stack of notes. 'Talk about easy money . . .'

'I saw your act.'

She did flinch. Her head jerked back. Through her existing glow she blushed fully. But her eyes kept steadily on Mark's. She said in a low voice, 'Well then. . . ?' He continued to try to stare down her gaze. She said, with an attempt at flirting, 'I did get a bit over-excited. But you *know* how I get. And knowing there were a hundred men in there mad for me, having paid to see me . . . it made me feel' — she hesitated — 'supreme! Like a god must feel. So I thought, I'll show them –' She caught the phrase and, to Mark's fury, smiled. He said, like ice, 'And so you did. I've never seen so much. Perhaps Mr Salerno enjoyed all that?'

'Yes', she said, head up. 'Of course. That's how I knew how to do it, against those ignorant girls from this dump.'

Her voice and flung-up face caused a stir. She was recognised. Heads swivelled in her direction. Eyes goggled. The shouting began: 'C'm on, sexy. Take 'em off again . . . we'll pay . . . Up on the bar top, luv. Let's 'ave another look.'

The manager smacked his fist on the bar so that the glasses leapt. 'I'll close this place!' he shouted. 'The police will make arrests.' He pointed, a feint, towards the main door. Heads turned.

Seizing the chance, Mark gripped her elbow, spun her round and drove her before him through the corner door into the dark tunnel. The door clanged. He turned her away from the club's red door towards the market where the filly waited. He pushed Tess in front of him faster and faster, cursing the encumbering saddle and bridle. 'Stop it!' she said, halting and facing him against the dank wall with its drooping posters and smell of beery urine. 'Listen Mark. I'm doing this for money. Every market day.'

'You are not!'

'For twenty minutes capering about three times that day, Mr Ali will pay me twice what poor old Sultan fetched, ten times what your sad farm can earn in weeks.'

'Then not with me.' He was trembling.

She put a hand on his arm. He shook it off. She said persuasively, 'Don't be silly. I'm doing it for us.'

'But that was disgusting!'

'"Disgusting?"' she mimicked, 'Now, that it was *not*. Everybody there thought it was beautiful. You saw them. Well, didn't they?'

'Beautiful! They wanted to screw you.'

She shrugged, 'Desirable then. Screwable, call it what *you* want. They still pay to look. And Mark', she grabbed his arm and squeezed it, 'What the hell is the difference between my posing for Pop for those erotic calendars and adverts, and these country geezers seeing me in the flesh?'

'That *is* the difference. You're there. It's *really* you. Pictures of things are just pretends.'

'So? Then it's better for them. And, I can tell you, it's ten times better for me, feeling that mass of lust. It's terrific. You hear actors, speakers, leaders quacking on about communication, about *feeling* their audience. So I've felt it now. Lust for *me*.'

He hesitated whether or not to leave her there. He stepped to one side of her and began to walk down the alley towards the market.

'Where are you going?'

'To find the filly', his voice boomed back. 'I'm going home.'

'Well, wait', she called, and he heard her small feet scampering after him. 'Let's have a meal first, Mark. I'm starving. I've worked. Really, I sweated. And we've money.' He waited for her. She said giggling, 'I've earned my first real money by my performance. I could eat and eat.'

They went to 'The Serenade' into which he used to peer, waiting for his school-bus. Never before had he been inside a restaurant.

Tess ate to make up for their months of starvation. The wine topping her victory made her garrulous. She was without shame. She wished like an athlete to go over again and again the pleasing strokes and winning movements of the day's play. 'And you know', she said ingenuously, biting off another pink lump of steak, 'I'd no idea at all they'd bring that final single white spot on from above! I was, you know, playing, in the dark, because I was that excited. I only just got my finger away in time!' She put her hand on Mark under the tablecloth. 'You're really ready', she breathed. 'You see it's good for both of us.'

He put his hand down onto hers. He said grimly, 'You'll not do this stripping so long as you're with me.'

'I'm afraid I'm going on with it. In fact, I'm not afraid at all. I'm delighted.'

'Then you'll leave.' He took his hand off hers. She left hers in his lap, and tapped him with a finger. That finger, he thought. She asked gently, 'How can you survive out there? On your own?'

'I shall. Because I must.' He was grim and knew he sounded pompous.

'You could come in to the town', she suggested, 'Get a job in the market perhaps.'

'No. I'm not leaving the house.'

'They'll drive you out one day.'

'Then that day I'll go. But I'm not surrendering now.'

'Surrendering!' She teased him. 'Hanging onto lost causes

167

isn't winning, for goodness sake. Winning's surviving.' She was still elated. 'It's using your talents.' He could not maintain his sternness. Looking at her, he slightly smiled, 'You're all puffed up like a little robin.'

She caught his warmth and pressed his leg. He put on a practical tone, 'It'll be easier on the place in the spring when I can get all the animals out. I can cope then. And maybe my father may be allowed out by next harvest. He might get strong –'

'But till then?' she interrupted with a real concern. He shrugged. She said, 'Listen. Compromise. I'll help you through the winter.'

'Doing those things in that club?'

'Yes. But on the farm all the other days. All right? Then we'll see.'

He knew by the feel of her hand and the look in her eye that she had already seen, that she had marked an end to them, that she genuinely wished to help him, and that he would be unable either to control her, or to reject her, or to keep her.

The cutting voice of his mother ran through his mind like one of her icy laughs when she had hurt him. 'That's growing-up.' He saw now that he had moved on several long strides and that something – he could not quite isolate it from a general jumble of regret – had been irretrievably left behind, had been deserted. 'Step by step', he murmured and squeezed her small hand. 'I've not much choice.' He had not meant it to sound ungracious.

'You're growing sensible, love – learning the ways of the big world. Come on, let's head for home. You've walked miles. And I've done my little dancing act twice and we've only the filly now between us. I'll walk the first bit back. While I'm still excited the road will spin past. I can do anything when I'm on fire.'

'Hmm', Mark grunted, puzzling over the writing and figures on the bill. 'Could you do this?' He pushed her money from Sultan's sale across. She left the right amount, calculated something and looked up at him like a merry urchin. 'That dinner cost no more than five minutes worth of my performance!' It was impossible and maddening not to smile back at her.

'I'll saddle up my poor filly', he said. 'She'll have to carry both of us now part of the way.'

37

The paddles in the potholed lane were not only ice-filled, but dusted with rime. Yet because the night was still and dry it felt not cold but bracing under the huge moon. They walked together by the filly's side until the last lights of the town were gone. Tess skipped, kicked flints over the ice and made owl noises into the enormous silence. At last, as the lane reached the ruined lodge by the old gates, she fell silent.

'Frightened?' asked Mark.

'No. I'm burned out.'

'You're like a terrier', said Mark fondly, 'All whizz and fizz then fast asleep.'

He put her up on the filly's back and gave her Sultan's saddle to hold on her lap. He said, 'It's very odd you're not frightened of the country. It's quite gone back to wilderness here.'

'I've never been afraid of those things', said Tess cheerfully. 'But that's because I've always won. People are only afraid of losing face, composure, their beliefs, their way of life, the pension they think they'll need.'

'You're mad to be so confident. The old gods will strike you down for it.'

The filly began to snort and to drag her feet. They had reached the place on the bank where Mark had found her abandoned. The feel of the spot and her own unease there rustled on her instincts. She shivered. Tess said, 'You know nothing about the filly's origins. Or mine. You're absolutely not curious. I can't understand that at all. All life is what happens to people. What they do to one another. How every person is slightly altered by another, like a painting by Pop, all the time.'

'I never – till you – except for my father, cared about any person.'

She dropped a hand lightly on his shoulder, but resumed her own line. 'About your own *history* though', she pointed into the forest. 'You can feel it back as far as the birth of those great trees.'

'Yes', Mark said, 'I care for them. Because I accept them as part of me.'

'The filly doesn't.' Tess tried to urge her forward, kicking with her legs, slapping her hard on her rump. Mark took the filly's head to lead her. 'Idiot', he said to Tess, 'that place is part of her past, too.' He wheedled her forwards. 'She *is* getting difficult', he admitted.

'Both your girls are', said Tess.

They walked on up the overgrown drive and saw a fox check, one pad raised, burning eyes turned towards them at the edge of the trees. He and the owl overhead were hunting mice by moonlight. Another fox yapped. Its high bark echoed. Tess reached down to touch Mark's cold ear by her knee. 'It's ridiculous', she said quietly, lest she disturb the myriad rustlings and squeaks of the frosty countryside. 'Here was I this afternoon flashing at all those rustic bums in that steaming little club room full of din and sex, and here . . .' She breathed in the icy air. When she exhaled, steam trumpeted from her flared nostrils. He would not interrupt to encourage her. He waited. But she was honest and her mind, temporarily diverted by the magic of the wild bright night, resumed its course. She concluded, 'And we're going back to live in a squalor ten times more primitive than any of that small town audience would possibly accept for one night! I don't know why I do it.'

'But you love me, I believe.'

'Yes.' She stroked his long hair and the rime flew off it like salt.

'And not just because I'm different?' Mark plodded on.

'One loves people *because* they're different.'

'I meant a freak', he said.

'Like the forgotten tribes I used to watch on television?'

She pondered. The filly's hooves brushed through the crisp moon-lit grasses. The saddles squeaked. Mark's feet padded. A little owl shrieked and there came piercingly the scream of a rabbit caught by a weasel. 'Perhaps that's true', she said honestly. 'My own particular savage? And quite noble too in his way. But I did fall for you a whole year before I knew all about this.' The great house, black as death against the milky indigo sky, loomed ahead.

'Ah well', he said, 'You thought I was rich.'

'Now that *is* nonsense. All the first year I thought you were a homeless gypsy, didn't I?'

He admitted it.

'I desired you', she said. 'You excited me. But I did love you, too. And for this strange world you came from.'

He turned to look up at her face white in the moon's flattening

170

beams. She added in a low voice looking steadfastly ahead at the encroaching army of the trees, 'You were part of something I'd never known. Thought lost, in fact. But which. . . .' She touched her heart with her sheepskin gauntlet. 'Which really pierced me here.' She did not look down at him.

'But you will leave in the spring', Mark said. His tone was casual, but he still looked up at her. She nodded twice. He nodded and walked on. She exclaimed, 'You are quite extraordinary.'

His shoulders shrugged. He began, 'I hear that heifer starting to calve and –'

She said, 'Months ago I'd have thought you crazy – and would have been exceedingly insulted – that you didn't fight and fight to keep me. But no. The horse man doesn't lift a finger.' She gave his ear a cat's cuff with her glove. 'But that was before I realised that, though *I* would fight, *you* are the great acceptor.' He stopped, turned and smiled up at her. His teeth sparkled in the white light, but the moon had given his cheeks a spectral pallor. A flicker of anxiety passed through her expression. She added, '*I* accept *that* now. So climb up on here and hold me. The filly won't mind.'

She did though. Uttering small grunts of disapproval she ambled on with the ostentatious slowness of a child sent on some irksome errand. But the filly's sulking was of no consequence to Mark and Tess. She sat before him, head against his shoulder, his arms round her small waist. They were, within the limits set for them, perfectly at peace with one another.

The fire was nearly out, but the room was lit by great white squares of moonlight splashing through the windows. Tess had fallen asleep against Mark's shoulder for the last mile home. Thus refreshed she had dashed about the farmyard as he plodded, feeding the last of the ravenous animals, helping the heifer calve.

'Wouldn't you like children?' He looked at her over the tottering black and white calf. His eyes felt gritty and his blood lead-heavy with exhaustion.

'Is that a proposition? Will you cover me to conceive?'

He shook his head. 'As you're leaving, that'd be foolish.' The calf began to suckle, clumsily at first, then drawing deeply. The calf and the cow were content. Mark asked 'Could Mr Salerno have a child?'

'No. Why are you smiling, Mark?'

'I would really have hated the idea of his child growing in you.'

171

'There's no risk of that. I may not be able to myself.'

He stared at her, 'Why? Why not? What's wrong?'

'Nothing so far as I know', she said, warmed by his alarm and therefore soothing. 'No panic.'

They settled under their blankets. Mark holding her to him all the way down, breathed into her ear, 'I would like to give you a baby, but I'm so tired. . . .'

She felt. 'You are', she said. 'I'm still excited.'

'Your energy. . . .' he murmured.

'I'm a survivor.' She moved a little from him. 'I'm the swimmer who keeps swimming from the wreck.' She turned back the blankets so that he could see her marble white under the moon's shafts. She said sensuously 'Think of me doing my performance.' She spread her legs and began to move her pelvis. His hands reached out, one to her breast, the other between her legs. 'Ah . . .' she whispered, 'That's beautiful. . . .'

So it was. She said against his hot face, feeling his lungs move in and out against hers like two fishes in the deep ocean, 'You see it's not bad, showing oneself off? It's a therapy, as Pop would say about his pictures of me. And what harm ever was there in desire?' But he, lips open and touching the tiny lobe of her ear, was fast asleep. She had her answer, mute.

When Mark woke, Tess was up. He heard her tiptoeing across the rotten boards. 'What are you doing?' Jerked from sleep he believed she was leaving him. 'It isn't dawn yet. Not even the cocks have started crowing.'

'I'm going to get Sultan back', she said.

Mark rubbed his eyes, watching her pulling on her old clothes.

'Steal him?'

'No, buy him back before the farmer could do that dreadful thing. You fell asleep on me and in me for a bit, and that was very nice. But I lay awake thinking about poor Sultan.'

Mark had sprung up. Naked he grabbed her by the pale grey window. 'I do love you, Tess. I'll come with you.'

'No. There's far too much to do here. Just tell me how to find the man, and I'll ride there.'

'On the filly? And lead Sultan back?'

'She needs exercising, it'll save time.' Tess, once resolved upon a plan, itched to activate it, and was brusque. She dashed about in the dark helping Mark feed and turn out the stock. The young cattle banged about uncertainly through the shadowy gateways. The moon had sunk behind the belt of dawn fog. The chickens hunched themselves morosely at their doors, refusing to venture out into dark danger. In the woods the geese, like vintage motor cars, honked out their protests at the unusually early activity.

The filly dragged her feet. 'I shall be firm', said Tess. 'Don't you hit her', Mark warned. 'Seriously, I'm not joking. She'll not move for the stick. You've got to coax her.'

'One sharp cut –' Tess began.

'You say that's the only way to treat females. But you don't believe it. Look how well we get on: I don't bash you.'

'Well not in that way perhaps.' Tess put out her tongue at him and rode off into the shadows, Sultan's bridle looped around her neck.

38

By noon an exceptionally warm sun for late winter smiled on the stubble field. Coaxed out by this and the good pickings of grain and beetles between the old wheat stalks, a flock of pheasants was deployed in force. Mouse-brown hens and gaudy cocks pecked among the stubble. Mark took his catapult, filled his old jacket pockets with smooth black pebbles from the mill stream and crept up the hedgerow to stalk. He had lined his pockets with bracken to stop the stones chinking. They lay in it like eggs in a nest. Rip, on his belly, too, crawled behind him. The grainy smell of the warming earth, the scents of the mixed wood stems of the hedgerows tangy and rich, and of the grasses and weeds of the headlands, were all sweet in Mark's nose. Resting before he darted across a gap, he patted the earth, picked up some chalky particles and crumbled them with pleasure between his fingers. He loved the place and was delighted by the morning. He would get two fine cock pheasants (he left the hens to breed now) to please the returning Tess.

As she looked for him, calling from the stable yard, she saw the cattle staring up at the far bank. Tess observed Mark and Rip crawling like two native hounds uphill in the lee of the hedge. She took their route quietly. When she reached the gap in the overgrown hedgerow she saw Mark's target. The pheasant flock, oblivious of the danger stalking them down wind, still strutted across the stubble. As she was looking at them, and wondering where Mark was, one arrogant cock suddenly fell over. It let out a spluttered squawk. One wing fluttered. Then it collapsed upon the ground completely still. Its fellows and hens hesitated in their pecking, eyed the phenomenon, but did not disperse. Then another cock in full feed was hurled sideways onto the ground. Only half off the stubble it began feebly to struggle away. Rip bore down swift as a brindle bullet. The flock, running into flight like ancient aircraft, departed whirring towards the shelter of the woods. Rip seized the wounded cock by the neck at full gallop and, completing a circle like a tent-pegging lancer, raced back to the wood's fringe. Tess saw Mark standing. She waved. He caught the movement and walked down the hill towards her.

She ran uphill to him, pink-faced, eyes sparkling, hair undulating goldenly behind her. He thought: of all this lovely day, she is easily the loveliest thing. These trees, these slopes will stay. She passes across them like a leaf. And she will go like one.

'God!' she exclaimed with awe. 'You're *deadly* with that catapult. You're a killer.' He had scooped up both pheasants and now presented them to her, blood-warm, with a bow.

'It's silent', he said. 'They don't see what's hit them.' He grinned. 'And the authorities can't hear either.'

'You're a real assassin', she said, stroking the bright sheen on the birds' backs and gazing up at Mark with dancing admiration. 'Practice', he said, pleased. 'Did you get Sultan safe? You've been hours.'

'Yes, and in one piece', Tess said smiling. 'It was coaxing your filly. She *crept*. She loathed leaving. She was hanging back for you. She loves you, you know. Too', she added.

Mark was delighted, but 'Didn't like leaving her stable more likely', he said gruffly. He was assuming not only his father's mantle, but his tone.

'I had to pay that farmer brute more than he paid you. I *said* you sold him too cheap.'

'Oh, come on, Tess. He just knew he had you desperate, clamouring to buy your pet back. He could have asked you anything and you'd have paid it.' Considering the source of her money, he gave her a severe look. 'Like the men wanting you in the strip club. You said it yourself: having what people want is power.'

She was piqued by the comparison, and said crossly, 'There was one of them there. A man who'd seen me.'

'Mr Ali, that oily creep from the city?'

'No. A rough farmer. It was really strange. There was a family group there for Sunday dinner and we were all squashed in the farm's little parlour while I was arguing about the price for poor Sultan. One man kept giving me bullock's eyes and trying to get against me.' Because Mark frowned, she said enticingly 'Men are always trying to rub against me in hotels, quite smart shops, and as for going up in lifts – I've really laughed sometimes feeling them at it. Anyway, finally, when I'm bending over to pay the farmer my money, I feel this hand behind come through between my legs, right up. This voice breathes in my ear,"You're the lovely little stripper." I stand up so sharply I nearly squeeze his hand off and glare at him. And I'm just thinking that part of the money I've just put down was paid by this baboon when he says, "I paid to see every little bit of you. And I did."'

'Fame', said Mark drily.

'But it was weird', said Tess. 'Finding this stranger out there who knew every curl of my little gold hairs.' She had felt this time only partly flattered. Even more so than with Salerno's pictures of her, she felt that she had been robbed. But she received no advice nor understanding from Mark. He looked coldly at her. 'Well, he didn't *know* my body, did he?' Tess continued. 'He'd only *looked*. But he might have been very close gawping up. I can't see anyone's faces against those spotlights on me, you know. And the early ones get right up under the wire. I do see their teeth and eyes shining.'

'Good looking?' enquired Mark, starting to walk on.

'No, I told you. Great rustic yob. But he kept goggling at me like this –' she pulled the face. 'And me with all these clothes on knowing that he knew exactly what was underneath . . . You don't think that's an odd feeling?'

'Should have given him a show in that parlour', said Mark angrily. Tess grinned naughtily. 'He asked what I'd want for a kiss and a squeeze in his old car.'

Mark was scornful. 'You're delighted by that.'

Tess shrugged, 'His sort of compliment, isn't it?'

'Nonsense.'

'Don't be so cross. I just *need* people. Girls need men to need us. I do. You're the exception. I want people around. You're so lucky to be content here.' Tess touched his arm. 'Tell you one thing. The filly really needs you.' Mark hesitated on the brink of a sulky retort. 'How d'you know?'

'Because she goes so much better for you.'

'Was she awful?'

'Not as soon as we'd got off this place. Then she settled for me. She went very sweetly. We got on well then.'

'Girls together', said Mark smiling now. 'They say the nice ones get along pretty well with each other!' He swung one long arm round Tess' shoulder. 'I had a good morning, too.'

'Mark's girls together', Tess said and kissed him. They walked back to the house.

39

The snowdrops faded and their leaves browned among the last smears of snow on the north side of the bare hedges. The lengthening days increased the span of work. Spring showed softly. The daffodils which Lincoln used to love sprang lemon and green through the overgrown thickets. Sowing progressed in a rattle of drills and clank of harness. And the new grass, the real worth of spring, which marked the time of Tess's departure, finally began. A rinse of green was tingeing the yellow tufts of winter meadows. But it was the first season that Mark could not rejoice in winter's passing and the first proofs of resurrection.

Old Lincoln seldom wrote now, and when he did the messages were incoherent. He was adrift in time and believed the filly had already won her races and should now be retired to stud. His short scrawls in their ominously shaking hand, recommended stallions long dead in distant parts. The filly, moody still, waxed fat, and ran out in the fields every morning.

'There must be some goodness in the grass now,' Mark said

reluctantly, kicking at a sod with his boot. Tess was sitting perched in the old iron seat above the grass-harrows. She had stopped her work to ask whether Mark wanted her to cross the field again at right-angles. Her harrowing tracks behind the workhorse laid broad swathes, like painters' mixing-charts, where the old dead grass tufts had been ripped out by the deep rusty prongs. Cow pats and horse-droppings had been dispersed to let the new grass spring.

She waited for Mark to look up, but he kept his head down, watching the torn toe of his old boot stubbing at the turf. He said, 'It won't really be for several weeks. . . . I couldn't get the stock out for at least three weeks. . . . After then, of course. . . .'

He turned and at last looked at her. He was not stricken, but essentially resigned.

'Could it be Easter?' she enquired politely. 'Just under three weeks, I know. But there was a card for me yesterday in the post office.' Her voice had the timbre of boldness overlaying guilt.

He asked immediately, 'From Salerno?'

'Not exactly. Look.' She pulled her leather gauntlet off with her sharp white teeth. Mr Ali insisted she wore gloves all the time to keep her hands smooth for her performances. She stuck the small hand into the sheepskin Mark had bought her, years ago it felt, at the winter's start. Out came a large card, slightly crumpled. As she passed it down to Mark, she turned it over and he saw reproduced on it in splendid colour Salerno's magical impressionist painting of the woods.

His muddy thumb and forefinger gripped it. Its image summoned up from seemingly decades earlier, that first full day with her in the haunted house; her body displayed on the balcony, all those posed pictures of her acting different roles, the mad electronic kitchen and the folder full of her. He remembered the feel of the paper round his thigh as he stole her angry portrait. He recaptured instantly his knowledge that Random Salerno was formidable as well as famous. Flushing, he looked up at her. 'So long ago.' He fluttered the card. 'And it's as if we've – as if I've grown up – and even been married to you since.' The fluttering of the card disclosed that it was double and contained writing. Cocking his head like a pointer, he raised an eyebrow. 'Go on,' she said, 'It's not private.'

Nor was it. The printed invitation from the great metropolitan gallery was to the Private View of Random Salerno's new exhibition of

Impressionist paintings, *'Nature's Way'*. Champagne would be served from 6 p.m.

'Champagne', he repeated, finding any other comment too hard. It was just another thing from that bizarre world of cities and aircraft which he had never experienced. Tess, dressed like a peasant and perched on his father's ancient harrow, was still a champagne girl.

Then Mark grew aware, staring at her, of what the invitation meant. He realised that he had been given, very cunningly, a mortal blow. He recognised as absolutely as that cock pheasant bowled over, that Salerno had by stealth and by the power of his art, entered into Mark's once private domain. And he had thereby recaptured Tess. Up till then Mark had believed that Tess could not leave him for ever, that one day she must return.

'*"Nature's Way"*', he repeated with ripe disgust. He thrust the invitation back up at her. Holding it out his arm trembled with emotion. The picture quivered. She took it and stuck it in the front of her sheepskin jacket, opening a button to sheathe it, so that Mark saw through her pink pullover her full breast and the tilt of its nipple. In less than three weeks, he thought in black despair, I'll never see her body again, except in awful pictures.

She said gently, 'He has done the thing we – you and I – both said he ought to do.' Mark nodded very quickly, like a soldier hoping to keep his head out of the whistle of the bullets. Tess added, 'Probably he'll never paint me again.'

She had meant it to sound like a new and better chapter of which Mark would approve in her resumed life with Salerno. But Mark snatched at the wrong straw. 'Won't you stay with him then?'

'Of *course*. Now that he's launched on these real pictures. It's what I've wanted him to do for seven years. He'll not be a commercial, sexy, artist anymore. But a real painter.'

Mark said, 'So that's why you were so excited when you got back from the town last night.' He added bitterly, 'I'd imagined you'd produced some specially erotic new act. What about the stripping and Mr Ali then?'

'It'll finish of course,' she said. 'I've got enough money now from the club for a suitcase and my train fare and some proper clothes at the other end.'

'Have you told Ali?'

'Why should I yet? He'll only kick up a stink. Goodness knows what he's made out of me. The club's twice the size since you were there. I'll tell him the day I leave.' She thought she saw disapproval in Mark's expression and burst out, 'Well, he *is* dreadful, as you say. He's just been a stepping stone, that's all.' She flapped the reins on the horse's rounded rump and clicked her tongue at him. The harrow, clanking and jerking moved off across the pasture. Mark watched her driving across the field like a charioteer. Stepping-stones were quite her thing, he thought. She crossed rivers. And I, as she says, drift down them. . . .

On the evenings after her performances reaction always set in and she was tired. Now, although the day stretched out and the birds were singing, Tess said she would not walk down to the river with him to try for a trout. She must tuck herself up and rest, she said, touching his upper arm. 'I know you think we should steal every minute, but I'd drop asleep on you.' He looked with yearning at the body which set her audiences on the boil, and then with hatred, for it had so easily earned her the ticket to leave him.

She said on the eve of Easter, quite casually, 'If you would take me in the trap for my last performance, I'll catch the train afterwards. I'd rather go straight from there.'

He could hardly answer. The days had dashed at him. Finally he asked, 'More convenient?'

'More suitable', she said, hugging him. 'I have loved you.'

He held off grimly, 'Stepping stone.'

'Certainly not! I've never stepped on you. Wouldn't have been able to. You're far too independent. And have I advanced myself with you by the tiniest step? Quite the reverse. I've drifted backwards with you. Look!' She pointed from one raised elbow all round the collapsing room, 'Not one thing has been altered. Not one empty pane has been filled. You never touched the saw and wood and glass I bought.'

'You did try', he said putting his mouth gently over her breast.

'Oh, I'd great hopes of changing you. Of bringing you forward.' She rubbed the back of his neck, pressing his mouth deeper round her nipple. 'Now with your tongue and teeth, please, so. . . .' She breathed deeply in. 'Aaah. . . . more. . . .'

'What about not having this with Mr Salerno?' he asked suddenly, against her breast.

'I've no idea.'

'You'd not mind?'

'I'd have to notice', she said. 'D'you know we've only missed eighteen days all winter.'

'You counted.' He was surprised and proud. 'You won't be able to go without.'

'I'll contrive', she said. 'I used to, after all. There were – will be other things. The launching of him. Feeling I've helped him. Me projecting.' She did seem content. Mark grumbled, 'I don't see how you *can* give me up – all this side of me.'

She pushed his head down, so that his mouth again found her erect teat. She murmured, 'It's like a holiday thing. Not that you'd know what the hell that nonsense is. I've simply made an expedition to the past. And all expeditions have a term.' Then she said, in a different voice and giving his long back a fraternal squeeze. 'I said I would jerk you into modern times.' He laughed against her. She said, 'What a flop. It's the same old ruin, as I call it. You'll never notice I've been here.'

He raised his head. 'I wouldn't say that.' He knew that everything had been altered by her. But he said only 'I could never have got through the winter.'

'Without me to feed the stock and muck them out? Romantic man you are.' He made a few protestations and she stifled them. 'And as it turns out, I am *delighted* that you and this place never changed!' Then she asked 'Would it be awful for you to keep Sultan for a bit? He'd not quite do in the city. You could use him on some farm mares, couldn't you? Leave you his seed as a remembrance of lost time?'

He began, 'I think that the filly –'

But she was recapturing the glory of that day when, bestriding the black stallion, she had felt him leap upon the filly. 'I felt *I* was creating then!' she exclaimed.

He thought of the violence of the act and her wild face. He said gravely, 'I think she is in foal to him from that.'

'No! Honestly? Mark, how marvellous. It'll be beautiful –'

'It could be dreadful. She's far too young. I really ought to try –'

'No', Tess spurted. 'Don't you dare touch her. If she was meant to conceive that magic day –'

'It could be very bad for her,' he repeated.

'I don't think so,' said Tess, and feeling his back and shoulders tense with anxiety, drew him gently onto her beneath the old blanket. She thought: only three days and two nights more of him and one of those will be the morning before my last performance. She thought, missing him will lance and lance, then leave an awful hunger gnawing. The days will grate and pine like empty rooms, like starving, scratching dogs. And then, she recognised firmly, gradually the need will slacken, the ache ease, the belly shrink. To stiffen her resolution she looked up at the ceiling above his shoulder and saw through its torn holes right up through two floors to the lost tiles in the roof and the early night sky of spring.

He asked, 'Will you send for Sultan then?'

'I'll come.'

'He'd not allow you.'

'He mightn't know.'

That was impossible, Mark knew, but he let out a growl of wild delight, and they fell to it furiously.

40

When summer came her departure, so long expected like a death, did not seem to have wounded him severely. She had said, 'If it would help to see the last of me in a bad light, come to the club for my finale. You wouldn't like the sight of that.'

Mark had said no, he didn't need that prop. 'I'd rather think well of you.'

'I'm glad', she had said and with those two suitable words echoing in the dank alley, vanished into the club clutching her brand new suitcase. Mark had not waited. He sent the pony and trap trotting out of the squat and grimy town. While Tess was reaching the crescendo of her last act, Mark was already at home in the fields banging in fencing posts with the savagery of an executioner wielding a joyful axe.

He knew the therapy. He worked till the moon was up and the hares ran in its weird glow. He drank half a bottle of old Lincoln's most fierce apple-brandy and did not wake till the cocks screeched into his headache and his hand, feeling for Tess, found only the wrinkles of the old blanket and one of her crumpled handkerchiefs.

He smelled the cotton, put it between his lips then, rising, cast it onto the ash of the fire. It browned, while he debated whether he should rescue this unremarkable memento. He watched it under heavy lids till it ignited. It flared, then disappeared among the pile of old ashes. He observed that he was rubbing his hands, but did not know whether from satisfaction, or for warmth, or from a desire to cleanse them of an old contagion.

The days were long and he toiled throughout them from the first lemon slit of dawn to the last orange flush of coming night. On top of all his usual daily labours he found others, so that his body never ceased to be in use, and so that his mind, like a chicken's head bent upon the chalkline on the floor, could think of nothing either side of his one dumb route. He ceased to shave. He swam in the mill pond only to exhaust that set of muscles in his lower back which he had not used since Tess went and which still ached for her. He ate the first berries and raw vegetables, cooked hardly ever and drank copiously of his father's spirits. His feet, legs and arms developed separate existences. He noticed them swinging to their tasks, but ceased to feel them.

When he paused at all, it was with the filly. She grew fat in foal. After Tess had gone she turned to Mark again and he to her. They became firm friends again. Their relationship, as of a marriage which had been threatened, was not better just because the intruder had been removed, but more aware and thus more sympathetic. They saw what they had missed. The filly stayed out night and day, grazing by night and snuffling to Mark when he came to hug her on his way back from his extensive, trivial expeditions to the woods. She lay basking in the morning sun and let Mark lie beside her, his arms about her neck, falling asleep beside her in a minute. She would not stir while he lay there and he, feeling her warmth beside him, and the sun's warmth above and the warmth of the growing earth beneath him, would glide away, rocked by her gentle breathing.

By the heat of midsummer, after three months as lonely as a hermit and as starved, the hallucinations began. As his limbs had grown apart through the continued slavery to which he had condemned them, so now his head more often seemed to be floating away from his exhausted body. Its lightness felt such that he frequently touched his temple, as a child pats down a wayward balloon. He heard, clearly but always behind his back, her voice saying some short sentence. Her words made perfect sense in themselves, but came without context. Nor were they ever directed towards him. Uttered with absolute clarity they were like captions to unseen photographs. 'It'd be better to take the brown,' her voice would declare. It meant nothing to him. 'Certainly, there's no such thing,' her voice would say. The tones reflected the mood of when she had spoken them, or would speak them: he was unsure where her voice came from in time. He knew only that he was overhearing part of her life which was not in the remotest way concerned with him. This saddened him immensely. He did not feel that her voice was of a ghost's returning. He felt rather that he was the spirit trying to return after death to someone adored, and finding her preoccupied, cut off with private matters.

As she spoke only behind his back, so he only glimpsed her, in the heavy buzz of midsummer insects, out of the fleeting corners of his eyes. In these visions, too, she was never looking at him. She was always in profile, drifting and sometimes dashing about her own business, whatever that might be, in the wood's fringe, in the barn with bats, at a blank window of the great house.

When it came to cutting the hay again Mark started to collapse. He would find himself lying in the middle with the mowing-horses grazing at the far edge of the field. In the centre of his unconsciousness it was always totally black but, on entering and leaving these periods of unknown time, he passed through a noisy kaleidoscope of trance. The voices of Tess, his father, Mr Salerno, Trapchek, the Inspector and sergeant, Mr Ali and the bar woman who were, effectively, all the human beings he knew, soliloquised separately in a din. Their images, too, became psychedelicly overlaid: Mr Salerno's hatted head too frequently spoke from Tess' naked body. The trances, lasting minutes, became hours of terror.

One vision continually recurred: Tess, monstrous with the black stallion sprouting from her loins, bestrode him. He felt his limbs spread and the stallion savagely enter him.

Because he had been unable to face the town again after Tess left, he collected no further postcards from old Lincoln. But one summer night as Mark sat cross-legged, swaying before the mountain of cold ash in the fire, the great owl Ozymandias flew in from his domed hall. Making a white circuit of the room he perched upon the cracked mantleshelf. The pale light from the sky of the warm summer night illumined the owl's eyes. It stared down at Mark from the marble ledge and very gently shuffled its wing feathers. There was a family legend in the great house that the owl came from its turret only as a portent of a death. The tale was as deep-rooted as that saga of the foxes of that northern castle who, before each laird's death, left their woods and padded across the lawns to sit howling beneath his window.

So Mark felt no great shock that his father's life must now be leaking away. What he suffered was the customary guilt of neglect. He regretted that even his thoughts, all through the last long time, had not attended to his father.

He saw then that Ozymandias was holding in one savage claw a small field-mouse. It was still alive. Its minute eye, bright with terror, gleamed like a glow-worm. Mark blinked and shook his head to clear his mind. The owl continued to stare down upon him. It came to Mark instantly, like eyes to the blind, that, just as the tiny mouse lay pinned in the owl's clutch, so was he himself held down by something equally enormous, old and terrible. If the mouse might escape, so might he. Without moving, lest he disturb Ozymandias and send him ballooning away, still clutching his victim, he stared up at the owl from his cross-legged squat on the boards. He willed and willed the owl to drop the mouse. The eyes of Ozymandias, yellow as a panther's, balefully stared back into his. They were full of the icy dispassion of nature and the wilds.

Mark had never entered a church nor prayed and had sworn only by hearsay on the old beliefs. But now he exerted a great prayer to the owl that the mouse might go free. He murmured to Ozymandias and making the old sign, ended 'Please' with a sibilant beseeching. The owl, without removing its gaze, released the grip of its horny claw. The mouse fell lightly into the warm ash, shook itself, paused even to clean its whiskers with a tiny paw, and scurried away through the broken wainscot. Ozymandias, as if the second purpose of his visitation was now completed, hoisted himself into the air with a mighty rush of feathers and blows of his wide wings. He flew directly across the room and out into the immensity of the night.

Mark was therefore in no way surprised next morning to hear the approach of the police truck. Its dust spread behind it in a grey wake. The sergeant alone descended and seeing the haggard, bearded man by the balustrade, hesitated and looked surprised. 'Lookin' for young

Mark', the sergeant said.

'Yes.'

The sergeant stared. 'By God! I'd never have recognised you! You look fifty. You ill?'

Mark shook his head. 'No. I've not seen myself. No looking-glass.' He caught his reflection in the glittering mirror of the truck and stared behind him for the elderly dishevelled tramp. He pulled at his beard and tugged his hair aside. 'Yes, I see. . . .' he said slowly.

'I've bad news, Mark,' the sergeant said, 'So you'll have to brace up.'

'Father's dying.'

The sergeant looked astonished. 'You've heard?'

Mark nodded. The sergeant raised an eyebrow and put his hand on Mark's arm in the gesture the living make to share their warmth when speaking of the eternally cold dead. 'It's gone further than that now, I'm afraid. He died last night.'

'Of course.' Mark inclined his head. He was about to enquire the time to see whether the owl's call had been merely coincidental. But he thought the sergeant would misconstrue such curiosity.

'So, was he ill?' Mark asked.

'Not as we were told. They don't say much from there as you know. But he was right old though, weren't he, Mark? And in his day a famous man in his way, so they say.'

'Oh, he was.' Perhaps the sergeant would be the only one to remember his father. 'Yes, he was. In his way. In his day', he repeated. 'True', he added to try to make it sound better. He realised that all the millions of the dead had, in their little ways, someone to praise them.

The sergeant hesitated. Mark said quickly, 'I'll not come to the burying. He'd no friends but me. I'd not want to see him put down by strangers.'

'Very well, Mark.' The sergeant looked along the long façade of blind and broken windows. 'I'll get that place for you in the Resettlement Camp; and quickly. For you'll die here, if you stay. I've never seen a man age so quick. Magic really. Like an ole spell. Or curse.' Mark did not reply. The sergeant said inquisitively, 'We'd heard a girl stayed here. Mr Salerno's daughter, some said, tho' *that* we didn't credit!' The sergeant laughed. 'Others said she was just a stripper from Ali's club.' He examined Mark closely, seeing with concern how vague and dim the man's old eyes had grown. The sergeant shrugged 'Seems that was crazy, too. Though you were a fine làd once. But it's plain as a pike no woman's touched this place in bloody years.'

Mark turned and looked at the great front of the battered house. 'No', he said, 'No woman's touched it.' His voice was firmer. His hands, which had been trembling, clasped one another in a sort of bond. The sergeant noted the stirring of some idiotic pride. Wishing to help, but having nothing to offer but a packet of cigarettes, he extended this. Mark simply shook his head. His eyes roamed over the buildings. He knew, absolutely, what he must now do.

'Thank you', he said courteously. 'For coming.' Perhaps something more was expected of him? He added, 'It's all quite clear.'

The sergeant, climbing back behind his steering wheel, called out encouragingly, 'I'll be back in a few weeks. Right?' and drove away.

As soon as his dust had safely settled, Mark walked into the farm buildings. He opened every door. The chickens, quavering at the gates out of their wired camps, cautiously darted into freedom. The pigs more resolutely squeezed themselves together, and burst out of their concentrated sties. The cattle plodded out to their liberty with calm assurance. Within the hour every living creature on the place except the filly and the stallion, was running free. Gradually, and in mounting spurts, the stock surged into the wild. As they left, scampering across the bowling green field, trotting down the overgrown drive, Mark shouted his creed and valediction: 'Fend for yourselves!'

He needed now only to deliver the stallion. He packed nothing, for he had nothing to take, but saddled the filly and put a headcollar on Sultan. The dog Rip sat and whined, deeply disturbed. His amber eyes looked longingly at Mark. 'Oh you shall come,' said Mark to him roughly. 'We must care for each other a bit longer, I suppose.' Rip's tail thumped the stones. His lips uncurled in his ridiculous grin.

'Come', said Mark, climbing onto the filly. Leading Sultan, he rode off across the hay meadow and up into the woods. He felt completely calm and, if not joyful (for he had not the energy for taxing joy) at least content that he had chanced upon his final solution. Indeed, he felt a gratitude to Ozymandias and to the police sergeant for so gradually setting him free. His weight was so diminished that the filly, although ten months heavy with foal, could still plod along and bear him. But she blew heavily as they ascended the hill into the

forest, and the eager Sultan bent his black neck trying to pull ahead
of her.

41

It had been Mark's simple purpose to release the stallion in Mr
Salerno's grand railed paddock. But when he reached the gate to it
from the wood he found it heavily chained and padlocked. His wits
had not expected any change in his remembered past. He sat upon the
filly, puzzling and staring across the spread of late summer grass.
Beyond it stood erect the proud turret of Mr Salerno's rehabilitated
farm. Out of the small hole at the tip of the tower there arose a white
emission of smoke. It came out first in squirts against the cerulean
sky and then in one long stream, as if fertilising particles of the gigantic atmosphere. Staring at the tower Mark thought of it so clearly
now as part of Mr Salerno that he murmured to himself, 'He'll not
keep that up', and let out a grunt.

The noise plucked him back to reality. That fire in the Salerno's
living-room must be being lit to warm them against the supposed chill
of the late summer evening. As he pondered whether he could therefore safely leave Sultan tethered to the fence, the figure of Tess
emerged on the rim round the shaft of the tower. She was clutching
the dazzling aluminium reflector and moving slowly round the balcony seeking the greatest concentration of the sun's rays. She seemed
bright with white light like a flashing star. As Mark gazed, he pressed
by reflex against the filly's expanded flanks and tugged at the
stallion's rope.

Sultan squeezed against the filly. She squealed and kicked out
sideways at him. She caught him a sharp upwards blow at the base of
his belly, and he let out a shrill scream, and then a roaring neigh of
anger.

The slowly moving light of Tess paused. She put down the
reflector. She saw Mark and the two horses at the distant gate and
waved. Mark's hand had shot up to wave back before he could start
to think. Not just his head, but his worn out body too now felt full of

the pale blue light of the sky. Inside, his heart beat like a bird, banging inside a thin drum of crimson skin.

Then Tess came running across the field. She ran barefoot. She had a little shirt half open and her breasts leapt as she ran. Her trousers gleamed expensively in the sun's rays. She waved a great black key. Mark sat completely still. It took an age for the running figure of the girl to cross the long field towards him. His heart's blows eased their drumming. He felt growing inside his body a great stillness. The stillness was a vacuum: it required most urgently to be filled.

When she could see him properly, she stopped. She let out a terrible cry 'What's *happened* to you?' She stared at him as if he were a spectre. The hand which held the key had flown up to her mouth in that old gesture. Then she ran forward again, much faster. She looked distraught. 'What's happened to you, for the love of God?' she cried, hanging onto the far side of the gate and staring up at him. 'You're desperately ill.' She was panting.

He shook his head. 'My father's dead.'

'When?' Her voice was high. It sounded shriller than he recalled, for the tones he had conjured up had been her loving murmurs and deep gasps.

'When?' he repeated foolishly. 'I don't know when.' He thought that it might have been months ago when Ozymandias had come with the field-mouse.

'But what are you *doing*?' Tess insisted.

'Bringing Salerno back', he said.

'Salerno?' She looked frightened.

'Your horse', he said looking at Sultan, and giving the rope an emphatic shake.

Tess looked down at the padlock, and began slowly to unlock it while she thought.

'Why?' she asked. 'Why now? Bringing Sultan back?' She glanced up sharply to see if he would now notice the name.

'I'm going away', he said simply. She had opened the gate and he rode through it on the filly, pulling the stallion behind him. She was about to shut the gate behind them. She had started to swing it. 'No', he said, gazing down at her, with such a yearning that his head followed his eyes and his body his head, so that he nearly fell forward down the flight of his desire. He shook his head. It was also to clear it. 'No, I can't stay.'

Neither moved. She stared at him. Her eyes were enormous. Her mouth was open. In it he saw her tongue tip flickering. She jumped up at him, stretching up her arms towards him, but reaching only his thigh. He dropped Sultan's rope and bent right down to her. Their cheeks touched. Tears coursed between their faces in a flood. A mixture of their salts ran into the corners of their mouths.

The stallion suddenly shrieked. He sprang away. The crack of a rifle flashed from the house. The stallion's black quarters had been gouged with a brilliant scarlet streak. Demented by pain he thundered off across the field. Then the next bullet smacked through the gate's top bar. The wood split whitely. The gate was swung backwards with the blow.

Mark had only raised his head. He stared towards the house. On the parapet of the tower he saw Mr Salerno bending attentively over a long black rifle. He was taking a third aim through his telescopic sights. The thick bar, jutting out, glittered in the sun. Mark gazed back at him across the length of the field. He was wondering how much the blow of the bullet in his body would hurt before it killed him. Tess clawed up at him like a cat. 'Christ! Quick!' she spat. 'Get me up. He'll kill us.' Mark was too weak to haul her up. But she, grabbing the filly's mane with one hand and Mark's thigh with the other, sprang, kicked, wriggled and lay across Mark's knees. 'Quick!' she urged shrilly. She punched the filly's off-side with her fists, and kicked into the near-side with her knees. 'Turn her, idiot', Tess cursed.

The next bullet struck the metal hinge of the gate and twanged away whining into the wood. The filly leapt, and alarmed by Tess' attack upon her, at last sprang into action. In spite of the weight of the foal within her and of the two human bodies on her back she galloped back through the gate and into the increasingly green dimness of the wood. Within a minute the thick sentinel trunks of the beech forest closed in behind them. Salerno distantly fired two more shots, but they heard no crack of the bullets. 'Wait', panted Tess. Her head was still down by Mark's right knee. 'Hoist me up.' Her face was scarlet. She sat herself side-saddle on the filly's withers and turned to Mark. Her eyes were dancing. 'He's absolutely mad', she said and flinging both her arms round Mark's neck, began furiously to kiss him. When she stopped, she stroked his bearded face. 'I don't like all this shaggy stuff.' she said. The lightness of her tone made it seem as if they had never been parted. '*Are* you ill?' she asked, this time with less alarm, and more concern. He did indeed look dreadful, had changed in months into a haggard man of many years, whose eyes, once so wonderful, now seemed sunk like pebbles in his skull. 'Where are we going?' she asked, leaving her palm against his hairy cheek.

'I'm going to the sea', he said.

Her hand dropped. He had certainly grown a little mad. 'Why the sea?' she asked. 'You've never been there.'

He nodded. 'I said I was going away.' He told her about the animals, that he had left the house for ever – 'How can you?' she exclaimed. 'How can you live without it? You can't exist cut off from that great root.'

'I must contrive', he said with faint irony. And, because she smiled, added, 'I must find stepping stones and cease to drift.' At this she laughed, until he demanded sharply 'And you?'

'What? Where I've been?'

'No.' He asked brutally, 'What are you going to do?'

So she looked away ahead of her over the chestnut pricked ears, into the patterned depths of the wood through which the filly was slowly bearing them. After several minutes she asked, without looking round at him, 'Aren't we both escaping?' She felt no response. She continued, exasperated, 'Pop was truly trying to kill us, you know, as he said he would, if he ever caught me even trying to see you again.'

Mark said quietly, 'Everyone wants to be rid of me.'

Tess was sharp. 'He was shooting at me, too. Trying to kill me. Well, wasn't he?' She whirled round to face him.

Then Mark shrugged. 'So what are you going to do with me?' She demanded. They had come at last to the western edge of the beech forest. It thinned. The hill ran down into the bracken sea. Below them meandered the lane leading to the old back gate.

Mark looked down on the derelict lodge where he had gone those years ago to catapult rabbits and had found the filly foal. His hand touched his deep poacher's pocket in which lay his catapult and clutch of stones. The lane trickled away engulfed by grass and bracken, towards the far main road and distant town. Mark said with only a peck of bitterness, 'You could go back to Mr Ali's club.' He felt her body stiffen in front of him. He asked, 'Or haven't you been doing any of that?'

'Nothing like that', she growled. He felt her tremble through her lungs with anger. 'I was living perfectly normally with Pop. His new pictures are generally acclaimed. He is infinitely happier —'

'Are you?'

'I was', she said fiercely. 'Till you appear again.'

'Oh come —' he began. Then 'Look!' he snapped. 'And don't talk.' He hissed at Rip who crouched. Mark took a firm hold of the filly's head to turn her under the nearest heavy boughs. Below them on the lane a large estate car was bumping up dustily towards the old lodge. The bangs of the car's suspension rose clearly. Tess had just uttered 'Pop — he's come round through the town', when through the window of the car appeared the swaying muzzle of a rifle held in a uniformed arm. Mark swung the filly back into the woods. As his heels drummed into her swollen flanks the rifle fired. Then they heard the clank of a door and another sharper rifle sound: several bullets ripped into the trunks of trees around them. Mark beat the filly's rump and kicked her desperately forwards. Tess lay along her neck. Mark pressed down on her. The darkness of the trees encircled them. They heard in the valley below the estate car moving forward again.

Mark felt Tess shaking under him. 'Are you all right?' He breathed into her ear. 'They'll go to the house. And find it empty. We shall have time to —' He had no notion what.

'I don't want to be killed.' She started to cry in floods. 'I am so afraid of death now. I've only started. . . .'

Mark put his mouth against her nape. He asked, 'Was the other man a security guard?' Tess nodded. 'He's official. Either could shoot us. They'll say we were a looting gang.'

The estate car had turned into what lingered of the drive. It was moving very slowly along it on their right over its grassy undulations and pot holes towards the house. Through the trees Mark caught the bright flash of the guard's binoculars. Then the car stopped again as a police vehicle roared up the lane, and halted by the ruined lodge. The Inspector, sporting his plaid coat, and the sergeant both leapt down. They too began to scan the woods above them. The sergeant's voice boomed from the truck's amplifier. 'Come on down, Mark.' In spite of the echo in the valley, the tone was intended to be inviting. 'Just give yourself up,' the sergeant boomed.

'There', Tess moaned. 'He's got the authorities as always. He's got the power with him.'

Mark asked, 'Do you want to go to them?' She hesitated. Weighing the odds, thought Mark bitterly. But she asked, 'To leave you more easily to get away?'

'Yes. You'd be safe. They couldn't touch you.'

'He would', she cried. 'He'd finish me. So, no, I'll help you.'

The origin of that echoing phrase reverberated in his head. The doors of the police-truck opened. More uniformed men got out. One held a tracker dog. Rip, sighting it, began to tremble. 'Sit, Rip. Sit.' urged Mark. He murmured to Tess. 'All these – it's ridiculous!' She said, 'They're determined to flush you out for ever. You knew it.'

'But I'm going', he said and began to laugh.

She turned to face him. 'Shut up!' She was as fierce as a vixen. She shook him. '*They* will lock you up.' She nodded at the police. 'And *he* will shoot you, and you're in no fit state . . .' She then repeated with resolve taut as a bow string, 'I am going to help you get away. To the sea. As that's what you say you want. After that, let's see. I shall be all right, I dare say, wherever I end up.'

Mark's laughter had escaped through a crack in the hard shell which had covered his strain. He now felt both energy and will seeping away. Argument, the finding of words even, was impossible. He just must escape. So he nodded his chin on her shoulder and said, 'We can go where no trucks can. And in the night we may lose them all together.'

He turned the filly deeper into the trees and dismounted. 'We'll walk in turns. To rest her,' he said. They trudged on. Soon the light hardly filtered into the green gloom of the woods. He turned away westwards again and emerged on the wood's lip higher up the valley. Outside the trees the clear light of a summer evening still rinsed the valley. There was neither sight nor sound of Salerno and the police. There was an abundance of bird noises, but no calls of alarm.

'Hop off', Mark said. 'We'll run down across the open valley.'

Tess slipped off immediately. He took the filly's bridle. She brightened as soon as she felt Tess leave her back. Mark stroked her neck and she nickered to him. 'There, love', he murmured to her, 'We've got to make speed now. So watch your feet.'

They rushed down through the clutching waist-deep bracken and across a green cropped space like a wood-god's lawn, where dappled deer were grazing. Then they were again into the bracken. The hill was very steep. The filly gasped. Mark's legs ached like lead. Tess took his other hand and pulled him.

'Rest?' She asked after a while. 'You'd better.'

'Daren't', Mark grunted. 'Must get over hilltop.'

So they did. But on the undulating lands ahead the wild protection of the forest and encroaching bracken sharply ended. Cultivated fields lay patterned. Occasional farm-buildings glowed pinkly in the descending sun. They could make out the run of country roads. There was no harbouring copse ahead this side of the far horizon. Tess and Mark lay down panting. The filly cropped grass. Rip crouched like a sphinx, sniffing for the rabbits out on their evening meal. Mark's gaze panned right across the landscape and stopped. 'There. The quarry', he murmured. 'Where father found the donk.' Ridiculously his eyes filled with tears.

'Cry', whispered Tess. 'Let it out.'

'I dare not.'

'Do.'

'I'm hardly strong enough', Mark began, and then the sobs burst out of him as if he were retching up the poisons of the past. Groans vomited from him. His body shook upon the short turf. The filly placed her soft muzzle against his jerking head. Rip drew close, turning his head askew in great anxiety. Tess, as if Mark were a frightened horse, stroked and stroked him, murmuring all the while. And at last it was over. And Mark felt neither exhausted nor defeated, but lighter in every way, as if he had in fact emptied himself of a sickness. He clutched her hand. He put his cheek against the filly's muzzle. Rip softly licked him.

'That's better', he said. All the front of his old shirt was soaking. 'Let's go on.'

42

They reached the quarry without being spoken to. But they had attracted attention. They seemed, with their poaching dog and in-foal mare and dishevelled clothes, a gypsy couple. The country people watched till they were out of sight, for the travelling folk who still remained free were particularly light-fingered.

Of the four, Tess and Rip strode out the boldest. Tess said, 'We are a mad couple together. We never have money.' She was buoyant. Rip, remembering the plump, incautious rabbits on the green quarry floor, loped eagerly in front.

But not only the dog had remembered the quarry. The Inspector, whose memory was infallible when etched by failure, soon recalled the stolen donkey, the mad logic of the farmer's wife, and thus the place. Infuriated by losing, he had been goaded by Mr Salerno's haughty references to his friends in central government. The Inspector declared he would have Mark picked up in the morning. 'I know the quarry where he'll be lying up. Just like foxes, these rustic creatures', he declared to Mr Salerno. He was surprised that the artist did not smile with him. Mr Salerno had stated that the man had kidnapped his model while attempting another robbery on his home. 'Tinkers' blood will out', the Inspector declared with satisfaction. The charge would serve to have him put away and that shambles of a mansion at last obliterated.

The cows stared at the strange visitors in the quarry. Then the sun, slipping down, took the warmth from the hill-top, and the herd moved away downhill from the quarry's edge.

Against the advice of Tess, Mark had simply unsaddled the filly with complete trust, looped her reins over her neck so that she could not get tangled, and then turned her loose to graze. She had promptly rolled and, being great with foal, had nearly lodged on her back. As she lay there, her fawn belly bulging, Mark touched Tess. 'Look, her bag's filling. She'll not be long. She'll only be days now.'

'You don't mind now?'

'She's all I've left.'

Tess waited. But when Mark continued it was only to say, 'I'd mind if I couldn't get her safely somewhere first. Safe to the sea.'

There were blackberries from the great thicket at the cliff's foot and apples on the wizened trees. These they ate ravenously, sucking in the sweetness. Rip chopped a baby rabbit and devoured it. The filly grazed.

'Why to the sea?' Tess persisted.

'It's as far west as I can go.'

'And your mother's beyond it.'

'Well, so she is', said Mark wiping his purple-stained mouth with the earthy back of his hand. 'But I'm not likely to see her with thousands of miles of ocean in between.'

Tess grunted, 'That's why you're going that way though', she diagnosed. He did not answer. She laid her head against his shoulder. 'Even you don't know yourself.'

'Do you?' he asked.

'I know what I want. That's even better.' She started to curl up against him like a cat. 'No', he said, pulling his catapult out. 'The rabbits are coming out again. I'll kill a couple. We'll need the food.'

'We,' she repeated to herself. So, 'Very well', she said and they crawled for cover under the thicket of blackberries. It was the spot where Lincoln had found the donkey's dead foal. Above them rose the cliff from which they had named the quarry Babylon. Mark looked up and picked out the grassy ledge on which the donkey mother had been stranded.

Rip growled softly. 'Silence', Mark swore, cuffing him. The dog lay still for a moment, then another muffled grumble rumbled from his throat. Mark kicked back at him, for five plump young rabbits were now almost in range. Behind them, however, the filly cropped the grass. Mark dare not loose a killing stone lest it ricochet and smash her leg. He turned back beneath the undergrowth to signal to Tess, with finger on lip, to stay hidden there while he edged round right-handed. As he turned, he saw Rip's hackles standing up like hedgehog quills along his back. The dog's head was turned and cocked up towards the quarry's rim high above. His ears were flattened. His mouth was just open, showing his teeth, in a snarl. Another suppressed growl rattled in his throat. His yellow eyes stared.

Mark looked upwards. Silhouetted against the darkening blue sky of early night he saw the wide-hatted head and shoulders of Salerno. He must be lying on the quarry's rim. Jutting out before him was the long barrel of the rifle. Above it, the end of the telescopic sight reflected a small circle of pale blue. The figure, which made it more ominous, was absolutely still. Its black bulk cut into the skyline like a metal target.

To stifle Rip before he could bark outright, Mark bounded forward under the briars. But the dead twigs crackled and the brambles moved scratchily over his head. As Mark seized Rip's neck to pin him down, to silence him, Salerno's deep voice resounded from the sky: 'I hear you down there.'

Tess, who had seen nothing from her side, let out a tiny cry of shock.

'And you, too.' Salerno's voice, directed downwards boomed about the quarry's amphitheatre like that of an ancient god. By wriggling forward Mark could get closer to Tess beneath the thicket. He could see her trembling. Mark rolled over quietly and stared upwards. To his left was a small gap in the thick mesh of brambles. Raising one finger at Tess, and dragging Rip by his scruff, Mark crawled underneath the opening. Now he could see Salerno quite clearly. He was not more than twenty paces, a short fall, above him.

'I want you out!' shouted Salerno.

Tess started to crawl fast and noisily towards Mark. Her mouth, just above the level of old dead leaves, was open in terror.

'Come out, you miserable stoat!' screamed Salerno. His black silhouetted face was turned down towards them, but because it was swinging from side to side Mark knew that Salerno had not yet precisely spotted them. Mark opened his mouth towards Tess and silently, urgently, besought her to keep mute.

'Come *out*, I said!' shouted Salerno. 'Or I will spray bullets into those bushes – I see you skulking, I see you –'

'No!' screamed Tess.

Mark grabbed her, loosing Rip, who made off on his belly. Mark shook Tess vigorously. The branches rattled, the briars quivered, the berries black and red danced below the downward pointing muzzle of Salerno's rifle.

'I said I'd shoot him', cried Salerno in triumph.

'You'll kill me', Tess screamed.

'Stand up then', boomed Salerno majestically.

Mark seized her throat and pinned her down as he had held the dog. 'Wait', breathed Mark. 'He'll not shoot.' Their breaths mingled and panted between them, but all else was silent.

'Well then?' Salerno sounded less certain. 'Listen', he called down. There came a rattle and click. 'Another bullet up into the spout', shouted Salerno. 'To smash your body into bloody pulp, Miss Tess.'

She opened her mouth, started to scream and Mark forced his fingers and knuckles into her mouth. He felt her tongue leaping inside, then her teeth came down, crunching onto his fingers. He put his other hand across her mouth and clamped it down. As he turned he saw the dog Rip emerge on the further lip of the quarry and begin slowly to stalk round the rim towards Salerno.

Mark whispered to Tess, 'Rip'll see him off. He's moving round.' Tess whimpered under his palm, but wriggled less. Mark said right into her ear, 'Just lie quite still. Trust me.'

But the dog's swift stalk had upset the filly. Refreshed and rested she started back out of the gloaming towards Mark and Tess. 'Oh God', groaned Mark and, turning to face her through the thicket, willed her to stop. But she trotted steadily on, her big belly wobbling as she approached their hiding-place and came into close range of the rifle. Salerno saw her. He gave his deep laugh. 'Don't worry, dirty horse boy. First I'll shoot your precious filly.' Salerno rose on his one knee the better to mark the filly and to look over into the thicket at the cliff's foot below him. As he did so he caught sight of the dog Rip creeping towards him like a wolf round the quarry's lip. He swung round on his good knee to face the dog. He raised his rifle to his shoulder and took aim.

'Don't!' bellowed Mark. '*Stop!*' He struggled to fight his way up through the scratching tangle of brambles and the dog, hearing his master's command, dropped to a crouch. He laid his grizzled head on his outstretched pads, watching the enemy Salerno with his amber eyes, but cocking his ear for another call from Mark.

Salerno, presented with this stationary, obedient target, maintained his steady aim and squeezed the trigger. The dog let out one grunt, like the explosion of a paper-bag, as the soft-nosed bullet tore through his chest and exploded steel and lead inside his lungs. The force knocked him back and upwards so that it seemed as if he were attempting some tragic dance against the skyline. His old paws beat at the unsupporting air, searching for his master's hand. Then he crashed backwards, a flopping mass of bones and flesh, down the dark cliff of Babylon.

Mark saw him fall only as a blur through the thorns of the thicket and could not stop one cry escaping. When he heard the dog's last fall, he moved his head and saw the body bent like a brindle rope and motionless. He felt a physical heat roar through him like a bonfire.

'There', Tess hissed. 'He *will* kill.'

Mark clapped his hand down on her mouth again.

Without a word, Salerno swivelled himself round on his knee through the right angle to face the filly. She, alerted by the crack of the rifle, the thud of the bullet, and the slithering descent of the dog's corpse stood still, head up, ears cocked. She was not in fear, for in all her life no man had ever yet attacked her. She watched the dog Rip fall and then looking up saw the kneeling figure of Salerno slowly traversing round to bring his rifle to bear on her keen head.

Mark struggled. He got his head up through the brushwood. He pulled his arm up through the thorns gripping his catapult. He got his other hand out, loaded a great stone in the sling, and stood up a little further over the surface of the thorns to take aim upwards at Salerno. The man under his wide hat was intent upon drawing his aim steadily at the filly's bulk. He presented in profile an adequate target.

'Pop!' screamed Tess. 'Look out! Pop, he'll —'

Her cry had only leapt half way into the dusk before Mark loosed the black stone from the mill-pond. Salerno had frozen. The stone flew true. It's black weight crunched into the corner of his jaw which had just left the rifle-butt. The stone was rising and yet still accelerating, and the smash of the crushed jaw rang out in the night. The blow hurled Salerno off his good knee and onto his metal stump. This, having no purchase on the greensward, began to buckle over. Salerno's body like a black sail on a smashed mast was slowly tipping over into the void.

'No, no, no', wailed Tess. She was fighting her way out of the thicket to get to the foot of the cliff. Mark stood upright, quite still.

Salerno's body was flapping like a scarecrow to resist its jerking pivot over the brink. As his hand went out to grasp a tussock and gripped only the empty air, he let out the shrillest scream. It was the cry of a female. It was a screech of total dread. His top-heavy body followed the stiff arm over, and began with desperately ponderous thuds and grunts to roll over down the cliff-edge. It moved faster and faster, like a felled log, until it struck the ledge on which the donkey had been marooned. Had he been lighter or with two legs, he might have snatched a refuge there. But on the ledge Salerno's body bounced. Then Salerno shrieked into the dusk above their heads, as he felt his body again flung into the air. It fell towards them, enormous against the night sky. Its arms, like pathetic wings, clawed at the rushing air.

Tess, tearing across, was felled by his body, hurled sideways, rolling like a small dog kicked by a horse. She was as quickly on her hands and knees again. She sprang back to him. He had crashed upon his back. His eyes were wide open. His big body lay straight, but his stump had been torn backwards. Both his arms remained stiffly extended to either side, crucified against the turf.

Tess reached him and bent over his face. 'Oh Pop, are you all right?'

He made some noise. Words, gasped out, emerged thickly. 'What?' begged Tess. 'What?' She saw Mark standing by the side of the thicket. She cursed him. 'You've killed him. Killed him!' she screamed.

Mark crossed to the body of his dog. It was a hairy bag of blood. He caught the filly by her reins, took them over her frightened head, and came coldly back to look down at Salerno. The big man saw him against the sky. His mouth opened. He strained to raise his head. He said to Mark, 'She saved me.' He repeated it. Victory and pride rode on the thick words. 'Tess saved me.' His eyes, enormous without his glasses, swung round towards her. His head, however, he could not move at all.

Mark nodded. 'Perhaps.' He had seen beasts pole-axed lying like this before the final slaughter, their eyes and mind alive, but their limbs terminally paralysed.

'Pop', Tess urged. 'Can you move your arms? Try . . . Just move a hand Pop . . . Oh God almighty, move a hand. Move a finger Oh God, Oh Pop, move just one finger.' She seized the hand with which he painted and tried herself to flex the fingers.

Salerno's heavy torso strained. But neither his one good leg nor either hand nor arm even flickered. The current of life had been cut off from them.

The moon had risen over the quarry. In its glow Salerno's face gleamed like a marble gravestone in the rain. He was wet with sweat. He ceased his efforts and his lungs rasped in and out like bellows of old stiff leather. When he could speak again, he grunted out, 'Can't move, Tess. Painting done for. Back smashed.'

She whirled at Mark. She struck his face. Her nails tore down his cheek and ripped into his beard. With her other flailing hand she fell upon the filly's eyes. Mark pulled the filly back. Tess saw Salerno's rifle glinting. She stooped, seized it and tried to cock it. All the time she was moaning and cursing Mark, 'You've destroyed him . . . all he could do . . . what he could add . . . greatness . . . now I'll –' She had the rifle at her waist and tugged the trigger. A bullet whistled past

Mark and the filly, exploded against the quarry wall and, striking rock, whined away into the dusk.

'Can't you speak?' Tess cried. She was fumbling with the magazine. Tears startled to throttle her. She shook. 'Can't you speak?' She blurted, 'Aren't you ever human?'

After a minute's struggling she saw that the magazine below the rifle had become loosened by her agitation. She banged it back in place with her hand and looked up. There was no sign of Mark and his filly in the darkness. She listened. The distant world in front of her was silent. Only from behind her rose the gasp of Salerno's breath.

'Where are you, Mark?' she called. Her voice echoed back, ''ark, 'ark,' like the cry of a gull over the sea. Then she heard the faint pad of hoof-falls, a tiny clink of flint and the far-off snuffle of the filly's nostrils. Above the furthest rim of the quarry the last band of day lay citrus yellow. Against this strip she saw Mark's head and the filly's rising side by side as they crossed the crest. She raised the rifle to her shoulder. They were walking quietly away together, his arm resting with fatigue, with love, around her neck. Tess took aim. The rifle's night-telescope brought out the two figures large and clear. She put the cross lines on Mark's body, trigger fitting against her finger like a ring. She needed to move the rifle a shade to the right. Her hands quivered, the sights jumped, and she hesitated. Then, as if she had been holding her breath for minutes, her lungs stung with pain. She let the air out and flung the rifle down.

She stooped right down towards the turf, as if she had been so gravely wounded in her belly that she was about to die. She hung there bent over like a willow. Then, 'Tess', groaned Random Salerno. 'Help me. Please.' She shuffled across to him, still stooping. Her shoulders were hunched like an old peasant woman's already accustomed to her daily burden.

43

Mark and the filly walked onward through the night. The last yapping farm dogs reminded him with tears of Rip. They died away behind as they left the cultivated lands and started the long climb towards the mountains.

In the dawn the lake where old Lincoln had come to find a foster mother for the filly lay like beaten pewter. There was no mist this time. No birds yet sang. The only noise was the slap of the small waves lapping the lake's dappled stones. The filly bent her head to drink deeply. Mark lay upon his face in the shallow water, feeling the slipperiness of the stones all along the length of his weary body. The coldness of the water was exquisite. He plunged his head beneath the surface and felt the water lifting and smoothing the tangle of his hair and beard. When he raised his dripping head he saw the filly regarding him with huge-eyed puzzlement. 'But look at your silly whiskers, love', he said. Her golden muzzle had been tinted by the water. Drops clung to her whiskers like sprouts of pearls bending them downwards and giving her the air of a clown.

The sun sent its first pale shaft over the saddle of the far mountains. 'Come on', he said gently, 'We must hide up all day or the police will surely find us.' He had no fear now of being dead, but his absence would leave no one to care for the filly and her foal. He remembered his father saying that the mountainside beyond the lake belonged to the military. 'Could you carry me a bit?' he asked. 'I'm awfully tired.' And because the filly did not actively refuse, he climbed upon her bare back. He let her walk round the shallows of the lake where his father had been years before. She had been lying at home with him then, struggling for this laboured life.

He was making for the hermit's cave, which would be their lair during daylight. But in the boggy ground of the valley the filly demurred. She would carry him no further. He swung off, his feet squelching into the sweet-smelling bog. The filly stretched her head round to examine her belly. 'Oh no', said Mark tugging at her, 'You can't have it here.' She hung back against him. 'Idiot,' he said, 'It's far too wet here. As well as too dangerous.'

The urgency in his voice bestirred her. She consented to resume the climb, but her hooves squelched heavily in the soft peaty turf. She was deliberately making heavy weather of it; a mistress whose burdens and impending risks were not appreciated. She laid her ears back resentfully. She did not care for his busy impatience, when what she desired was his full solicitude.

The sun was already flashing across the lake when they reached the cave on the mountain. He had feared that she might be unwilling to enter it, but when she heard the water running from its spring she quickened, and pushed him aside at the narrow mouth. She was blowing heavily. She walked without fear into the dark cleft of the mountain and drank deeply. Then she paused and looked round at Mark, eyes glowing in the gloom like a woman who has chosen well. She sighed and started to sniff around the dusty floor of the cave.

'If you roll here, you'll get stuck.' He found the old branches which had made his father's bed and crossed them into a barricade across the entrance, so that neither could she leave him, nor could they be surprised. Then he stood, knuckling his brow, scratching at his beard, wondering what best to do. For rest he must, immediately and for hours. He swayed. Seeing him she went down on her knees and sniffed the ground again. 'Nothing for it then', he said thickly, for even his tongue sulked in his mouth. His eyelids were lead-heavy, his head rocked and his legs felt as soft as the river-lilies. He lay down in the middle of the earth floor and, looking up at her, mumbled, 'Don't you dare roll on me.' She pushed at him with her muzzle, attempting, gently to roll him over. Feeling her nudge and her warm breath confused his blurred brain with the touch of Tess beneath those old blankets. But he could not respond. He felt that he should hold out at least a hand to tell her that he was unable. But nothing would stir. He tipped into the lap of sleep.

But the filly was determined to make him give her room. He was rolled over and into the space provided she carefully lowered her huge bulk. Feeling her bulging body he started awake, for if she rolled now she would crush his ribs against the rock wall. But she had no intention of lying flat out. Folding her forelegs neatly beneath her chest, she placed her head lightly on Mark's shoulder-blade and sighed.

They were both awoken, the filly first, by the whistle of mortar shells on the firing-range below, and the thump of their explosions on the belly of the mountain. Mark, restraining the filly, crouched behind his barricade across the entrance. The explosions recalled for the filly, too, the acts in the quarry. She shivered. He stroked her neck. 'Nothing to do with us', he said, but as his words emerged, he realised for the first time in his life, their basic falsehood. 'Well, then they shouldn't be', he said as if arguing with the filly or with Tess. 'We're nothing to do with them', he declared firmly, but vainly. He would never be able to delude himself again.

The explosions jetted up dark fountains of damp earth. One, off-target, burst near a flock of mountain sheep and caught a pregnant ewe unable to scurry off as quickly as her sisters. The sheep's fat body, woolly as a toy, was lofted high into the air before crashing down, amazed, to death. From below erupted the merry laughter of the soldiery.

Then a more terrifying shouting split the slopes. Animal growls and screeches thundered and squealed up the mountain. Mark looked down. From a long wooden gibbet twelve sacks were hanging. They were ridiculously garbed in the uniforms of one of the nation's enemies. Into these swinging sacks waves of leaping, screaming soldiers were plunging the short stabbing crowd-control bayonets at the ends of their automatic rifles. Round them, like huntsmen goading on their packs, uniformed persons in authority thrashed the air with sticks and thwacked their soldiers' buttocks, bellowing them forward; 'Carve 'is bloody guts out there! Twist that steel. Boot in 'is bloody balls there! Kill! Kill! *Kill*!' The soldiers in greater frenzy lunged, stabbed, kicked and bayonetted the silently swinging mocking sacks. 'Kill-Kill-Kill!' they screamed with voices hoarse and panting in the cause of duty. They were maddened by the sacks' superior dumb insolence.

His father in his day had felt disgusted by these sights and sounds. But Mark additionally felt guilt. He knew that when he had aimed at Salerno on the quarry's lip, voices in his mind, too, had shrieked 'Kill! Kill!' He too had desired the threat extinguished, Salerno dead.

The filly moved beside him. She peered from the cave's crack down the mountain slope, and watched the gibbering antics of the soldiers. 'It was to save you', said Mark and gently pulled her soft ear, as in those old days he used to pull the teats of warm milk cows. 'He would certainly have killed you. As sure he killed poor Rip.' The filly, enjoying the sensation, slightly dropped her head. 'And me, too, of course. He'd not have shot the girl. He still needed her. Will for ever, now, I suppose.' The filly breathed contentedly. Mark said, 'They're both in each other's traps now . . . poor wretches.'

'I wish I hadn't had to do it.' Hearing his words aloud, he wondered if judges in those courts which daily sentenced thousands would have regrets if they saw their sentences enacted. Did they ever have doubts about acting against one individual for the intended benefit of others? 'No one else in the whole world,' he remarked to the filly, 'Would think even a thousand of you to be worth one Salerno. They'd use your hooves to make his glue. But to me you were worth more than the man Salerno. And I was there to sling the stone.'

The screams below abated. The soldiery, their galvanising current cut off by their superiors, slumped upon the ground. They lit cigarettes and, their catharsis completed, they talked like humans. The stuffed sacks, only trivially ripped by all that force, still swung gently from their gibbets.

Mark said 'I only killed him to protect you. I never even wished him harm before. I didn't hate him. I wasn't jealous, you know. I was disgusted when I caught him on top of you, but only because I thought that you were – she was his daughter. I didn't rage when I knew she'd return to him. I didn't mind her performances in the club. Not only didn't mind', he corrected himself, as one who caps another's argument, 'I lusted for her. I longed to mount her I longed to mount you there with all those men.' His thoughts recaptured the dazzling image of Tess arched backwards in a golden bow in the piercing spotlight. He heard the greedy roars. He said reasonably to the filly, 'But that's part of all of us. She was part of all of us. Which we all share.' And then, slapping the filly's neck in what he hoped was a breezy manner, he declared, 'But you I loved. I love. Because you still depend on me.'

Whistles blew below. The soldiers reformed into straight squares on the curving belly of the hill and, with much unnecessary shouting, were marched away to waiting transports. The chug of diesel-engines and their fumes wafted up the mountain. 'And I depend on you', said Mark. 'Let's start again.'

44

The days dragged achingly on their long journey to the west. The hills were high, and the tracks sharp with granite. Mark's shoes were soon tattered into fragments. The filly's hooves split at their toes and she hobbled. Soon she was starting to tire after only an hour's climbing. There were only occasional small streams yielding trickles of brown water. She should have been sustained by oats. There were none. The grass on the mountains was coarse, unpalatable and did not restore her. Mark gave her eggs taken from plovers' nests and sucked them raw himself. Otherwise he ate nothing but berries. He was so weak that at each dawn his body glided like a shadowy fish in and out of sleep and dreams and fantasies. He became barely able to force it up out of the heather to plod on. There were no farms left on the highlands. Sometimes they came upon the ruins of a croft now engulfed by nature's sea of gorse and heather. 'Like the haunted farm', said Mark, 'Before the mighty Salerno came.'

Mark dozed with nothing above his head except the pale stars and the silence of the universe. In his mind the day in the hermit's cave exploded with the boom of shells and the screams of the men and his own urging thoughts. He kept encouraging her. 'It'll be better, my love, when we reach the sea.' At the end of the land he believed they would find their peace.

He crouched down by the filly as she lay, bloated, ribby and old. She looked a ruin. He knelt by her bony head which had once, to his young eyes, seemed so beautiful. Her eye regarded him. In its pupil he saw with awful clarity, and distorted only in their outlines, the figure and head of an ancient bearded man. He sprang up. The blood sank from his head and he tottered. He peered around. No one stood behind him. Against the faint blows of his heart's hammer, he again knelt down by the filly's head and peered another time into her weary eye, and saw himself again.

This time he gently touched her soft muzzle. 'Oh we are so old, love. So old now. What have I done to you? And what have we grown old for?'

He remained for some time kneeling while his mind groped for an answer, as blindly as Rip had tried to snap the swiftly darting bats at dusk.

The filly's eyes had closed again. His horrible reflection was terminated. Her breath sighed softly in and out like surf upon the shore.

'It'll be better, love, I promise, when we reach the sea.'

He put his arm and shoulder beneath her chest to help her rise. She staggered up.

'Better, all be better at the end.'

She must have doubted him, for she was walking even more slowly. Her bag was enormous. Her teats were waxing up. 'Please', he begged her. 'Please try.' In a few more days when there was still no sight of the sea, he saw what he had been dreading: from her nearside teat emerged a drop of milk. By the evening's slow walk and rest and plod and pause, the teat was dripping milk from its grey bag. She would foal now within a day. She grew restless and uneasy. Twice she lay down. Sweat started on her poor thin neck and flank. She rocked on the ground, stretching round towards her womb. Spasms of pain came, then passed. When she seemed quieter again, Mark coaxed her up and forward. There was no shelter anywhere in sight on this bleak heath. No water ran. No trees gave shade. Only sharp rocks stabbed at the sky, like smashed memorials in a deserted cemetery.

At last one noon when they were climbing a ridge the filly stumbled, fell down and lay still. Her eyes had dimmed again. He feared she was dying. He staggered in the heat up to the crest to look for some covered resting place. There was a wind with a strange smell on it as he neared the top. He sucked it into his dry lungs. It tingled the back of his nose. He looked down from the ridge and saw below him, filling half his vision, the emerald and turquoise immensity of the sea. Across it lay, glittering and dancing like the light hurled from a million aluminium foils, a brilliant silver pathway running on westwards, still ahead of him. The sun's path danced on like a continuance not only of his direction but of his spirit. It did not cease until it reached the grey blurred rim of the far horizon, and there it merged with the colossal sky. He turned and tottered back calling 'It's there, love! There.' He knelt by the filly's head and coaxed her. She raised her head, but it was only to turn with alarm towards the sharp pain in her uterus.

Her muscles down there were sending out waves rolling towards its neck, which was now starting to dilate. He crawled behind her to hoist her up. She looked at him sadly, but rose at least onto her forelegs. 'One more heave', he murmured, trying to place his shoulder under her girth. Finally she staggered, wobbled and rose to her four feet. Mare's milk was running from her nearside teat.

'You can smell the sea', he said. 'It's marvellous.' He ran a little ahead of her as Rip had used to run on before him, coming home at last after a long day's hunting. The filly did not halt again, but came matronly, ponderously up the last rise. She did indeed snuff the air and cast her head up for the first time in weeks and cock her chestnut ears. 'Look', he said, 'All down hill.' The air was cooler. He would get her somewhere before the evening when she would surely foal.

The turf was very thin. Stones pierced it. The sun's heat during the day on the solid rock beneath made all the turf warm as a body beneath their feet. The new breeze on their bodies and faces gave off the scent of hay and blue cornflowers, small cow-parsleys and a pattern of white and purple clovers. Butterflies, bright blues and dusty browns danced in the scented air. 'We're so nearly there.' She stopped again, once more lay down, and three more spasms, like breaking rollers, passed through her, shuddering.

Then they both heard the first strange rumbling, the distant thunder of the sea. As they plodded closer down the slope they heard upon the breeze a high singing. It was like the mourning vibration of many violins which he had heard once in school and which, to the others' scorn, had set him forlornly weeping for something lost.

The singing sound moved over the bass grumble of the surf as the swirling air spun over the depths of the sea. The lightness in it was like the lightness in his head over the rhythmic plod of his old body.

The ground started to fall away sharply. Rocks thrust through the turf like the snouts of prehistoric monsters. The ocean's noise became deafening. Over the hiss and shush of the wind spinning off the sea came the clap and crash of waves on rocks, like giants' hands slapping upon monstrous bellies.

Then he realised with despair that this green path led not to a gentle coast, or inviting beach, or to any haven under the rocks but to a dizzily towering line of cliffs. Had he the strength he would have wept. Then slowly he walked to the edge as if going to his execution. He looked far down at the white gulls flying on and on beneath him across the heaving emerald and purple surface of the sea. There were rock-pools a long stone's crash beneath, bright-green with weeds but leapt upon by the snarling waves. He saw now that the waves formed themselves far beyond his dreams, that they shimmered in from the distance like the first faint stir of thought, growing in noise and height, power and violence until they smashed into the cliff's roots like maniacs. Salt spray spumed up. White clots splattered his face. He crouched down upon the cliff's edge like a primitive man, and his head fell between his knees. The drumming thunder of the sea overwhelmed him.

He saw beneath his nose, between his bare feet a tiny pink flower. The booming in his ears erased thought. He gazed upon the flower's rosy labia. They appeared to him to be growing, to be gradually and tantalisingly opening. He thought with anguish: if only I could still lose myself in there. Under his concentration the drumming of the ocean receded. Then he heard from some mousehole in the wainscot of his mind the sound of a piano. He saw again the fat greying woman playing it at school with tears running down her puckered cheeks. He heard her voice read out again, and end again in a choke, Liszt's superscription on his symphonic poem: 'What is our life but a series of preludes to that unknown song?' The woman in playing had ceased to sob and had looked up with shining eyes. Then he had been mystified. Now he comprehended. He gave a great sigh. A silence grew round him which had no rim. Then the cold began. An urge stirred in him that he must, however arduous the task, stave it off for a while. The chill was dulling him more each moment. He heard his voice, sounding very deep, pronounce from somewhere: 'I will go on.'

He shook himself. He heaved up his head. When he rose up his mind was spinning still but now with the rumbling of the sea. He was dazed. He looked for the filly and saw no sign of her. He thought: she has gone over. He began to run along the cliff, a worried old man, looking into the sea below and bleating with terror. The gulls shrieked at him as he tottered on, moving on the swirls of air without a flicker of their hooped white wings. He started to cry out for the filly in a voice almost as high as the gull's shrieks. But the sound of the surf tossed away his little old voice like spume.

Then he reached the saddle of a headland where the cliffs towered so blackly that he could not bear to approach the edge, let alone look over it. He shrank away from the brink, and pressed himself on hands and knees on the tilting turf. He was in shadow. The sun was sinking. He crawled onto the saddle of the promontory. And the scene changed. A narrow green valley with a brook in its groin ran down towards a small beach. The westering sun no longer left a path across the ocean, but limned the sand in a pink wash. There was a small whitened building. A smooth turf track wound down to it. And on the track, walking slowly down and swaying, was his filly. He ran after her downhill on his burning feet, as if he flew. He caught her, touched her neck. But she gave him only a sidelong glance and kept on walking. In the cool swirl of the evening air from the sea, she was sweating on her neck and on her chest. The sweat was dark and her hair curled under it. She was in pain. It was the onset of her final birthpangs.

There was an old stone bridge over the stream, and beyond it a half open barn under a thatched reed roof. A stack of reeds lay in the barn. The filly crossed the bridge and turned to stare down at the water in the brook, but did not go down to it. She slowly climbed the further slope and entered the open barn. Using her head and hooves she spread the rushes across the dusty ground. She stood splayed. Her water broke. As her placenta ruptured, Mark saw the quick emergence of the pale yellow liquid which had been surrounding the foal within its membrane. The filly pawed at the rushes desperately and then went down, half-rolling, trying to speed the passage of her foal from her exhausted body into uncertain life. She rose again, crept closer to the whitewashed back wall of the barn, and again went down, this time with her back to the stones, seeking its support. She strained and strained. She seemed in agony. Mark crouched by her head, murmuring, murmuring, stroking her neck. A convulsion passed through her. He saw the ripped placenta bursting out. Within its pale and slimey transparency he saw the outstretched black hooves and forelegs of an enormous foal.

The filly heaved and groaned trying to force this monster out of her. But she was weak and starved and weary as far as life's last milestone. Mark gripped the foal's legs and pulled. They came out a little further. He could see the foal's head, shrouded in the grey placenta like the owl Ozymandias, like the ghost in the ruined farm. He could now reach the foal's elbows. He took a slippery grip, dreading that he might hurt them or the quiescent filly. But he pulled again until he could see the foal's huge black shoulders tearing the filly open.

'Help me, Tess!' he cried. 'Help me. Push.' But there was no movement from the filly. 'I can't. . . .' he was heaving. 'I can't . . . on my own. . . . I'm tired, too, Tess. . . .'

The foal burst out on the reed bed. His dark head thrust through the placenta as if through a bag. Within a second of doing so his forefeet, already freed of the bag, were pawing at the rushy floor to claw his way entirely free of her last hold. As his hindlegs at last came out, his umbilical cord was stretched as tight as a bow string. It snapped. The foal was free and shining black all over and alive. Mark stood up shaking and saw the filly's head. It was flung back on the reeds against the wall. Her eyes were open. But so was her mouth. And in the snarl of painful death.

He flung himself down by her and felt for her heart beneath her sweaty golden skin. But there was no beat, no breath in her. He tried to close that eye in which he had over the long years seen his ageing self again and again reflected. He caressed her neck. He heard his voice murmuring. Above the gaping mouth he kissed her muzzle. He could not cry.

In the silence he heard a rustle. The black colt foal was stirring on the rushes. He rose and went to him. 'Cold', he said. He looked down on the quivering black body. 'Murderer?' He heard himself mumble 'Or survivor?' Without thinking he had taken off his old torn sweater and, as he and his father had done so many times since the days of the first shepherd, he slipped his scrap of clothing over the foal's body. 'To keep you warm', he said, and, as a shepherd hoists an orphan lamb, he stooped and raised the foal in his long arms. As he rose he turned and saw to his amazement that it was evening, and that the low, scarlet sun was illuminating a small figure, quick and lithe as his father had been, hurrying towards him.

Mark stood holding the foal and leaning against the stone door pillar for support. He saw that the figure was a girl and that in her haste she was skipping the odd stride, as his father had used to do.

The girl said in a strange soft accent 'We've milk in the croft and a bottle. We'll have to feed him now. Or he, too, will die like his mother.' She put her small arm inside its fisherman's sweater around Mark's waist to help him forward. He saw that the croft had a huge outside chimney-stack in which a wood-fire was glowing, fanned by the salty wind of the now gentler sea. The flames of the old hearth danced against the darkness of the small end wall of the cottage. The girl noticed his surprise. She said 'The chimney you're looking at? It was part of a great old house once, now long pulled down. Keep the colt warm in your arms by the hearth now. And I will fetch out the bottle to him with his milk.'

Mark sat holding the foal, and then hugging him to his body for warmth. The open hearth was sheltered from the sighing ocean by the croft's low bulk. A wide skirt of grey ashes, still warm after years of quiet burning, spread out from its warm and leaping glow. A holly stick leant against the wall close by the fire. When the girl comes back, Mark thought, she will crouch over the ashes with that stick, as my father did, and make those two lines in them, one forceful, one trailing away and ask if I think that together we can save the foal.

And how may I answer that this time? How can I say what will happen? When I can't speak, and can barely move and need only this hearth's warmth and tomorrow's sun and this little body to cling to for the present?

The girl came out of the croft with a bottle full of milk and Mark saw without surprise that her eyes, too, were very blue and wide apart. 'Open his mouth a little', she said, 'with your finger. That he may suck.' Mark did so and she slipped the teat into the small mouth. She squeezed it, and the foal began noisily to suck.

'There', said the girl smiling. 'You've both had a long journey.' She was crouching by him, with her body a little twisted. So he took the bottle from her, and she rose to ease her legs. He heard his voice say, 'I do see now that, each time, *if you are careful*, that you do get a little bit further on along the way. . . .'

'Yes.' The girl nodded. 'Oh, yes.' She took the old polished holly stick from the wall and squatted comfortably above the great sweep of ashes round the hearth. Without looking up at Mark she drew the first firm mark through the white ashes. Mark waited upon the movement of the end of the wooden staff. She drew it towards her again and made, not a faint trail, but another bold stroke, firm and true this time, by the side of the first. She looked up and said quietly, 'Together, you and I, we can save him.'

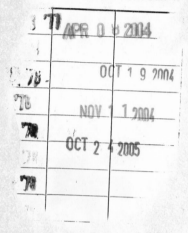